BROKEN TRAIL

BROKEN TRAIL

ALAN GEOFFRION

PINNACLE BOOKS
Kensington Publishing Corp.
www.kensingtonbooks.com

PINNACLE BOOKS are published by

Kensington Publishing Corp.
850 Third Avenue
New York, NY 10022

Previously published in a trade paperback edition by Fulcrum Publishing.

ISBN-13: 978-0-7860-1992-2
ISBN-10: 0-7860-1992-1

First printing: July 2008

10 9 8 7 6 5 4 3 2 1

Printed in the United States of America

For Danielle and Donald

Prologue

The little stallion turned his head into the wind, gently flared his nostrils, and inhaled the night air. He smelled the budding sage, the thawing earth, and the faintest hint of the scent of carnivores. Clouds scudded past a waning moon. Spring had come early to the mesa, and with it the rhythms of the changing seasons. Wolves ventured south, vying with the coyotes for the pronghorn fawns and any early foals on the Owyhee Range. Spring stirred the young colts, emboldened with hopes of having mares that would be coming into heat. This would be the stallion's ninth year on the range. He had covered this band of mares for the last four seasons, protecting it from predators and colts eager to challenge his claim. He was acutely aware of the world around him. It was all encoded deep inside him as it had been in his sire and all the other stallions going back to the little Spanish horses that swam ashore from the galleons off the shores of Hispaniola almost four hundred years before.

A sorrel mare, heavy with foal, had been up and down for hours, positioning the unborn inside her.

The sounds of her labor and the smell of her afterbirth would soon be on the night air. Again he breathed in the night, deep into his synapse. The air was thick with the smell of the sage that the horses had trampled on. The buttery moonlight shone on his spring coat. He quietly moved out into the darkness, feeling a nagging twinge in his hock. In the darkness out beyond the band of mares, he pawed the earth and snorted loudly to the seen and the unseen.

A flat gray line of morning fog and smoke from cook fires hung evenly over the village. The damp morning air awakened the timeless scent of a thousand years of dust and dehydrated animal and human waste. The nameless village lay in a nameless part of the western Guandong Province of China. Mud huts surrounded a compound of deteriorating walls. inside the walls gathered people as dreary and desperate-looking as the land they lived in. The village headman watched as his verdict on the man who knelt before him was carried out. Roosters scratched and pecked at the litter on the ground. A cord tied fast around the man's thumb was pulled as two men held the wretch and forced his hand on a stump. The headman nodded and a third helper dropped the axe, severing the hand from its shaking owner. The villagers looked on in silence. Poverty had long ago ground away all their emotions. Their presence was merely a requirement, much as was their daily toiling in the fields of a thankless land. A woman sobbed as three children clutched about her. Her anguish was as much for what her future held as for the wretch whose bloody hand lay before them.

The sergeant major strutted up the middle of the dirt road, which was lined with a dozen tin-roofed buildings. Lydesdorp had been the provincial capital of northern Transvaal. Swagger stick held under his left arm, his boots powdered with dust, he marched toward a detail of soldiers. The men were using mules to drag dead horses beyond the village. It was an hour before sunset, and still the sky was filled with soaring vultures. They glided in big, looping circles on thermals that rose from the African bushveld.

By the time the sergeant major caught up with the working detail, they had just removed the rope from around the ankles of a stout dun. The gelding lay with a distended belly, stiff legs, and its mouth open on its side next to a pile of thirty or so dead horses.

A soldier knelt beside the animal and brushed the horse's dark forelock to the side of its face. Its big, beautiful dark eye stared at nothing. The soldier turned his head at the sound of the sergeant major's footsteps.

"Cramer, no time to be sitting on your haunches. I want this mess cleared up before retreat," said the big Yorkshireman, pointing to the carcass with the swagger stick. "There's nothing you can do for them now, laddy. They've served their purpose," he said, tucking the stick back under his arm.

"You mean Lord Kitchner's. There must be three thousand dead 'tween here and Fort Edwards. They say Kitchner's lost two hundred thousand horses, and he still can't catch the Dutchmen," said the soldier as he rose and wiped his hand on his trousers.

"Steady on there, boy'o. Talk like that will get you in front of the provost. Aye, he's a wee one," said the sergeant major, nodding to the dun.

"He's a mustang, sergeant," said the soldier in a low voice.

"What's that, soldier? Speak up," snapped the sergeant major.

The soldier straightened and in a clear voice said, "He's a mustang, sergeant major. From America."

"From America? Ah, well. Carry on."

Chapter One

Print Ritter had to quit. His body knew it even before he did. The imperceptible pains worked to slow his steps across the ground and the aches spoke to him as he sat astride a horse. He refused to see it that way, but it was the truth. He adhered to the old saw that "it was better to wear out than rust out."

He removed his hat and wiped his brow. From above his eyebrows, his forehead was as white as a fish's underbelly; below, the look and color of tobacco. His white moustache drooped to his jaw. He ran his fingers through his silver hair before he replaced his hat. He had a paunch, but that was it. He carried no extra weight. His clothes were worn but tidy. He squeezed his wiry legs and the big chestnut moved out at a ground-eating trot.

Long flying wedges of Canada geese passed overhead, and wherever there was water, it was covered with pintails, most of them with their heads underwater and their pointy little asses in the air. Spring was sure coming early this year, he thought. And that made him think of empty stock tanks and dry creek beds. It seemed to him that early springs meant waterless summers. Then again, maybe not.

He was about halfway from the OO Ranch, heading to the Gap Ranch in the northern corner of Harney County. Those honkers will make it there before I do, he thought. The waterbirds had converged on Silver Lake, resting on their journey up to Canada and on to the Arctic Circle.

It was just north of the lake that the war chief Buffalo Horn had met his maker during the Indian Wars in eastern Oregon. Print had been working for the cattleman Peter French back in the summer of '78. He had been hired on to "sort out" young colts, but he was up for any chore Mr. French assigned to him. The two had struck it off from the first time they met. Print liked the way Peter French handled his men and his cows, and French liked the way Print finished off his horses. They and about a dozen hands were working over on the Diamond Ranch, branding, when Coon Smith raced in yelling that "about twenty-five" mounted braves were heading for the branding camp. It had been at the Diamond Ranch that a band of Bannocks had earlier on burned out George Smyth and his son, forcing them with intense barrage from their repeating rifles back into their cabin, where father and son burned to death. From then on, everyone got anxious anytime there was a sighting of two or more Indians in the countryside.

French, being the only one armed at the time, ordered all the hands to make a run for it back to the P Ranch. They threw the Chinaman, their cook, up on a horse and made a straight line for the P. French took up a position and started taking potshots at the approaching band. When they got close, he took off until he found a new position that offered some cover, and started dropping more of them as they advanced. He continued this until his men were over the trail crossing at McCoy Creek and the Bannocks felt that he was taking all the fun out of their day. The Chinaman had not lasted long on the galloping horse and had fallen off. The band caught the cook and put him to a gruesome death so that their entire day was not a loss.

Later, Print and Peter French and other cowhands joined up with a Colonel Bernard and made a fight of it at Silver Lake with the joined forces of Bannocks and Paiutes under Buffalo Horn. French had said that "it wasn't required and it was strictly on a volunteer basis." Print didn't care one way or the other. He went because Peter French had asked. It wasn't because of the Bannocks and Paiutes, or the Chinaman, or old man George Smyth and his son who got roasted in their cabin. He had left that kind of thinking a lifetime ago, back in the Valley Campaign, chasing Phil Sheridan up and down the Shenandoah. He went because this man he considered a friend had asked.

In the end, four troopers were killed and nearly fifty braves, including Buffalo Horn. He had been a handsome devil, even in death, thought Print. And a crafty one too. He had convinced the governor to give his braves more guns and ammunition so they could hunt for themselves, as the beef allotments from the government weren't enough to live on. Politicians. Worse than lawyers. Skimming money from the government beef fund, then allowing the tribes to arm themselves so that they could go out and kill ranchers trying to raise enough cows to feed the country, including the Indians. Print spat.

And now at his stopover at the OO Ranch, he learned from the Hanleys that his old friend Peter French had been murdered. They said it was over cows. There ain't enough cows in Christendom to be worth getting killed over, thought Print. But then maybe it wasn't really about cows. Maybe cows were just an excuse, and there was another issue. And there were issues in life worth making a stand over. They said that the fella that had done it was indicted by a coroner's jury that had been convened at the Sod House spread. Due to a low-set bail, and a firm of brass-buttoned lawyers all the way from Portland, the culprit ducked out of the justice he deserved. Politicians and lawyers. Print spat again. Forget it. Push on. Follow the honkers, the pintails, and terns north.

The following morning, the sun rose on his right. The clumps of manzanita cast long shadows across the range floor. The day would warm up quickly. Definitely an early spring, he thought. The waterbirds were high in the sky, winging north. A frantic jackrabbit darted left, then right, and disappeared into the brush. He had been in the saddle since before first light. He was betting he could make his destination before breakfast was over. He hadn't wanted to waste time making a fire, not even for coffee. He liked riding at this time of the day, especially when the weather was good. He could always have coffee, but not good weather.

He pushed Bob Tate into a lope as he sighted the Gap Ranch compound. A half an hour later, as he eased the big chestnut up at the approach to the ranch quarters, a spry man stepped off the porch to meet him.

"I'm lookin' for a Tom Harte," said Print.

The spry man said nothing. Print took his measure. No rudeness was implied.

"I'm his uncle," Print added.

The spry man nodded, removed a toothpick from his mouth, and pointed to the corral. "Over there," the man replied.

Behind the fence of lodgepoles, lariats were flying through the air. Calves bawled amid the dust and smoke as they thudded to the ground. The men wrestled a bull calf to the ground while another man slit open its scrotum with a pocketknife, tossing warm testicles into a wooden bucket. One gland missed the bucket and instantly a thin cattle dog snapped up the warm morsel. The branding iron bit into the thick hair and hide. Smoke billowed and another "new" steer struggled to its feet, its backside still smoking. A big bull calf threw himself against the poles, trying to escape. Once. Twice. The third time, he landed on the top pole, snapping it and two more. He somersaulted over, landing on his back. He scrambled and was off before the cowhands could clear the broken fence.

With a slight squeeze of his legs, Print had the big chestnut off in a shot. In one fluid motion, Print uncoiled his riata, played out a loop, and tossed it around the bull calf's hind legs. He dallied up as Bob Tate set himself for the force and the calf hit the end of the rope. Horse and rider took the impact as Print sat deep in the saddle. The calf hung suspended in the air for a moment, then hit the ground. The big cow pony backed up just enough to keep the tension on the rope.

Several hands scrambled over the breached corral, heading for the struggling calf. One of them stopped and looked up at Print.

"Uncle Print?" he asked.

He turned to the spry man who had followed Print.

"This is my uncle, Print Ritter. . . . Prentice Ritter."

Print and the spry man exchanged nods. Tom loosened the rope around the calf's hind legs as the other hands took over. His shirt was mottled with sweat and dust. Tom was lean and, like most of the Ritter clan, had bright red hair.

"What brings you out here? Thought maybe you'd died."

Print smiled slightly at the notion. "No, son, not yet. But your ma did. She passed away."

Tom said nothing. Neither did his face as he coiled another loop of the rope. "Did she say anything?" he asked.

"No, son. Her hired man found her in the vegetable garden," replied Print.

"Is he looking after the place?"

Print sighed. His wrists crossed over the horn of the saddle. "He is . . . I need ta say something straight out: she wrote a will." Print tugged at the glove on his left hand. He looked straight into the face of his nephew. "She left it all to me."

He raised his gaze momentarily, watching the cowhands wrestle the bull calf back over the broken opening. Then he looked back at the silent young man. "I don't know what was cros't between you two, but she done it. The land, the livestock, ever'thing. It ain't a fortune, but it's legit."

Print released his end of the rope from the horn and let it slip away

"That's it?" Tom asked, his face as lifeless as his departed mother's.

Print reached inside his coat and removed an envelope, offering it to his nephew "She did leave this for ya."

Tom stepped forward, took the envelope, looked at it, and stuffed it unopened into his shirt pocket. The two men looked at one another. Tom coiled up the last of the rope.

"I don't feel good about this, Nephew, not at all. I always figgered that it would all go ta you."

Tom tapped the coiled rope against his chaps. Print continued.

"That's why I come out here. I wanted to talk. Ya

see, your mother made me the executor to her estate. That means I have to carry out the orders of her will. She left ever'thin' ta me, 'cept there was a codicil. You can buy the old Fairbairn place—the three sections that run down from Steens to the Mahluer from her estate—if ya've a mind to.'

"I can buy it?" Tom asked.

Print nodded. "Market price."

A bitter Tom turned to walk away

"Will's on file over ta Burns'," Print called after him.

Tom stopped and turned to face his uncle. "Sonnuva bitch. That's mother's milk for ya."

Print nodded in agreement. "More like hind tit, son."

Tom looked over at the spry man and then back to Print. "Any more good news for me, Uncle?"

Print shifted in the saddle, "Look, son, I don't like this any mor'n you do, but I got this idea . . . might work out for both of us . . . maybe. I got this idea ta take horses back to Wyoming."

Print extracted a newspaper clipping from his coat pocket. "Listen ta this: Wanted: Hot- or cold-blooded horses. Sound and disease free. Three to eight years of age. Proof of ownership required. Purchase price commiserate with the quality of stock. Contact William or Malcolm Moncrieffe, Quarter Circle A Ranch, Sheridan, Wyoming—Agents for Her Majesty's War Office, British Empire."

Print looked up from the paper to gauge Tom's reaction. He continued. "Why don't we take some of yer ma's money an' buy a big string of horses? Might be a handy way ta increase our capital."

"You mean your capital. They ain't got horses in Wyoming?"

A vexed Print pursed his lips. "Try not ta get all swolled up an' just think about this fer a minute.

A fella name of Haythorne was out this way last year. Tried ta hire me to help drive a herd of five hundr'd head back ta Valentine, Nebraska. He had a contract with the Indian Agency ta supply horses for the Rosebud Reservation—"

"How many? An' what kind?" Tom interrupted.

Now yer gettin' it, Print thought. "I figger we could handle easy five hundr'd, maybe more if we took on a couple a boys. I'm thinkin' tough, high desert mustangs. Easy keepers. They kin go unshod and oughta be fairly broke by the time we get ta Sheridan."

Print could see that Tom wasn't as sold as he had hoped.

"An' you think I should quit here an' help make you richer than my ma already has?" Tom asked, looking over at the spry man and then back to his uncle.

"That's not my intention."

"We'd do this on shares?" Tom asked.

Print nodded. "I figger fifty/fifty split on the profits after expenses and loan repayment."

"Loan repayment?"

Print shifted again and Bob Tate responded by shifting his weight from one hind leg to the other. "That's right, loan repayment, ta the bank. I'd hafta put the ranch up as collateral."

"What the hell kinda deal is that? Yer gonna hock the family place to buy horses?"

Print was beginning to lose patience. "Well, that's one way a lookin' at it."

"What's the other?" asked Tom.

"No disrespect meant, but ain't you spent enough time cuttin' the nuts off another man's cows for chuck an' wages?" replied Print, first looking at the spry man and then to Tom.

Print continued. "Keep it up an' you'll be walkin'

aroun' like a crab, all stove up along with all the other bachelor cowhands from here to the Dalles—no disrespect meant."

Tom walked away. Print dismounted, flipped the stirrup over the saddle seat, and loosened the cinch strap. He lifted the saddle and moved the saddle blanket forward. Tom turned and walked back to his uncle.

"Here," he said, handing him the coiled riata.

Print took the rope and his eyes followed Tom as he walked around to the off side of the horse. Tom stared across the seat of the saddle at his uncle.

"Still ridin' old Bob Tate, I see."

Print smiled. "You bet," he replied.

Tom turned to the spry man, who nodded and took the toothpick from his mouth and pointed to the bunkhouse. Tom looked back at Print and said, "I'll get my stuff."

Having reset the blanket and saddle properly, Print tightened the cinch strap, dropped the stirrup back down, and said to the spry man, "Guess I'm gonna leave you a man short."

The spry man stuck the toothpick back in his mouth. "Tom's a hell of a hand. Hope things work out for you two."

Soon Tom returned with two horses, one saddled and the other with a packsaddle and his gear. He swung into the saddle.

"Maybe we'll see ya next spring," Print said to the spry man.

The spry man nodded and replied, "Keep yer nose to the wind, 'specially in that Green River country. There's desperate citizens that populate that land."

The two men turned their mounts and started off. The sun was now high, reminding Print that he hadn't had any coffee this day.

Chapter Two

The following month Print and Tom spent going from ranch to ranch buying horses. They ranged from as far south as the 3 Mile Ranch at the bottom end of the Steens to the Juniper place, then back over to Barton Lake, where they put up their stock in the big round barn that Peter French had built back in the early eighties, which was the talk of the countryside. After a lifetime of "excitement," Print found he still had a curiosity about things, even if it was only what the next week might bring.

They were sorting through some of the stock at French's barn. Print pointed to a red roan colt that Tom had picked out from stock over at the Venator Ranch that was penned up in the stone corral. "How rode out is that one?"

Tom shrugged. "He ain't no Bob Tate, but he'll do," he replied.

Print tossed a loop over the colt's head. He didn't fight and stood quietly as Print saddled him and slipped on a hackamore. In a side pen were four cows that they had picked up along the way and were planning on leaving there. Print said they would let the owners over at Ruby's know about them when they passed through.

Print quietly swung up and then carefully settled in the saddle. The cow pony stood stock-still. He then walked over to the pen with the strays in it. He opened the gate from atop the horse, passed through, and closed it from behind. At the far end of the pen, the strays bunched up. Tom took a seat on the wall of the stone corral to watch. Print approached the strays, moving in on a white-faced cow. The bunch broke and the pony cut right, splitting the cows. The half with the white-faced cow darted off to the side and then doubled back to the far end. Print and the pony were right on them. Two jumps and the pony had "whitey" separated. When the cow tried to bolt, the pony jumped right up and cut him off. Then he'd ease off to give the cow time to think it out. As soon as the cow moved, the pony was on him. No matter which way it turned, the pony would sweep left or right. Finally, the cow gave up and shut it down. Print wheeled the red roan and trotted over to Tom. He stopped and rested his crossed arms on the horn.

"Yer right. He ain't no Bob Tate," he said, smiling. "But he'll do."

They camped in the stone corral that was really a long chute entrance to the round barn. They stayed up late that night and Print told his nephew stories of the vaqueros who had broken horses under that round roof. And of horses that had broken some men.

They mustered their growing herd at the Hanleys' Bella A Ranch and headed west to Wagontire Mountain and Bill Brown's place. "Wagontire" Brown raised horses and sheep. He was hard on his help and spent long periods having to run his place on his own. He wrote his checks on wrapping paper and the bank in Burns accepted every one of them for almost forty years. He tended his flocks out in the bush and lived on nuts and raisins with a pinch of strychnine. "Just enough to kill the appetite, not the cook." He raised exactly the kind of horses Print wanted and needed.

When they had ganged over five hundred head, Print took off for Canyon City and John Day and then back to Burns, taking care of the paperwork, finances, and provisions.

Early on the morning of the fifteenth of May, with four extra men to help get them started, Print and Tom emptied the pens to head for the Moncrieffe brothers' in Sheridan.

"Let's wheel 'em to the right!" yelled Print.

Slowly, the milling horses started in a counterclockwise direction, shoving and bumping, some rearing onto the backs of others. The men did a good job keeping them turned in. Clouds of dust rose, obscuring the men and the herd. From high up where the geese flew, it must have looked like a giant turning mandala.

Print rode around the herd counter to its movement. His blood was up. It pumped through him, and he didn't feel any aches. He felt strong. He wasn't thinking about making money or bank loans or squaring things with his nephew. He rode in close on the turning horses, close enough that they bumped his leg. It may have looked like mayhem, but he controlled it. He felt solid. And young again, or at least younger. He pulled the kerchief down that covered his face.

"Let 'em go! Let 'em go! Head 'em east an' let 'em go!"

The men eased off, and as they did, the circle expanded until the lead mares broke free and more or less headed off to the east. The circle undid itself. Once the herd straightened out, all the boys had to do was keep up on either side. One man with the packhorses brought up the rear far behind. Five hundred and thirty-six horses charged into the rays of the morning sun.

Chapter Three

The clipper ship plowed down the deep troughs and then through the cresting waves of the South China Sea. The captain stood behind the helmsman on the shifting quarterdeck. Spray from the waves breaking over the bowsprit soaked everything topside. The captain grabbed the rail of the quarterdeck as the ship laid heavy to port and slid down the lee side of a huge wave. All her sails were reefed save one spritsail to help her keep her heading. The helmsman struggled with the great wheel. The captain stepped forward to help him. Together they headed her almost directly into the wind. As she crested the next wave, her bow all the way to the keel came out of the water. Then down she plunged, thrusting her nose into the gray-green ocean covering her fo'c'sle.

"Good God, man, keep her inta the wind, man!" the captain screamed. "It's gunna be an ugly night. I'm going below!" he yelled to the sailor.

He noticed that the wind was rising as it caught the tops of the waves and skimmed spray off them. He opened the hatch and descended the ladder, sliding the hatch cover closed behind him.

"Bagwell! Bagwell!" the captain shouted.

From the darkened companionway, the first mate appeared, his slicker already in hand.

"I want you topside at the wheel. Take two men to help. She's gonna have her teeth in us tonight."

"Aye, aye, capt'n," he replied.

"An' get all hands going on the bilge pumps, port an' starboard."

"Aye, capt'n," answered the mate, slipping on his foul-weather gear.

The captain made his way forward along the companionway until he got to the next opening and descended the ladder to the next deck. Then he reversed himself, heading aft along that deck's companionway to the next opening, and braced himself against the bulkhead as the ship rose up and hove to port. He could hear the transom groan as the sea pressed on all sides. At the bottom of the ladder, a lantern swung, barely lighting the hold. With all the portholes and air shafts secured for the gale, the stench in the compartment was retching. Even with a lifetime at sea behind him, the captain gagged as he took the lantern down and made his way forward.

The captain had a flinty face and a flinty heart. He held the lamp high as he walked to the motion of the ship. Secured to the ship's bulkheads were large containers with bolted doors and barred windows. He held the light to one of the windows and leaned close, bracing himself as the ship rolled to port. The swaying lamp revealed young Chinese girls huddled together. Some so overcome with sickness from the storm lay on the floor of the container, exhausted from retching. The wooden bucket used as a toilet had overturned in the storm and its contents sloshed back and forth. He looked into all the lashed containers and then returned the lantern to its hook and doused the light. He ascended the ladder, wondering how much the storm would affect his calculated arrival date in San Francisco.

Chapter Four

After a couple of miles, the herd had thinned out and was now a long stretched-out line. The pace had slacked off some, so the riders urged them on. Print wanted to make sure the herd understood that slowing down or stopping was always going to be his idea, not theirs. They ran along the East Fork for a half an hour with a stout, flea-bitten gray mare in the lead. Tom rode close to the front of the herd, watching the mare. He had already decided she wasn't going to be sold in Sheridan. He was keeping her for himself. As she crested an incline, she eased into a trot, and Tom did the same. Soon all of the herd was at the trot.

Print rode up to Tom. He was glad to see that his nephew was taking to sharing the decision making already. Tom nodded to him as Bob Tate pulled alongside.

"Nothin' like a five-mile romp ta knock the edge off 'em!" yelled a smiling Print.

Tom nodded and pushed his horse just a little ahead of his uncle's big chestnut. Print responded by pulling up even to Tom.

"Figger out who's gonna be the caporal of this mob?"

Tom pointed to the lead horse churning out in front, "That gray mare!" he yelled. "Maybe the piebald next to her. Either one."

Print nodded at Tom's assessment. "You can ease up a bit, but let's keep 'em moving. We'll water 'em at the north end of the lake. I want 'em good an' tired when we make camp tonight."

Print peeled off and headed back toward the rear of the herd, checking with the outriders.

That afternoon the herd walked into a meadow on the north edge of Malheur Lake, tired and ready to graze. The men went about setting up camp for the night, while two stayed in the saddle, slowly walking around the herd, easing back in any that wanted to feed elsewhere.

Print had already tended to the packhorses and was busy cooking as the cowboys hauled their gear around the fire. It was still hours until sunset, but the day had worked up an appetite for both the herd and the men. Tom and another hand dropped a load of wood beside the cook fire for Print.

"Hope you boys are hungry. Thought I'd do 'er up a little special tonight. Figger this'll be the last company we'll have for a while."

The coffeepot was passed around. A pot of beans bubbled beside the fire, and set in a ring of coals off to the side was a Dutch oven. A big skillet filled with beefsteaks sputtered as Print sliced an onion and sprinkled the rings over the steaks.

"Trick to makin' a good pot a beans is a quarter stick of Mexican vanilla, a big slug of blackstrap molasses, an' a strong jolt of bug juice," said Print as he stirred the pot. He lifted the wooden spoon, licked it, and then stirred the pot again.

He stood up and looked to the south. A creek

where the horses watered ran into a marsh and beyond that was the lake. Snowy egrets and cranes stalked about in the salt grass. Hundreds of terns would take flight and then immediately drop down again as another flock would take off and then land. Pintails wheeled in the sky overhead, and way out on the lake a vee of Canada geese crossed over. Beyond that lay the Steens, their ridgelines and crevices white with snow. He reached down and tossed a couple of pieces of old juniper on the fire. With a long fork, he flipped the steaks as the wood caught fire and popped.

The men sidled up to the fire with tin plates and forks in hand.

"Looks like first-rate grub tonight, Mr. Ritter," said one of the hands.

"Boys, the culinary procedures I have implemented tonight do not fall under the category of 'grub.' Nor 'chuck,' for that matter. No, sir,"replied Print.

Using his wadded-up kerchief, he pulled the Dutch oven from the coals and removed the lid to reveal big, puffy brown biscuits. With the long fork, he slapped grilled steaks onto each man's plate as they helped themselves to beans and biscuits. Print wadded up the bloody, brown paper that the meat had been in and tossed it into the fire.

The camp grew silent save the clinking of forks on tin plates as Tom approached.

"Grab a plate, son," said Print. "Havin' beefsteak for supper will be few an' far between on this trip."

Tom took a plate and fork and helped himself. "I hobbled those lead mares. I think they're all tired enough, but we might as well take advantage of the extra help tonight to watch over 'em," said Tom, piling beans over his steak.

He sat down and took out his large pocketknife

to cut up his steak. Print poured drippings from the skillet into his plate and hooked crispy onion rings onto the big fork. He sat down and sopped up the drippings with a biscuit, ate the onion rings, and licked his fingers.

"Boys, we'll be passin' north of the Circle Bar 'bout noon tomorrow. Guess that's the best jumpin' off spot for you," said Print, popping the last of the greasy biscuit into his mouth.

"Mr. Ritter, would ya mind if Bob an' I skinned outta here after supper? We'd like to pull for the ranch tonight, if ya don't mind," said a tall, tow-headed lad.

Print looked at them and then smiled. "Guess not, boys. Can't be you're in a hurry to catch up on yer chores?"

"No, sir," smiled the lad.

"Couldn't be there's some pretty felines in Princeton needin' attention? Well, be careful boys. . . . Remember what happen'd ta Adam at the apple sale."

"Yes, sir."

"I'll get you yer wages," said Print.

"That's all right, Mr. Ritter, you can settle up with Pete. He'll get it to us."

"You boys are in a sweat. Good enough. Thanks fer the help."

"See ya in the fall, Mr. Ritter."

Print nodded and touched the brim of his hat. He turned to the others. "A meal this fine oughta be that the cook don't hafta clean up. Gentlemen, it's all yours."

Print took out his penknife from a vest pocket and a piece of wood to whittle on. Soon the camp settled down. The fire was fed. Overhead was the sound of snipes in flight, and out on the lake a trumpeter swan called out in the dark.

"Lonely drake out there," said Print to Tom.

Tom nodded.

"Not bad for the first day."

"For the first day," added Tom.

A breakfast of leftover beans and coffee and the men had the horses on the move as light was just seeping into the eastern sky. By noon they had gotten the herd to just north of the Circle Bar Ranch. As they approached, they saw a lone figure mounted and waiting for them in the brush. Tom brought the herd to a stop and, with Print, rode over to the waiting rider.

He was turned out like much of the rest of the hands, still wearing his winter woollies chaps. He looked pale and raised his hand to motion them to stop when they got close to him.

"Morning," said the young man.

"Not much of it left," said Print.

"Name's Billy Via. I thought ya might be looking for help."

"Well, Billy Via, I'm Print Ritter, and this is my nephew, Tom. We're not local. We're headin' ta Wyoming and we're not takin' on any hands at this time."

"Yes, sir, I know. Bub Waters told me. They came in late last night . . . from Princeton."

"No worse for the wear?" asked Print.

"No, sir."

"Sorry we can't help ya, son. We're workin' on a kinda tight purse on this deal," said Print.

"I understand, sir, but I won't cost ya much. I could really use the job, sir."

"You in trouble?" asked Tom.

Tom and Print waited.

"Not exactly. . . . See, I had a pretty bad wreck a couple years back. A bad'n went up an' over on me. Busted my appendix. Doctor got that taken care of, but my gut was torn and he couldn't stitch 'er, so he left a hole."

"A hole?" asked Tom.

"Yes, sir. Thing is, it never really healed up."

Again the men waited in silence.

"It never did sort itself out an' now it just leaks."

"Leaks?"

"Yes, sir. It leaks."

"What's it leak?" asked Tom.

"Shit, mostly, sir."

"Shit?"

"Yes, sir. Mostly."

"I really don't see how we can help ya, son. We ain't doctors," said Print.

"No, sir. I don't need a doctor. I got it under control. I keep it covered an' change the towels regular. I am clean in all my habits, sir. My problem is the smell, sir."

"The smell?"

"Yes, sir. It's a heinous odor to it. Ungodly, really. I'm used to it, but it is hard on others. Can't hold a job being anywhere 'round other hands. Not even sleepin' out in the barn."

Tom shifted his weight in the saddle and looked at Print. It was all they could do to keep from grinning.

"Well, we ain't deprived in the smelling department either, son," said Print.

Billy looked away and then back at them. "No, sir. I know that, but I figgered an outdoor job like this might work out okay. I'll stay off by myself. Make my own camp away from you. Tend ta myself. I'll stay downwind of ya. I can handle horses with the best of 'em. Ask the boys. They ain't got it in fer me, they just can't stand the smell."

Print looked at Tom for his thoughts and then at Billy "I don't know, son. I'd like ta help, but I just don't know . . ."

"I'm about at the end of my string, sir. I'll make it work for ya."

"An' if it don't?" asked Tom.

"You'll get no argument from me. I'll move on."

"Just like that?" asked Tom.

"Yes, sir. Just like that."

Tom turned to Print. "Your call, Uncle."

Print brushed his moustache with his finger. "Okay, Billy Via, we'll try it out for a while. Come on."

The young man grinned and got some color back in his face.

"I'll just stay here 'til you've settled up with the boys."

Print and Tom turned their horses back to the waiting herd.

"What if the wind changes in the night?" asked Tom.

Print chuckled. As they approached, the men gathered around them. "Guess it's time to pay you, boys."

"Yer gonna have yer hands full, Mr. Ritter. Sure ya don't want us to go along? At least for a few days?" asked the rangy cowboy.

"I think we got a handle on it, boys. 'Sides, I just took on a man."

"Billy Via?" asked the cowboy.

Print and Tom both looked over their shoulder at the young man on his horse where they had left him. They turned back to the cowboy.

"He's a good hand, but . . ."

"But . . . ? Ya mean the smell?" asked Tom.

"Sir, it's like dummy foals. There's some things that just wasn't intended to live. I'd say Billy's one of 'em."

Print looked at the man for a long moment. "We'll see."

Chapter Five

The figure stopped in front of Old Saint Mary's to strike a match. He lit the cheroot and puffed as the church bells rang out the hour. The heavy fog that had rolled in seemed to flatten the pealing of the church's bells. He puffed again and looked up at the cathedral's facade.

By the light of the street lamp, he read the words chiseled over the entryway: SON, OBSERVE THE TIME . . . AND FLY FROM EVIL. He flicked out the match, took another puff, and turned up the frayed collar on his coat. Another figure, much shorter, came up to him from behind. The smaller man stopped only momentarily and then seemed to glide across the street. The first man stepped off the curb and crossed Grant Avenue, following the little man. He disappeared into the fog and the darkness. He could hear the clanking of the streetcar over on Powell Street. It was all he could do to keep sight of the little specter. At one point it stopped, waiting, and then moved on, heading for Chinatown.

He could smell the cooking from the Asian quarter. It masked the tainted air of Chinatown. The little specter stopped again, waiting, then ducked into an alley that led to another. He turned the last corner and heard a knocking sound. A door opened, and a light shone on the little Chinaman who had brought him there. He entered, then turned to see his guide slip away. Two Chinamen motioned him to follow them down a hallway that led to a door behind which stairs descended to a large room.

The room was filled with Asiatics. There was a line of shivering, naked girls in the process of being washed and scrubbed by several old women. The steamy room smelled of lye soap. Other women were dressing girls, scolding and chattering as they outfitted the young women. A woman shuffled over to the visitor.

"You come to buy?" she asked.

"I have," he replied.

"Good, good. You got money, I got girls."

"I got money."

"How many you want?"

"Five," he said, raising his hand with spread fingers.

"Good. Any you want?"

"Five virgins. Virgins. Guaranteed. Five. You understand?"

The woman nodded. "No problem. Can do. Five virgins. You pick."

He stepped forward, inspecting the girls who cowered, dripping and frightened. If they turned away or covered themselves, he would jerk them around to stand and face him.

"I'll take this one . . . and her." He pulled them out of the wash line. He turned to the girls who were dressed. He opened the front of their pajamas one at a time. One girl clutched her robe and he slapped her hard across the face. The woman who was selling stepped between them and slapped the girl even harder. The woman opened the front of the girl's pajamas.

"You like?"

"She's a virgin?" he asked.

"Absolute. Absolute virgin. You like? Pretty girl. She make you much money. You like?"

"Maybe."

"You like her. I know. I make you good price. She lucky girl. Make you lucky man."

He moved on, picking three more girls. "All virgins. You guarantee."

"Yes, yes," the eager woman replied.

She waved two old hags over to her and pointed out the girls. The old women sat one of the naked girls on a chair and spread her legs apart. She poked and prodded and peered about the young girl's crotch. She nodded and another girl was seated. When the fourth girl was inspected, the crouching old woman said something to the seller and the girl was yanked away.

"No virgin. No sale. You pick," she said. "What about lucky girl?"

The woman dragged the girl to the chair and sat her down. The girl had seen what had happened to the other girls and still she struggled. All three of the older women slapped and hit her about the face and head. The frantic seller growled something at the girl. The girl reluctantly complied. The women checked her carefully and nodded yes.

The seller tried to compose herself as she turned to the man, who was thoroughly enjoying the medical exam.

"She make much moneys for you."

"I'm not sure."

"Oh, yes. Lucky girl for you. I give you very good price."

The man smiled. His mouth was full of rotten yellow teeth.

The woman reached inside the folds of her robe and pulled out a small leather flask. She pantomimed opening it and tipping its mouth on her forefinger. She turned to the "lucky girl" and opened the front of her pajamas. The girl struggled; her pants were still around her ankles. The woman grabbed the left breast of the young girl, squeezing it hard. Tears of pain came to her eyes. With gritted teeth, the woman mimed rubbing the flask's contents on the girl's nipple.

"Good time, boy. Kiss, kiss. Love, love lucky girl."

The man stared at her.

"Good time, boy, kiss, kiss," she said.

She released the girl's breast and at the same time snapped her fingers loudly. She closed her eyes and cocked her head to the side as if she were asleep. She then looked up to see if the man understood. He grinned and nodded.

"Nipple knockout drops," he shook his head. "A Mickey Finn from mother's milk," he laughed.

The woman didn't understand him but laughed even louder. She handed the flask to him.

"You take. You take. Five girls. Take. Take." She pressed the flask to his chest.

"Okay. I take. How much for you?" he asked.

The woman looked confused.

"Now how much for you? You. You," he said, smiling at her.

The woman's eyes were locked on the rows of rotten teeth in his mouth. She forced a smile.

"You got no humor, lady."

"You funny fellow."

"Yeah, me funny fellow. I better be a "lucky" funny fella, you old Chiney whore. If these girls ain't on the up-an'-up, I'll buy your bony ass from

Wu Ta and take you down to Bodie. Those miners 'ill wear you out in a week, old woman."

The woman acted as if she didn't understand him. Her eyes darted from his teeth to the long billfold he removed from his coat. Then back to the rotten teeth and then to the billfold.

"I'll be back for them tomorrow night."

"Yes, yes."

He paid her off and took the flask. He followed the two men back to the door at the alley. They opened it and the little phantom was there waiting for him. He started into the foggy night. He called to the little man to halt. He unbuttoned his pants to relieve himself. The alley filled with the odor of his urine. He could smell the rum in it that he had been drinking most of the day.

Chapter Six

The herd was on the move with Tom moving up and down one side and Print flanking on the other. Billy brought up the rear with the packhorses. The plan was to head in the direction of Jordan Valley. Print had decided to bypass the Crowleys' place by heading a little more south and pushing to get to the river's edge of the Owyhee to let them graze. Print rode through the moving herd and over to Tom.

"W're makin' great time, but we're gonna have ta ease up in the next day or so. We got no idea what the forage will be like out there. The Moncrieffes won't pay for hide an' hoof?"

"I ain't pushin' them. They seem plenty up for it," replied Tom. "They're mor'n up for it. Thing is, they don't care what price they bring."

Print looked up at the sun's position. "Let's keep movin'. No stoppin' at noon. Let's wait until two an' then they can have a good, long graze. Billy okay?"

Tom shrugged. "He seems content to eat dust. I figger he'll let us know when he's had enough."

Print moved back through the herd to take up his position on the other side.

Not long after two in the afternoon, Print brought

the herd to a halt. He raised up in the saddle, looking around to get his bearings. He sat back down and trotted off to the south. A couple hundred yards away, he waved for Tom and Billy to move the horses to him.

As the horses milled about, Tom rode over to his uncle while Billy hung back. The trailing dust washed over them.

"Plenty of grass here. We'll call it a day. Let's set up over there," he said, pointing to a deep cut in the ground.

"What's that?"

"A cave. Camped here many a night. Nice an' cozy."

"Not too cozy, I hope," said Tom as he looked over his shoulder in the direction of Billy.

"I'd only sleep in it if the weather turns. No, it's just a good spot to camp. I'm gonna ride out a bit while you two set up."

"Sure ya don't need company?"

Print smiled. "No. Just pay attention to the prevailing wind."

Print squeezed Bob Tate and headed off to the east. He liked prowling around while the others set up camp. It was one of the few rights he felt he earned with his age.

The grass was good here, and the herd needed all they could get. He had no idea what was ahead for them. The spring sun felt good on his back. High overhead raptors were riding the thermals. The range was really budding up, he thought. Purple clumps of Russian thistle mixed in with yellow rabbitbrush stretched out as far as one could see. Desert primrose was in abundance. Way off the forms of several pronghorns undulated in the heat waves rising off the basin's floor.

It is so big out here, he thought, you didn't even

have to think. Its vastness just sops the thoughts right out of your head. To him it was bigger than anything he had ever seen. Bigger than the prairies east of the Rockies. Bigger than the ocean. He had been to Seattle once, but never to sea. That was another thing his curiosity had wanted him to do. He had often thought that he was a sailor. He knew why seamen thought and talked of their ships in the first person. He had talked to all the cow ponies whose ears he had looked between and steered all over the endless West. Of course, it wasn't endless, but then neither were the oceans. But somehow the desert range of the Great Basin seemed that way. It left a nice, quiet ache in you. The older a man got, the more he seemed to go for plainer and simpler. He let Bob Tate pick his own way. The sun worked its way through his coat. His mind just bled out.

"'Bout time the cook got back," said Tom as Print dismounted.

He untied a bunch of wild onion he had picked. With one hand he undid the cinch strap and hauled the saddle off the big horse's back. He walked to the fire, dropping the saddle and handing the onions to Tom. He went back to his horse and removed the blanket and slipped off the bridle. The chestnut stood for a moment and then took off to go give himself a good roll in the dirt.

"One day he might take off for good."

Print turned to his nephew. "Not as long as I keep givin' him my fritters soaked in bug juice. Let's see what we can whip up tonight."

The day had turned to evening, but the ground still held the sun's warmth. Print had fed them boiled pork with chopped-up onions, prunes, beans, biscuits, and gravy. Tom poured a cup of coffee as his uncle tamped tobacco into his pipe.

"Did ya take a look in the cave?"

"Not much."

"If ya go way back in there, they say there's a lake with blind fish in it."

"Ever eat one?"

"Na. Don't think I could work up much of an appetite for blind fish."

"Saw some figgers on the walls. A few bones. Lotta soot from fires."

"Been all sorts of folks through here. Know how this range got its name?"

"Not really."

Print poured a little whiskey into his tin cup from a bottle under his saddle blanket. He offered it to Tom, who declined.

"Takes the ache outta an old man's hands. It was Frenchys, French trappers that come into this region long time ago. Seems they'd bought a string of native fellas from the islands off a sea captain down the coast. Captain had swapped 'em out for some truck he was freightin' back from the Orient."

"How much of this am I supposed to swallow?" asked Tom as he tossed a few sticks on the fire.

"All 'r none. It's up ta you. But it is the truth, historical truth."

Tom stretched out, laying his head in the seat of his saddle. He tilted his hat over his face. "Go on. I'm listening."

"Well, the old salt puts in somewheres down near San Francisco. This was a long time ago, near a hundr'd years ago. So the Frenchys swaps a hefty load of beaver pelts for this gang of native boys."

"Why would they do that?"

"I'm gettin' there. They was plannin' on bringing them up north ta skin out and tan the hides an' pelts they took. Give the dusky boys the dirty work."

"What would they know about beaver pelts?"

"Well, there ya go. 'Course they didn't. They had

no knowledge or need for beaver pelts, or any other fur, for that matter. They come from a nation of nearly hairless people, 'cept for their heads. There's more hair on a hen's egg than was on those folks. 'Sides, it's so damn hot back in their lands, they hardly have need for any clothes."

"Sound like poor folks for the fur trade."

"Tell that ta the Frenchys. Had they been after fish, or seashells, or coconuts, they might have been on the right track."

Print belched slightly. Tom tipped up the brim of his hat to look over at his uncle. Print shrugged and puffed his pipe.

"Ain't much callin' for coconut peelers up here."

"Somewheres in all this, you're gonna reveal how the range got named?"

"Well, the frogs brought those poor lads up here. Guess they started them in on jackrabbits an' coy'ot, 'cuz things was pretty thin in the beaver department 'round here."

Both men chuckled.

"It ain't really funny when ya think about it. Imagine what was goin' through the minds of those poor souls. Never seen a snowflake back home and they get hauled up here just in time for winter."

"So what happened to them?"

"They lasted 'bout as long as spit in that fire. They never made it to Thanksgiving in their new country, I'm sure. But leave it to the frogs to put a shine on their endeavors, even their screwups. An' they are an arrogant people when it comes to other folks' language. They named this the Great Owyhee Range after them pitiful, brokenhearted lads from Hawai'i."

Print sipped the last dram from his cup.

"You gonna have a story every night, Uncle?"

"I might. You might wind up a fairly educated fella 'time we get to Sheridan."

Tom pushed his hat back and sat up. "Think I'll have a touch of that," he said, holding out his cup.

Print poured whiskey into the cup, looked over at Billy, who was sitting off a ways. "He's a respectful lad, I'll say that."

"He don't seem to have much choice. Have ya got a whiff of him yet?" asked Tom, looking at the cowboy finishing the last of his supper.

"Nope. Maybe it ain't that bad."

Print struck a match and sucked deeply on the pipe, puffing a thick cloud of smoke around his face. He flicked the spent match into the fire. "Hey, Billy, how 'bout some more chuck?"

The young cowboy, sitting cross-legged, looked up. "Thanks, Mr. Ritter. Think I've had my fill."

"Well, come on over and get yerself some coffee. I hate wastin' coffee."

Billy rose and came over to their fire and squatted to get the coffeepot. Instinctively his hand went to his side. He poured himself a cup and stood. Tom was the first one to get a whiff and then Print. It wasn't as bad as he had thought it would be, but it wasn't that good either. Both men tried to pretend that they couldn't smell him. But Billy was keenly sensitive to how his presence affected others. He took a sip, then said, "I'll stay up with the horses. You fellas get some sleep."

As he walked away, he turned, "Thanks, Mr. Ritter, Tom."

"You bet, son. Check the hobbles on those lead mares."

"Yes, sir."

Print took out the figurine he had been whittling on from a vest pocket and then his pocketknife. Tom rolled a smoke.

"Don't be too free with those invites, Uncle. That's enough to make yer eyes water."

Print took a puff and scraped the little wooden horse with his blade. "I smelled worse, lots worse."

"Like what?"

Print quit whittling and looked into the dark at the departing young man. "Oh, like a dozen men cut ta pieces by a round a grapeshot. They done more than just leak shit. Yes, sir."

Tom lit his smoke and Print looked up into the evening sky.

"Somethin' about a starry night that just jerks yer head up, ya can't help it."

Tom exhaled and looked up too. "He seems like a pretty good hand."

"Yes, he does."

Print took a sip from his cup and Tom poked at the fire.

Chapter Seven

They were making good distance, considering the bleak land they were traveling through. They had crossed Duck Creek, the Owyhee, and Cow Creek. They had put Jordan Valley behind them and crossed into Idaho. They had done all that without losing a horse, although several were gimpy. Billy was more than pulling his own, and most of the time, uncle and nephew hardly knew he was there. The weather had held. They did get snowed on just south of the Mahogany Mountains. It was just a dusting and kept the herd fresh,

They made camp on the bank of Reynolds Creek and could see the lights of Silver City off to the east. Print dropped a load of broken sagebrush on the fire, then stepped back as it popped and flared.

"Time to reprovision. Thought we might go inta town in the morning. Hey, Billy, think you can handle things if we go into town for supplies in the mornin'?"

Out in the darkness, Billy called back. "Yes, sir. No problem."

"Anything you want while we're in there?"

Silence.

"You already got wages due ya, son, whatta ya need?"

"I could use some cotton cloth or towels if they got any, sir. Some makings maybe."

"That's it?"

"Yes, sir."

"How 'bout a pretty little hurdy-gurdy gal?"

"No, sir, Not unless she's got a busted sniffer."

"What about one of them squaws that's had their nose cut off? Would that do?" asked Tom.

"I don't believe so, Tom. I think you'd just have two people that was fairly unattracted to one another."

"That doctor didn't take off mor'n your appendix, did he?"

Silence.

"We're just givin' ya a little raze, son. No slight intended."

"Yes, sir. I know."

"Well, when we're in town, we'll do an inventory of the felines, an' if we find one with a malfunctioning snout, we'll set you up. How does that sound?"

"I'd be most grateful, sir, but I won't hold my breath waiting." Billy laughed at his own joke and the men joined in.

The next day Print saddled up the red roan he had ridden back at the round barn and Tom rode a mousy gray. Billy was picking up firewood as they rode off. It was a raw day that kept threatening bad weather. The herd was bunched up with their asses into the wind. The two rode in silence most of the way to town.

Silver City was a mining town that sort of ran uphill in several directions. It was past its glory days but still an active camp.

They walked their horses up to the front of the Idaho Hotel where a clerk was sweeping its front boardwalk. They watched as the man swept dirt and kicked dried chunks of mud into the street. One good-sized clod landed between the feet of the mousy gray. The gray snorted and the sweeper looked up.

"Gentlemen."

Both men nodded.

"If it's rooms you want, we're all booked up. Mine engineers out from Minnesota, here all month. Might try the War Eagle down the street."

"No rooms, thanks. We're here for supplies and a quiet drink."

"Whiskey and quietness we got. Constable an' the deputy board with us, so we never have trouble."

"What about supplies?" asked Tom.

"Mister, this is Silver City. We got four mercantiles, two hotels, three churches, a brewery, an' a carbolic acid factory—let alone the parlor houses and emporiums."

"Real up to date."

"If it's supplies you're lookin' for, Cosgrove's should have what ya want. He don't gouge too much. . . . About that drink. We got good rye whiskey right through them doors." He pointed with the broom handle to the entrance of the hotel. Both men dismounted and loosened their cinch straps.

"Nephew, it has occurred to me that I have overlooked an important item for this trip, and that's a decent shotgun. There's too much game on the wing for us to be passin' up. We can't be stoppin' in every town along the way ta feed ourselves."

Print took a coin purse from his vest and handed Tom a gold double eagle. "See what ya can find and I'll meet you over at this Mr. Cosgrove's, the man that don't gouge too much," he said, looking at the hotel clerk. "An' get plenty of shells too."

"Might try the constable's office. He complements his town salary sellin' confiscated weaponry. He don't gouge too much either," interjected the sweeper.

Print looked up at the clerk. "You'll speak up if ya see us doin' business with any fellas that *does* gouge too much, won't ya?"

"Surely."

Tom walked up the street, leading his horse in the direction of the constable's office. Print went in the other direction with the red roan.

Shortly, Tom emerged with a long-barreled side-by-side that had been well taken care of by its previous owner, a gentleman from Indianapolis who thought that because he was out West, it was acceptable to urinate in the street, even on Sunday morning when folks were going off to church. Short on cash, the reasonable constable of Silver City accepted the thoughtless pisser's shotgun to cover his fine.

The cold weather had given way to a warming sun. Tom flipped open a saddlebag and took out a soiled rag and stuffed two boxes of shells inside. He broke open the shotgun, wrapped the cloth around it, and tied it behind his saddle. First the stock and then the barrels. From down a side street, he could hear someone plinking on a badly tuned piano. The sound reminded him he was thirsty. Leading the mousy gray, he decided to investigate.

The magistrates of Silver City had obviously done a lot of thinking when laying out the town. The churches commanded the high ground, and the objects of their Sunday sermons were more or less confined to down below, symbolism not lost on their parishioners.

The keyboard music emanated from a building that wore a sign, "The Lemon Drop." Under that, in slightly smaller lettering, "Fresh and Tart." Tom set his course for the hitching post in front.

Parked at a slant in front of the Lemon Drop was a wagon. It was a cross between a prairie schooner and a city freight wagon, four iron hoops topped with canvas with its sides rolled up. Inside sat four Chinese girls. They looked road weary with more than a sprinkling of dust. Tom barely gave them a look as he tied his horse directly in front of the window. He made sure that he could keep an eye on him from inside.

He entered a long, deep room seemingly lit by the light from the windows and doorway. Business was slow at that hour, with only a card game in the back and one other cowboy at the bar. Several women in the back, dressed as if they were expecting a hot spell, watched the card game that seemed to have come to a halt as a rat-faced fellow with a stewpot hat was showing off a small Chinese girl to the card players. Tom could not hear what was being said, but his sense of it was that the men were more interested in getting on with the game but listened patiently. Tom turned to the bartender, a balding chap with a clean apron tied fast.

"Whiskey, please."

"Glass or bottle?"

"Glass."

The bartender placed a thick glass between them and poured. Tom emptied the tumbler. Neither fast, nor slow, but completely. He placed it on the countertop. The bartender slightly dipped his head in the direction of the empty glass. Tom savored the full effect of that first jolt and then nodded yes. The barkeep lifted the glass and wiped the bar with a rag. He set the glass back down and filled it to the brim. Tom placed a silver dollar on the bar and drank the second whiskey at an even slower rate.

He looked out the window. The mousy gray was

still tied and sleeping. He ordered a third round as one of the girls who had been watching the game sidled up to him.

"Buy a girl a drink?"

Tom looked down at her, trying to calculate how much longer his uncle would be shopping. "Why not?"

She raised her hand to the bartender. "Otto?"

She was pretty enough. More than pretty. It was hard to put an age on her. Her yellow curls were gathered up on top of her head and she wore a kind of clothing that Tom was not sure was outer- or underwear. She had a black ribbon tied around her throat and wore dark purple stockings that were striped. She had an uncomplicated face, and when she smiled, she seemed to be in possession of all her teeth. She had big, billowy breasts whose primary job seemed to be that of holding up her dress. She smelled of lavender. Otto the bartender interrupted Tom's assessment.

"Here."

"Lemonade?"

She lifted the drink as if to salute. "Fresh and tart."

"One more whiskey."

Tom put another dollar down and they clinked glasses. As they each sipped their drinks, the lavender lemon drop reached down and ran her hand up the inside of Tom's thigh. It came to rest on his crotch and she left it there. Tom felt the heat rise in several different regions of his body.

"How 'bout some bareback ridin', cowboy?"

"Can't, I got people waitin' for me."

"Oh, come on. What's yer name?"

"Tom. Tom Harte."

The hydromechanics of Mother Nature were starting to work on Tom. She squeezed the growing bulge in her hand as she looked straight into his eyes. "Well, Tom Harte, I can have that sanded down in no time."

Tom was turning red from the neck up. It had suddenly gotten very warm in the darkened saloon, and it wasn't all from Otto's liquor.

"Damn it's been a while since a fella blushed over me. Come on, Tommy, let me take the tension outta your britches."

Her hand and the whiskey were making it hard for Tom to calculate the time he needed to rendezvous with Print. She kept a hard grip on his crotch and started making a circular motion with her wrist. "Come on, cowboy, that critter needs exercise."

Tom's problem with the math was giving way to her sense of logic. He finished his drink and, holding his hat in front of him, followed the yellow-haired lady who was so full of common sense. They walked toward the gymnasium out back, past the stalled card game and the rodent-faced man with the little girl.

Print was surveying the contents of Cosgrove's Mercantile, waiting for the proprietor to finish up with two round women wearing bonnets that were several years behind the current fashion. He looked at a basket of turnips on the floor. He pulled out a stub of a pencil and a piece of paper and made a note.

The ladies, with laden baskets, passed Print.

"Can I help ya, mister?"

"Yes, sir. I need flour, bacon, salt pork . . ."

"Whoa, hold on there. How much and what kind?"

"How 'bout ten pounds of flour, the kind that don't have weevils. Whatever configuration yer bacon an' salt pork comes in, I'll take ten pounds of that, each. Then six bags of Arbuckle's, two dozen sticks of Mexican vanilla, a sack of chili beans, six cans of evaporated milk, couple of jars of whatever jam ya got handy . . ."

The clerk was writing as fast as he could.

"Three tins of cut tobacco. Three plugs too, an' four boxes of therapeutic papers. Oh, yeah, I'd like a bag of yer turnips."

"Will that do it for you?"

"Whatta ya got in the way of cotton? Like toweling?"

"Right now, all I got is a bolt of cotton muslin. Got some bunting, but that's gonna cost a lot more."

"Got somethin' I can put all that in?"

"Will flour sacks do?"

"They'll do just fine."

"Three cents apiece."

Print gave him a hard look but said nothing. "Do you sell whiskey?"

"No, sir. Bug juice you can get 'round the corner at the Lemon Drop."

"How are their prices?"

"I wouldn't know. I'm of the Baptist faith. I do know a man's got the right to make a profit on his labor."

"Town seems ta be adhering to your way of thinkin'."

Print paid up. Weighted down with twelve cents' worth of flour sacks and goods, he carried his load out to the red roan. He tightened the cinch on the saddle and then tied the provisions to either side of the pony's shoulders by way of the horn. The young horse came to life and snorted.

"Easy there. Now ain't the time to get scar't of a couple of sacks of beans an' jam."

He stroked the pony's neck, waiting for him to relax, and when he heard the pony exhale in a way he wanted, he untied him and went in search of the Lemon Drop whiskey emporium. He saw Tom's horse tied up outside. He secured the roan and noticed the girls in the wagon next to him.

As he entered, he brought in a wisp of light and a smell of the old manure that had been ground into the dusty street baking in the sun. He saw Tom talking to a short woman with yellow hair. At his approach, Tom straightened up as if he had been waiting for Print for quite a while.

"Uncle, this is Miss Lucy Highsmith. Miss Highsmith, this is my uncle, Prentice Ritter."

Print tipped his hat. "My pleasure, Miss Highsmith. This coltish lad ain't leading you astray, I hope?"

"He was just givin' me a lecture on horsemanship."

"You be careful 'round him, ma'am. He tends to get overmounted at times."

"He was very enthusiastic in his demonstration, but he was quick about it."

Print shook his head. "As they say, 'Youth is wasted on the young.'"

"If you have something you'd like to add to the subject, we run a pretty fine equestrian school out back."

"Thank you for the offer, Miss Highsmith, but I better get my nephew back ta camp 'fore he signs up for yer next equitation class."

"In that case, I'll leave you two as I got new students waitin' for lessons. Giddyup."

The two men watched her disappear toward the back of the room.

Print turned to Otto. "A whiskey, please. What about you, mister bronc rider?"

"Sure."

Print sniffed. "Interestin' shade a lavender yer

wearin'. Or is that lilac?" He sniffed again. "No, definitely lavender."

"How long am I goin' to have to be hearing about this?"

"I figger at least 'til Lander."

They downed their drinks, ordered three bottles to go, and paid up.

Outside, Print shifted two of the sacks to Tom's horse. They mounted up and headed down the street that led to the edge of town.

"Tell me, nephew, did ya have ta wear yer spurs? Looked like a lot of spirit there."

"She was a nice lady, Uncle."

Print laughed out loud. "If she was a lady, she'd be tampin' a tambourine 'stead of a mattress."

With the lights of town behind them, they turned back to camp. They never even noticed the wagon filled with Chinese girls that bumped along to the east.

Chapter Eight

Print was ladling beans and rectified prunes onto plates with thick strips of bacon and biscuits. "Come on, boys. Get it while it's hot."

Tom took a plate and Billy, standing off a bit, came forward to take a plate and pour a cup of coffee. He walked away to sit on an old log by a clump of hackberry. The men ate in silence.

"Interestin' town there," said Print as he wiped his plate with a half a biscuit. "They sure seem preoccupied with who's gouging who." He took the biscuit for one last round on the plate. "It's been my experience that when ya come across people that are so concerned with other folks' transgressions, ya better watch out, 'cuz mor'n likely, that's what they got in store for you."

"Maybe it has to do with being a mining town. Men underground gouging rock outta the earth and the rest of the residents aboveground gouging the refined and minted ore outta the topsiders."

"Now that's a damn good theory, Tom. Gougers versus miners. I like it. I can see yer gettin' more educated by the mile."

"I think I came out all right on that shotgun."

"Ya did indeed. That's a fine piece of avian artillery ya picked up from the constable."

Tom placed his plate and fork into the big skillet that doubled as a washbasin and rummaged through the flour sacks until he found a box of therapeutic papers and headed off for his own clump of hackberry bushes.

Print added his plate to the skillet, stood up, and poured himself some coffee. "You fellas trying ta triangulate me?"

"How's that, Uncle?"

"Well, I got Billy leakin' off ta my right and you on my left, layin' cable just a little too close ta camp. I know we're on the trail, but ya might try an' make your privy farther from where we sleep."

"I think you'll survive."

"Survivin' ain't the point. By the way, the man guaranteed me those papers got no splinters in 'em."

"Beats buffalo grass or corncobs."

Print took a handful of grass and dirt and went to work on the skillet and plates. He then took the water bag and rinsed everything.

"Billy, get that little roan I rode yesterday up for me. Think I'll give Bob Tate another day off."

"Yes, sir, Mr. Ritter."

They had the herd moving, and by afternoon, they were coming off the Owyhee front. They skirted north of the Nickel Creek Mesa and were about to cross the confluence of Corral Creek and Currant Creek when Print heard a mustang stallion calling out from up in the rocks. Looking up he saw a little bay stallion with a band of about a half a dozen mares set back from him in a stand of junipers. He gigged the red roan into a lope in Tom's direction. He pulled up short beside his nephew.

"Look at that," he said, pointing up to the pile of big rocks that lay strewn below the mesa.

"Where'd he come from?" asked Tom.

"Wild mustang. See his mares off in the trees?"

The stallion called out again.

"He's bold as brass out here in the daylight."

"He figgers he's safe enough up in the rocks. Probably wants ta add to his harem."

"Not unless he's got cash money he ain't."

"If he makes a run at the herd, yer gonna have ta drive him off. Either that or shoot him."

"Why wait?"

Tom pulled out his cut-down Remington Rider from the saddle scabbard. He thumbed back the hammer to full cock, rolled the breechblock back to expose the chamber. He slid the big cartridge in and eased the breechblock back in place. He swung down out of the saddle and handed his reins to Print.

"Not sure that's necessary, Tom."

"I'm not gonna shoot him, just scare him off. I don't want to have to be looking back all day."

He raised the rifle, sighted down on the rock facing, above the bay mustang. The Remington roared and Tom was enveloped in smoke. The slug ricocheted off the stone wall, sending shards of granite flying. The stallion bolted toward the mares that were already flushed from the trees. The red roan was backing up with Print, who was trying to hold on to Tom's horse.

"Whoa, whoa. Easy there, easy."

Print looked toward the back of the herd for Billy. Billy was standing up in the stirrups. Print yelled to him. "It's all right, Billy. Don't let 'em run back on ya!"

Tom and Print watched the mustang and his mares disappear into the boulders.

"That oughta take the edge off any amorous ideas he might have."

"I'd rather scare him than have to shoot him."

Tom slid the Remington back into the scabbard, took the reins from Print, and mounted. The shot had sent several of the horses running off from the herd and they turned to gather them in.

That night they camped by a slow-moving little creek that had a small draw next to it that made it easy to keep the horses penned up. There was enough wild ryegrass for a night's grazing. With the packhorses and Bob Tate picketed behind them and a good fire going, they settled down for supper. Tom noticed that Billy was making his camp closer to them every night but still kept a respectful distance.

It was a moonless night, and downwind from the campfire, the little bay stallion breathed in an array of scents and odors. His girth was streaked from serum and puss that oozed from a wound on his withers. A strong colt had challenged him and kicked him high. A well-placed hoof had caught him at the base of his neck. He finally drove the determined suitor off, but two nights later, he came back. By then the swelling had turned into a corruption beneath the skin and it was so painful the stallion couldn't lower his head to graze. The challenger was content to leave with one mare.

The infection had eventually broken open, pouring down his sides. With it went most of the pain. The green-head flies were vicious and eventually drove him to roll in the deep sand of the creek bottoms. The wound was crusting over and the sharp pain had given way to a dull ache. Tonight he sniffed the air. He pawed the ground and called out to the herd in the draw.

All three men looked up at the sound of the little stallion. Billy walked over for some more coffee. Print filled the bowl of his pipe.

"Think I'll set up a while with ya, Billy. That ol' stud has got ever'thing on edge tonight."

"Whatever you like, Mr. Ritter. Mind if I change out my towel for some of that muslin you bought?"

"Help yourself."

Tom was field dressing the Remington. Print lit his pipe.

"Ever thought of upgrading ta somethin' a little more modern, like a repeater?"

"I'd rather spend my money on a new saddle."

"Well, how about somethin' that at least burned smokeless powder?"

"It serves my needs."

Print blew a puff of smoke and took out his knife and wood. Billy ripped off a length of the rough cotton and headed off for the darkness.

"Hear that?"

Tom looked up from his gun cleaning.

"Sounds like a curlew."

A two-note whistle followed by a rattle came from the direction of the creek.

"There he goes. Down in the cattails. Know the difference between a curlew and the snipe?"

Tom had gone back to cleaning his rifle. "No. Not something I think much about."

"Maybe ya should. Some knowledge of ornithology might come in handy."

Tom ran the oily rag down the length of the barrel. He looked over at his uncle. "Ornithology?"

"Sure, ornithology. The study of birds."

"The study of birds."

"Why sure. Think 'bout it. Next time ya pay a visit ta Miss Lucy Highsmith, ya can tell her all about the spoonbill an' the titmouse an' the red-headed woodpecker—not to be confused with the red-cock woodpecker. Might even throw in a dissertation on the double-breasted bed thrasher."

Tom was forced to chuckle.

"Why, ya got that sexy species, the sparrow. Ya got

the seedeater, the dickcissel, an' the soft-tailed. Probably no need ta bring up the thrush an' the western peewee."

Tom stared at him as he kept wiping the gun. "Where do you come up with all this?"

"I read, son, I read. *Audubon's Guide to Land and Water Birds.* I always got somethin' close at hand ta read."

Tom shook his head.

"Bet she's tired of hearin' all the theories of bareback ridin'. She might welcome a conversation about birds. Ornithology. Think about it."

The curlew called out again from the creek bank. Tom changed the subject. "Did you get a good look at the stallion today?"

Print stopped whittling and relit his pipe. "It's the Spanish in 'em. Mosta the wild horses ya come across out here is stock that was turned loose 'r wandered off. But he's the genuine article."

Print gestured with his pocketknife. "Bit of a Roman nose, big, high-set eyes, an' a great front end."

"Wouldn't mind coming back here an' catching some of his children."

"They been on the loose for a long time. When the Indians first laid eyes on 'em, they called them God Dogs."

"Maybe we could spend next summer up here gatherin' up some."

"Sure. But let's get yer herd delivered first."

"It's a damn sight more your herd than mine."

Print put away his pocketknife and figurine. He knocked his pipe against the heel of his boot. "I don't feel that way an' I don't think your ma would've either."

Tom pulled out the letter that Print had given him back on the first day. He opened it and leaned closer to the light of the dimming fire. He read aloud. "Tom, as you seem to have little interest in the homestead, I see no reason to burden you with its ownership. You are free to seek your own opportunities. Your mother."

Print let out a long, slow sigh, tugged on his earlobe, and looked off into the darkness. "Not very generous."

Tom folded the paper, slipped it into the envelope, and then into his shirt pocket. Print watched him. Tom looked up.

"She was plenty generous with the cane."

"Never knew the warmin' of a lad's backsides ta be the ruin of him."

"She enjoyed it a little too much. She never forgave me for runnin' off to buckaroo."

"Losin' yer pa made her a hard woman."

"She was hard before that."

Print said nothing.

"I always sent money home after every season."

"We get these horses ta Sheridan an' we'll come on up here next spring."

Billy had finished changing and walked off toward the herd. Print slipped off his boots and britches and untied his kerchief and stretched out. The fire had turned to coals. The night sky glowed with green bands of light that danced and waved overhead. Ribbons of red and soft yellow lit up between the green waves. The aurora borealis was putting on quite a show as the two men watched from their bedrolls.

"Whenever I see them lights up there, I think the old man up there ain't happy."

Print smiled to himself. "Funny. I always got the feelin' it meant he was sorta pleased."

Print pulled the bedroll up to his chin. "This is a great life—when it ain't rainin' or snowin'."

Chapter Nine

Print was riding at the head of the herd with Tom flanking off to the right and Billy not quite in the drag position, as the horses were tending to stay more or less bunched up. They were following an old wagon road that would eventually tie in to the north branch of the Oregon Trail.

They had crossed the Bruneau uneventfully, except one colt got to scrambling on the far bank and had pulled something and was pretty lame. He would either sort it out or not. Print never expected to get to Sheridan with all the horses.

They slowly hazed the herd up a long incline. As Print crested the brow of the low-slung rolling hill, he looked down, and in the distance, he could see what looked like a light freight wagon moving east. Off to the left, a hawk was skimming across the flat land. There was a puff as he hit a dove or a pigeon. He banked and slowly headed off with his meal.

Even at a slow pace, the herd was gaining on the wagon. In a half an hour, the herd was coming abreast of the wagon on its left. Inside, Print and Tom could see five young Chinese girls and a man at the reins wearing a stewpot hat. He brought the two mules pulling the wagon to a halt and looked over at the herd. Print waved to Tom to join him as he loped over to the wagon.

The girls sat silently in the back of the wagon, watching the two riders approach.

"Afternoon," said the driver with a mouthful of yellow teeth.

Print nodded and then looked over at the girls. "You off ta church?"

The driver grinned even wider, revealing gaps where several teeth had rotted down to the gums. "No, sir. No indeed. Name's Billy Fender. Capt'n Billy Fender."

Print continued to watch the girls.

"How 'bout you boys?"

Print turned to look at Fender. "Print Ritter. This is my nephew, Tom Harte."

"Quite a herd ya got there. You goin' ta Fort Hall?"

"No. You?"

"Well, gentlemen, I purchased, at great expense, five virgin exotics in San Francisco, direct and intact from the Celestial Empire. I got another two in Sacramento. I'm headin' ta the mining camps, where hard men will pay good money for the opportunity to deflower these little Mongolian blossoms."

Bob Tate stomped at flies on his leg. Print shifted in the saddle.

"The boys linin' up for seconds, thirds, an' fourths 'ill pay well too. I'll let you boys punch the sirloin. I aim ta make a tidy sum workin' the tenderloin."

Tom kept looking at Fender's mouth and thinking that he would probably stand a better chance being bitten by a rattler than having this fellow sink his incisors into him.

"We seem ta be headin' in the same direction. Mind if I share the trail with ya? Conversation's been a bit thin," he said, jerking his head in the direction of the girls.

Print looked at Tom. Tom shrugged. He looked back at Fender. "We're workin' a faster pace than you. You'll be in our dust most of the time."

"Dirt never bothered me."

"Suit yerself."

He struck Tom as the type who had a deep-seated aversion to soap and water.

Print and Tom turned their horses back toward the herd. Tom pulled aside Print. "Why let him tag along?"

"What's my choice? I can't rule him off the range. I'd rather know where a fella like that is 'stead of worryin' where he might pop up. He'll tire of our dust soon enough."

Print kept the herd moving for the rest of the day, rather than stopping early to let them graze. The distance between the herd and the wagon grew, and as the sun cast long shadows out in front of them, the wagon was out of sight.

They had made camp and were cooking two good-sized rabbits that Billy had picked off when they heard the wagon approach in the dark. Fender called out, "I'll set up my own camp over here."

Print gestured with the wooden spoon he was using to stir the pot of beans. "Just don't spook the horses. Might want ta tell those girls ta steer clear of the herd."

Fender laughed. "I'd have better luck talkin' ta them mules. Don't worry 'bout the Celestials, they'll nest right under the wagon."

"We got a couple a rabbits if ya want ta join us," said Print.

"A kind offer, Mr. Ritter. You fellas pull a cork?"

"I'll have a sip at night. Good for the arthritis."

Fender had the girls pulling wood from the

cooney, slung under the wagon, and soon had his own fire going. The girls seemed to know the drill and went about preparing their own supper. Fender joined Print and Tom. He offered a bottle of whiskey, pouring some into the men's tin cups. He drank from the bottle.

Print took a sip and then ladled out beans on a plate. He added biscuits and a leg of cooked rabbit. Fender took the rabbit and tore into it with his rotten teeth. Warm grease dripped down his chin. "Oh, that's good."

He sputtered as bits of food flew in the direction of the fire. He held the plate to his mouth and shoveled in beans and stuffed a whole biscuit in behind the beans. Mashed food seeped out of the corner of his mouth, which he wiped away with the back of his hand. He licked the residue with his tongue. He took a long pull on the bottle, looked into the fire, and gave a loud belch. "Ya'll set a fine table."

"What about the girls?" asked Print.

"Pickier eaters y'all never find. Rice eaters, but that's okay, I didn't buy 'em for their eatin' habits."

Print took another sip and Tom placed his unfinished plate of food by the fire's edge.

"There's a lotta expense attendant ta these gals. They're dumb as dirt at understandin' English an' want ta wash themselves ever' day. Ha! I'd like ta see them out on the prairie soapin' up their little powder puffs come the new year. They'll learn. But that won't be my concern as I'll be cashed outta this deal by then."

Print took out his pipe and tobacco. Tom sipped from his cup but didn't return to his plate. "Thought you said you bought seven girls."

"Did. Had ta sell one ta help with the travelin' expenses and one just up an' died on me. As a businessman, ya have to expect som' percentage of spoilage of yer inventory."

Fender rose and recharged the men's cups. He took a swig and raised the bottle. "Travel with equals or travel alone, I always say."

Print saw that the girls were watching them closely. He took out the little wooden horse he was whittling and went to work on it with his knife.

"How'd you come to be a capt'n?" Tom asked.

"Well, it's more an honorary title given me for services rendered with the home guard back 'n Arkansas."

Both men took him for the liar he was. They all looked up at the sound of Billy approaching in the darkness. Tom noticed the girls draw together. "Billy, grab a plate. Want a short snort?"

"No, thank you, sir. It tends to irritate my problem."

"Billy, this here's Capt'n Fender. Fender, Billy Via."

"Captain Fender," said Billy as he piled on the biscuits. "I'm gonna go back to the horses. They're acting a bit edgy tonight."

"It's the mules," said Tom.

As he carefully walked away with coffee in one hand and his plate piled high in the other, he glanced over at the girls, who were watching him. Coyotes yapped out in the night.

"Nice young man," said Print. "Got a leakage problem. That's what that smell comes from."

Fender looked up from his plate. "I don't smell nothin'. Stench don't bother me a'tall. 'Cept rancid butter. A whiff a rancid butter'll turn my insides every time."

He tossed his empty plate on the ground and picked up his bottle. "I don't mind tellin' you boys I got a problem. These girls was all virgins when I bought 'em, but since leavin' San Francisco, I've deflowered two of 'em, cuttin' down on their enhanced value considerably."

"Enhanced value?" asked Tom with a look on his face as if he smelled something a lot worse than Billy.

"Sure. Uncharted territory. A one-time prize. Must be an acquired taste, I like a gal that already knows what she's doin', but some men will pay well to take the first slice of the cake. So, ya see, now close ta forty percent of my existin' inventory is slightly used."

Print took out his pipe and tobacco. Tom had never been to San Francisco and wondered if it was populated with more rodents like this Fender.

Fender took another swig and offered the bottle to the two men. Both declined. Fender rolled on, oblivious to the fact that the two men in front of him were drawing some hard and irrefutable impressions of him.

"Now that littlest Chink, with the itty-bitty feet, cost as much as two of the others. Those Mongolian bastards break their toes an' fold 'em under an' then bind 'em up tighter than Dick's hat band. Now is that heathen savagery fer ya?"

"Guess they're lucky to have you come along an' save 'em," said Print without looking up from his carving.

"Well, I guess they are. They claim it gives 'em stronger sex'al urges. I have been assured that the men in the camps'll pay premium for her. Ain't much on independent locomotion. I wind up carryin' her ever'where."

Fender finally realized that he had been doing all the talking and that the other men seemed inordinately quiet. He gave them both a long look.

"If you boys are interest'd, I let ya have a stab at the 'almost' virgins for a dollar apiece."

Neither Print nor Tom said anything.

"Married men?"

They shook their heads.

"Bachelors? Well, I'm all fer bachelors. I always say that bachelors know more about women than married men, else they'd be married too."

Fender roared at his own joke and finished off the last of the bottle. He tossed the empty bottle back in the direction of his wagon. It hit the ground but didn't break. The girls flinched at the sound of the bottle. "Nother dead Indian."

With considerable effort, Fender rose and headed back to his wagon. The girls cringed at his approach. He attempted to dance a jig and nearly fell.

> "Oh, whiskey is the life of man.
> Always was since the world began.
> I'll drink it from an old tin can. . . ."

He slurred the words. He jumped to click his heels and almost fell again. The girls pulled themselves under the wagon. Tom turned to Print. "Hope you ain't planning on sharing the trail with him much longer. You think he really bought those girls?"

Print shrugged, looking over at Fender as he rummaged in the back of his wagon. "We'll put the distance on them tomorrow."

Fender threw back a canvas tarp and extracted another bottle of whiskey. He clenched the cork between his rotten teeth and pulled. With his back to the other camp, he removed from inside his coat the flask given him in Chinatown. He poured from it into the bottle. He slipped the flask deep in a pocket and turned and headed back to Print and Tom, pushing the cork into the bottle.

"Gentlemen, another bottle." He paused to dance a step. "I do love to dance."

He poured into Print's cup.

"Last one fer me,"

"Me too," said Tom, tossing the butt of his smoke into the fire.

"Of course, gentlemen. Let he who sins while drunk be punished when he's sober, I always say."

His little ferret eyes gleamed in the firelight. Print pressed the pocketknife against his thigh to close it and slipped the little wooden horse back in his vest pocket. I gotta stop being so friendly out here, he thought. Shit-bird like this one is nothing but trouble. Too bad about those girls.

He raised the cup to his lips and swallowed its contents.

Chapter Ten

Print dreamed he was sleeping in a hearth. It was cold and there was a terrible pain in his head. His mouth was full of cinders. It was the fireplace in the cabin of his youth. The cold would not let him sleep. He was looking up the chimney. It was long and dark with sunlight at the top. His bladder was full. He squinted and the chimney gave way to gray light. He rolled over and pain ran through his head. He thought he was going to be sick. He forced himself up on an elbow and looked around.

The herd was grazing, unconcerned about the change in weather. He saw Fender's wagon and the girls still huddled there, looking over at him. He rolled over onto all fours and rose. I'm gettin' too old for this shit, he thought. He looked down and saw Tom out to the world. He staggered away from the camp and unbuttoned his pants to relieve himself. The weather surely had changed. A cutting wind from the north had chilled the land. He buttoned up and felt for his money belt. It was gone. He felt again and turned back to his bedroll. His feet were swollen and hurt from sleeping with his boots on. He reached down and lifted the bedroll and shook it out.

"Tom! Tom! Wake up! That shit-bird stole my money belt."

Tom looked up at his uncle from his own dream. He heard him yelling, but he couldn't understand him. His uncle left, and he stared up at the sky. A moment later he returned and was pouring his canteen on him. He sat up.

"Tom, boy! Get up. That slit-bird Fender doctored the bug juice and swapped stock on us."

Print was filling the palm of his hand and slapping water in his own face, Tom stood, looked around, and then trotted gingerly in his stocking feet over to the girls.

"Where the hell's our money and our horses?" he screamed at the terrified girls.

"Easy, boy. They sure as shit didn't take 'em." Print slowly turned a complete circle, scanning the land, "Go get Billy."

Tom returned to his bedroll, "That spivvy li'l' shit took my boots!"

He whipped back his bedroll to reveal his carbine and their sidearms. "At least we're still heeled."

"Go get Billy," Print repeated.

Print tossed sticks and wood on the embers of the fire and tossed the dregs of old coffee out of the pot. He rinsed it out and reached for the sack of Arbuckle's. He looked over at the girls. They seemed not to have moved since last night's supper. What am I gonna do with you little daughters of joy? he thought.

The fire started to come to life. He heard Tom yelling from the other side of the herd. He rose and looked across the horses, who swung their tails back and forth. He trotted on his bandy legs around the herd. As he came up on Tom, he stopped. Tom stood looking at him and he knew it was all wrong. Billy lay on top of his bedroll. He slowed to a walk and saw that Billy's head was covered in dark, crusted blood.

"He killed him. He stove his head in. He killed Billy."

The wind had blown his kerchief up and it had stuck to his cheek. His hat rested beside him. His sandy hair matted in the blackened blood. His pockets were turned out. His boots were gone.

Print's mouth pursed. His upper lip twitched. He sucked air through his teeth. "Looks like he took a couple of horses. . . . He took Bob Tate."

Print looked out at nothing. "I am such a fool. A damn fool."

He looked down at Billy and then back out at the skyline. "I get older, but I don't get smarter. Check the rest of the horses an' get some coffee."

Tom walked away and Print looked down again at the dead cowboy.

Print had the fire roaring when Tom walked back. He poured a cup of coffee and handed it to his nephew.

"Looks like he took three, maybe four horses. Guess they're not gonna tell us what happened," he said, looking over at the girls.

"We know what happened. Notice anything 'bout them?"

Tom walked a few steps toward their camp and looked. "There's only four."

"Yep. Must a took one for company."

"Or he stove her head in too and stuck her someplace."

Print took his kerchief from his vest pocket and lifted a pot of bubbling beans from the fire. He walked over to the girls and pointed to the pot. "I know you ladies can't understan' a word I'm sayin', but you must know what food's about."

They stared up at him, afraid to move. He squatted in front of them and placed the pot on the ground. "I'll let you figger it out."

He walked back to his fire as Tom was buckling his gun rig.

"What're you doin'?"

"I'll need some of that food yer givin' away."

"What for?"

"I'm going after our money an' horses."

"What makes ya think you should go?"

"'Cause that's the only way I'll ever get my hands on what shoulda been mine."

He took off his kerchief and placed a handful of dried prunes in it. Then some jerky and three biscuits from last night's supper. He rolled it up and placed it in his saddlebag. He put a box of cartridges in the bag on the other side. He slid the carbine in the scabbard.

Print sat down on the ground and pulled off his boots, tossing them at Tom. "They'll do you more good th'n me."

Tom stood on one leg and then the other, pulling on the boots. He wiggled his toes. He had never realized how big his uncle's feet were. He tightened the cinch strap, slipped the canteen over the horn, and mounted. He shoved his hat down tighter and pulled his coat collar up against the wind.

"I'll get it back. Bob Tate too."

"I c'n get another horse. It's nephews I'm shy on. You just make sure you get back."

Tom looked down at him and then over at the girls. The pot sat where Print had left it. They hadn't touched it. He put his pony into a walk, skirted the herd, and headed north into the rising wind.

Print watched him go. He was a tough enough of

a kid. He never knew him to do stupid things. He seemed to be well thought out in all things he did. He had been that way even as a boy. Print turned and hobbled back to his fire. He poured a cup, sipped, and saw the pot of beans where he had left it.

He walked toward them. Their faces were grimy with trail dust, and they looked like they hadn't slept all night. "Ladies, I guess it's time we was introduced."

He squatted, the pot between them. He lifted the cover and took out the wooden spoon and ate a mouthful. He offered a spoonful to the girls. They neither moved nor spoke. He tipped the brim of his hat back. "This just ain't gonna do."

He put the spoon in his mouth and then extracted it and pointed to the little girl on the left. "Yer gonna be Number One. One. Number One. Say 'One.'"

The girls pulled closer together. Their baggy pajamas looked like one garment and they like a four-headed person. The biggest girl snapped at Print and the spoon that he was pointing at them.

Print leaned back. "Oh, no. Take 'er easy. I ain't gonna harm you. We might just be stuck with one another for a while, so we gotta figger out some way of talkin'."

He noticed the big girl, who hadn't taken her eyes off the spoon. He quit pointing it at them. He held up his other hand, palm toward them. He modulated his voice. "This must be a pretty scary deal for y'all. I don't know what yer story is, but if you was in the company of a sack a shit, I'm sure it wasn't good."

He shifted his position and the girls cringed. He kneeled on his right leg, crossing his forearms and resting them on his raised left knee, the wooden spoon pointed toward the ground. He paused, hoping that if he went slowly they might start trying to listen to him rather than act as if he were going to harm them. He relaxed his face and smiled slightly, even though the kneeling position was already starting to bother him. He took a breath and sighed. "I know ya can't understan' a word I'm sayin', so let's start again. Yer Number One."

He pointed to the littlest girl on his left. He held up his index finger and repeated himself. He said the word "One" slowly. "Yer Number One. One . . . One . . . One . . ."

The girls looked at one another and then back at him.

"Com' on now. You can do it. One . . . One. Yer a smart little girl. One. Just gimme a 'One' one time."

The little girl moved her head a little closer to him, "Ong."

"There ya go. One. Yer Number One," he said, nodding his head. He smiled at her and she almost smiled.

He turned his face to the second girl. "Now yer Number Two. How 'bout it? Gimme a Two. . . . Two . . . Two," holding up two fingers each time he repeated himself.

The little girl on his left managed a tentative "Twu."

"No, no. Yer Number One, she's Number Two," he said, changing fingers each time.

The big girl started talking excitedly to the others. She nodded her head vigorously. She was explaining to the others what it was that Print was trying to do. She spoke rapidly, mostly out of fear, Print thought.

"There ya go. You listen ta her. Yer One an' yer Two."

He pointed to the big girl. "Now yer gonna be Number Three. One . . . Two . . . an' Three."

She repeated the words out loud, "Ong . . . Twu . . . Tree."

"That'll do 'er. An you, little cherry blossom, are gonna be Number Four. That's right. Four. One, Two, Three, an' Four."

The last girl reacted violently to Print when he held up four fingers.

"He is giving us numbers for names, that is all. It means nothing," the big girl, Number Three, said to the last girl.

"No. No. Four is the number of death. No."

"It is only a word. It mean nothing to us here. Be brave."

"No. It is death."

Print had no idea what was going on but let them talk it out. Number Three turned to him and held up her hand with her thumb and fingers spread wide.

"Oh. She don't wanna be Four? No problem. We'll make her Number Five. Five . . . Five." He held up his hand with all fingers spread. Number Five nodded excitedly.

"Fii . . . Fii."

"Sure. She can be Number Five, and when Tom brings her li'l sister back, we'll make her Number Four. So, let's get this right. One . . . Two . . . Three . . . an' Five. Now get it right or I'm gonna paint numbers on yer backs."

Print tried to rise, pushing off his left knee. It was a struggle, as his other leg had gone to sleep. He grunted and staggered slightly. The girls reacted in fear. He righted himself and turned and walked back to the fire. Using the spoon as a baton, he called out to himself, "One, Two, Three, Four, an' Five."

He tossed the last of the wood on the fire and kicked a piece that missed with his bootless foot. "Now that we all know one another, there's work ta be done."

Chapter Eleven

The temperature continued to drop and Tom felt the sting of snow flurries on his face as he rode into the wind. He had cut for sign early on and had picked up the trail not far from camp.

Fender didn't care much about being followed, or he didn't know how to cover his tracks.

They had set a good pace in the beginning but had slacked off. Tom assumed that Fender had tired of the sobering aspects of hard riding or thought that no one would come after him. Rats can be cunning, but they aren't always smart, he thought. There was no way he was going to lose that money, and then there was Billy. He had held his thoughts when Print took him on. It was too early on the trail to start crossing swords with his uncle. But Billy had turned out to be okay. He was a good hand, just like he said he was, and he hadn't been any trouble. Actually Tom was getting used to getting more sleep at night. He was like a working dog, always out on the edge, doing his job. You didn't have to talk to him much, but when you did, it was short and usually pleasant, depending on how the wind was blowing. He remembered what the cowboy had said to them about Billy: "There's some things that just wasn't intended to live." That may be, thought Tom, but it ain't up to no cowboy nor no shit-bird Fender to make that call.

Print had put the girls to work gathering rocks to help cover the dead boy. He was going to wrap him up in his bedroll but decided that it would be better used for the girls, as it seemed that Fender had provided nothing in the way of bedding for them.

He had gone through Billy's belongings to see if there was any clue to a family that might want to know what happened to him. He found nothing other than a small leather-bound Book of Common Prayer. It was frayed and wrapped with a string to keep it together. Inside was a handwritten inscription:

To William V. McKay
From his grandparents
Marshall Johnson
Ellen DeButts Johnson
Malvern, Arkansas 1887

On the facing page, written in a different handwriting, was scrawled,

There abides in us faith, hope, love, these three; but the greatest of these is love.

He was a sweet boy, Print thought. There had been many kind and thoughtful lads back in Virginia. Like Billy they had been maimed and blown apart and wrecked. Like Billy they had learned to live a different way. To sign their name with their other hand. Or turn the plow at the end of the furrow with only one arm. To put on pants that only half of you filled. And to go on as best a ruined and damaged lad could.

At least they had given him a chance. He would make inquiries when they got to Sheridan. He fashioned a cross out of two sticks and placed pebbles at the foot of the grave that spelled out Billy Via. He knew it wouldn't last, but then, what did? Maybe an Egyptian pyramid. Maybe not even that.

The front was really bearing down, and he turned his attention to getting more wood, as he had no idea how long Tom might be gone. In this matter the girls were as tractable and willing as they had been in gathering rocks. He threw up a picket line for the mules and piled green juniper along the windward side of the wagon for protection. He had the girls snug it up with small limbs of long-needle pine. He slipped on an extra pair of heavy woolen socks, as his toes were starting to feel numb. It seemed to him that although the girls were not gleeful, they did appear more relaxed. Keeping them busy seemed to help.

The flurries had turned into a full blow The change in weather was not surprising for this country, but it was a damn nuisance when tracking, especially wearing someone else's boots that didn't fit. Tom tightened the stampede string on his hat to keep it in place. Fender's trail edged around a butte that was in its last millionth-year disintegration. Scattered ponderosa ringed its base. Tom was staring at a fresh pile of horse manure that still gave off a little steam. Tom dismounted, took out his carbine, and proceeded on foot. He was careful, even though the wind muffled his approach. He walked around the lee side of the hill to where the wind kicked up again. In a small stand of evergreens he saw horses tied, their butts to the wind. Beside them was a sheer rock outcropping, about twenty feet tall. The snow was blowing left to right and cut way down on visibility. Tom tied his horse to a fat juniper bush and walked on. As he got closer, he could make out figures lying on the ground. One lay on top of the other. He was ten yards from them before he could hear the girl's sobbing over the wind.

The grunting Fender dug tracks in the snow with Tom's boots as he tried to get a better position on top of the struggling Chinese girl. She cried out in pain, and that excited him even more. His feet slipped in the snow. He tried to gain more traction. His lip curled upward and his eyes rolled back in his head at the very moment that he felt the cold barrel of the Remington pressed against the base of his skull.

Print, with the help of the girls, had gotten the camp pretty well buttoned down. There was a good pile of wood and a vigorous fire going. He had made a stew of beans, flour, and cut-up jerky. He had tried to interest the girls in it, but they seemed to prefer the rice that Number Three had made. He had found a piece of tarp in Fender's wagon and had placed it around the girls to try keep the wind off them. Always wary they took the canvas and pulled it close about themselves.

"Wonder if y'all get snow in yer part of China? This ain't unusual a'tall. Sweatin' one day, freezin' the next. It won't last. T'morrow it'll be gone an' sunny again. . . . One . . . Two . . . Three . . . Five," he said, pointing to each girl.

The girls repeated their new names.

Print stoked the fire and added pine boughs to the side of the wagon to protect against the wind. The girls watched and talked quietly.

Number One asked the oldest, Sun Foy, where she thought the other man went. Sun Foy thought he had gone to get Ye Fung back and that they should do nothing to make these men mad. *"This old man has fed us and kept us warm, but none of them are to be trusted."*

When Tom reached down and grabbed Fender by his collar and yanked him halfway to his feet, the girl rolled away and scrambled into the gathering darkness. He let Fender hang, suspended, thrashing about and gagging for air. He looked to see where the girl had gone, so he didn't see the knife Fender had pulled and then tried to plunge into Tom's thigh. Because he didn't have any footing, his aim was off and the blade cut across Tom's front leg. It was a wicked weapon and sliced through the leather chaps and cut deep into the meat of his leg. He dropped Fender, who took another swipe at Tom, missing, and nearly stabbing himself. Tom brought the butt of the Remington down on Fender's face, between his upper lip and nose. It knocked Fender senseless. He coughed up blood and a badly rotted tooth. Tom kicked the dropped knife away and placed his boot heel on the side of Fender's jaw. He put his weight into it and turned his heel until he heard Fender's mandible snap.

Print ladled water out of the wooden keg strapped to the side of the wagon to thin out his stew into something more like soup and arbitrarily spooned it over the girls' rice. They watched in silence.

"Go on. Eat up. Eat. I got no idea a what ta do with little Mongolian girls from the Celestial Empire an' sure won't know what ta do if ya get sick on me. Don't care if it don't appeal ta ya. Go on, eat."

He looked at them staring at him. He pantomimed eating. Snowflakes landed in their black hair and then melted. A drop of water ran down Number Five's brow. Whether Tom got their money back or not, this was a hell of a deal that he had gotten them in and it was going to take more than jerky stew to get them out if it.

As Fender curled up in a ball on the ground, gargling and whimpering at the same time, Tom bound his long bandanna around his thigh, which was oozing a good flow of blood. Fender turned his head to look up at Tom. Blood bubbled from both corners of his mouth. His lower jaw was offset and gave him the appearance of a man who had suffered a stroke. He made nonsensical noises. The burning feeling from Tom's leg wound was already turning into a sickening ache. Fender reached out to grab the bottom of Tom's chaps. He whined gibberish. Tom pulled his leg away and brought the heel of his boot down on Fender's wrist. Fender screamed and choked.

Tom limped off in the direction of the girl. He found her crouching at the far end of the rock. She was shaking violently from fear and the biting wind. He removed his coat and stepped toward her. She pulled back, and he knew she was going to bolt on him. He heard Fender groveling where he had left him. The captain was searching the ground for his knife, or maybe a sidearm, Tom thought. He dropped his coat on the ground and limped back to Fender.

"You so much as twitch and I'll stake you to the ground."

Fender whimpered and cursed at the same time. Tom returned to the girl. He picked up the coat and carefully extended it to her. She made no move. He let it fall at her feet. He stepped over to Fender.

"Get your coat off."

Fender blubbered.

"Get it off and my boots too."

Fender managed to squirm out of the coat but could not pull off the boots, as the hand that Tom had stomped on was no longer working. Tom bent down, grasped a boot heel, and tugged. Off came one and then the other. He reached down and removed Fender's leather belt. He secured it over the bandanna, which was soaked.

"The money belt."

Fender pointed to his chest. Tom ripped open the front of Fender's shirt, unbuckled the belt, pulled it out, and slung it over his shoulder. He looked back at the girl. She had put the coat around her. It was now almost dark as Tom rolled Fender over onto his stomach, facedown. He walked back to where he had tied his horse. The belt had slipped and he tightened it more. He led his horse back to Fender and the girl. He removed his rope and played out a small loop from the hondo. He slipped it over Fender's head and tightened it around his neck. Fender squealed and frantically turned to face Tom. Tom pushed his face back into the dirt. He flung the rest of the rope over the rock face. He led his horse away. Fender tried to see what was going on without moving his head. Tom walked around to the other side of the rock and picked up the rope. In the darkness he saw a stout aspen sapling. He walked the rope around the tree and back to his horse. He dallied the rope around the horn of the saddle and snugged it tight.

He led the horse away from the rock, and Fender

felt the line tighten and then start to pull him. First toward the rock, and then up. He flailed about, clawing at his neck. The rope tightened against his own weight. His eyes bulged. He couldn't even gag. Snot and blood came out of his nose. A thick blue-black tongue stuck out of his mouth. Tom moved the horse slowly. He didn't want to snap Fender's neck. The taunt rope jumped at Fender's movements. He patted the horse's neck, making sure he would stand, and then limped to the edge of the rock and looked down. Fender was quickly starting to fade. He kicked and the soles of his feet slapped the ground. Tom went back to his horse and had him take two steps forward, leaving Fender completely airborne. Tom stroked the horse's neck with one hand and held the other on the taunt rope, feeling the vibrations lessen to naught. He slackened the rope around the saddle horn and finally tossed it to the ground. He led the horse back around. Fender sat like a child's doll, legs splayed out in front, head cocked to the left and slightly down. His face was the color of raw liver. One eye bulged almost out of its socket.

Tom picked up Fender's coat and walked over to the girl. He tried to trade his coat for Fender's, as the dead man's was much too small for him to wear, but the girl was having none of it. In the end, he took the blanket from under the saddle on Billy's horse, which Fender had stolen, and got her to wrap herself in it and give Tom his coat back. He resaddled the horse and got her up on it. He knew that without the blanket, the saddle would probably gall the horse on its withers and back, but he figured it would have time to heal before they got to Sheridan. He mounted, grabbed the lead rope on the girl's horse. He looked back at her. She was cold and shaking, but at least she was alive, he thought. He walked past Fender the rag doll at the base of the sheer rock.

"Dance now, you son of a bitch."

Like many of these spring snowstorms, it put on a good show but never really amounted to much. As Tom led the horse and girl back to his uncle's camp, the wind was still howling, but the snow was easing up.

He dismounted and limped over to the wagon. The fire was all but gone. He helped the girl off the horse. On the lee side of the wagon was a snow-covered canvas tarp that covered a large pile. He kicked the pile. He kicked it again.

Print pulled down an edge of the tarp. "Tom? You all right, boy?"

"What ya doin', Uncle Print?"

"Hell, I'm tryin' ta stay warm, son. What're you doin'?"

Tom tossed a pair of boots on the tarp. Print pulled the cover down farther, revealing the heads of several of the girls.

"Returnin' the loan of yer boots."

Their voices woke the other girls, who peered out and saw the shivering girl beside Tom. They started talking, and Number Three slid out from under the tarp and went to the freezing girl. She talked excitedly to her and led her back under the canvas covering.

Print saw the blood-soaked chaps. "Want me ta take a look at that?"

"I packed it in snow. I want to sleep."

"Well, crawl in here. The herd ain't goin' anywhere tonight."

Chapter Twelve

A trickle of water ran down a crease in the canvas. Snow was melting in the morning sunlight. Summer had returned, and you could hear driblets of melting snow everywhere. Tom pulled back the canvas and closed his eyes to the bright sun. He smelled the wood smoke and the bacon. He raised up and immediately felt the dull ache in his leg turn to a stabbing pain. Print was squatting by the fire and looked over at him.

"You're lookin' a little peak'd, Nephew."

Print rose and walked over to Tom, who sank back in his bedroll, covering his eyes with his forearm. He felt clammy and hoped that he wasn't getting a fever.

"Made a poultice fer your leg. First let's skin them chaps off ya."

The belt Tom had put on had slipped loose in the night. He untied the bloody kerchief. Print grabbed the bottom of each leg as Tom undid the buckle. Tom winced as Print jerked the chaps off and kneeled down for a closer look. He poked his finger into the sliced pants and long underwear. He ripped both for a better look. He poured water from a canteen over the wound, which started to bleed a little.

From his tin cup he swiped a big glob of gray grease and swabbed it on liberally with two fingers.

"Made a poultice outta Slippery Elm, some fire ash, an' bacon grease. Wish I had som' bayberry or comfrey but this'll do. Wound's not deep enough to stitch up. 'Sides, you'd probably rip 'em out anyway ridin'."

"This ain't gonna lay me up."

It was a question as much as an answer.

"No, but it's lucky the captain left us a wagon. You can drive that for the next couple a days."

"What about the herd?"

"I'll work the herd. You bring up the rear. We'll go slow. It shouldn't be a problem. Thing is, I don't want this to turn sour on you. Give it a couple a days' rest. Let's get ya on your feet."

Print extended a hand to Tom and pulled him up. He helped him over to the fire. He eased Tom down to a sitting position. The girls were busy gathering more wood. Except for the girl Tom had brought back in the night. The girl that would soon be called Number Four. She sat across the fire from Tom. She made no eye contact. Tom sipped coffee.

"Did she eat this morning?"

"Not much. None of 'em much, 'cept for rice, an' it looks like we're gonna give out on that soon. Naw. She didn't eat hardly anythin'."

Print handed a plate of food to Tom. "Was he sober?"

"What?"

"Capt'n Fender, was he sober? 'Member, he said, 'If ya sin when yer drunk, y'll pay when yer sober.'"

Tom blew on the cup of coffee. He was looking over at the girl. "Sober enough."

The girls returned with wood and dumped it on the pile beside Tom. He looked at them, and they looked at him. Mostly his blood-soaked pant leg.

"Ya ain't been introduced."

Again pointing with the wooden spoon, this time at Tom, "This here's Tom . . . Tom . . . Tom. Come on, now. Say, 'Tom.' Tom."

Little Number Five, the girl with the bound feet said, "Tahm."

"Ther' ya go. Tom."

The other girls mouthed the word. Number Four was silent and seemed unconcerned with what was going on.

"This here's Number One, Number Two, Three, an' Number Five.

"The little one you brought back is gonna be Number Four, but I think we'll wait a day or so ta work on that. Think the big on', Three, is the one that's in charge."

"What do they call you?"

Print turned to the girls and thumped his chest with the spoon. More or less in unison, they said, "Honkle Pren."

"So, whatta ya think?"

Tom looked up from his plate. He laid it beside him on the ground. He reached and got the coffee-pot and poured a cup. "I go and get our money and horses back, and had to stretch a man to do it, an' you've gone and set up a school for Chinese girls."

Tom reached inside his shirt and pulled out Print's money belt and tossed it to him. Print picked it up and looked down at his nephew. The smile on his face was gone.

"You all right, kid?"

"Yeah. Sure, I'm all right. Had to leave my rope back there."

"Man like that ain't worth the food he eats, much less the price of a decent rope."

Tom nodded and sipped his coffee.

Chapter Thirteen

A chipmunk scooted up a ponderosa at the sound of the approaching horses. From a limb, he gnawed on a small grasshopper as the herd passed by. They had struck camp, with Tom driving the wagon. The girls rode in the back, and Print led the herd slowly. Sometimes he would drift over to the left flank and press the horses in on themselves. Then he'd ease back to the front and later repeat the process on the right flank. Because of the snow the night before, the wagon wasn't subject to drifting dust.

Print was back on Bob Tate. He was more than a little relieved that Tom had made it back. The lad was lucky. The wound was the kind that could go septic easily if not tended to. He was glad his nephew had retrieved the best horse he'd had in the last twenty years.

He had had a dream that night, with the girls all huddled up under the canvas. He had dreamed of her. Ann Blackwell. Ann Cetia Blackwell. Actually he had dreamed of the little girl, and Ann came and went in the dream. It was mostly about the little girl, and like all dreams, it was vague. Not all dreams, he thought. Some were so real and profound that they hung about him for days. But this one was vague. He hardly ever even remembered his dreams anymore. The little girl stood on a porch of a house. But the house was his papa's house back in Virginia, and that couldn't be. She wore little black button-up shoes, and he had brought her a zebra pony for her birthday, and that couldn't be right either. Ann came out of the house and took the girl inside. He could tell she didn't want to go. He could tell that Ann was not happy with him. He didn't think she had ever really been happy with him, but maybe she had never been happy period. Happiness was too elusive a thing to spend your life trying to chase, he thought. But he did think of the little girl with curly auburn hair. In the dream, she went to the window to see him and the zebra pony. Her mother came up behind her and led her away from the window.

A zebra pony. He shook his head. No wonder he hardly remembered his dreams anymore.

At the noon rest, they ate biscuits from the morning and jerky. Tom got down from the wagon to limp off and relieve himself. When he returned, Number Three was sitting up in the front of the wagon.

"Thought ya might give 'er a lesson on drivin' the wagon. Hopefully you'll be back on yer horse in a day or so. Som'body's gotta drive."

Tom struggled to get on board with his stiff leg. He held a biscuit between his teeth and took the reins in his hands.

"Remember, she's Number Three, the jigger boss of this sorority. I think she'll do pretty much whatever ya show her."

The mules started up and rocked the girl backward. Tom put his arm behind her and nodded for her to repeat what he had done. She did, and again the mules moved forward; this time they kept moving. He removed his arm from her back and let her go. He could hear the girls behind him, talking. Number Three said, *"Be quiet and pay attention. Pay attention to everything."* The mules drifted off to the left, and Tom took her right hand and showed her just how much she needed to correct them. He looked over his shoulder and saw that the girls in the back were watching him, except for the girl he brought back from Fender. She was curled up, as if asleep.

The afternoon was hot, and that kept the herd at a slow pace. All traces of the snow were gone and the footing was good. The girl drove the mules with a look of concentration on her face. If she saw a good-sized piece of wood, she would bark to the girls and either Number One or Number Two would jump out of the back of the wagon and retrieve it. Running beside the wagon, she would toss it into the cooney that was slung beneath the wagon. With the help of the other girl, she would climb back on board. Number Five, the little one with the bound feet, couldn't participate, and Number Four spent the day sleeping.

They camped late in the afternoon, so the herd could graze on good, hard grass that they came upon. Tom forced himself to walk around on his stiff leg. The girls helped with the firewood and even hauled water from a nearby creek. Print took the shotgun and put a handful of shells in his vest pocket. He slipped out of his chaps.

"Think I'll scare up somethin' for the pot tonight. How's the leg doin'?"

"It's sore as hell but mostly stiff."

"Well, don't walk on it too much. Ya gotta give it time ta granulate."

With his leg straight out in front of him, Tom lowered himself down and finally plopped on the ground. Print, carrying the shotgun in the crook of his arm, walked off away from the herd and the camp.

He walked along the side of the creek, feeling stiff himself. They had pitched camp on the west bank of Sailor Creek, and he was trying to calculate how far they had ridden since that first camp on the north shore of Malheur Lake when a pair of wood ducks beat it out of a line of gooseberry bushes beside the creek. It startled him and he broke open the shotgun and slipped two shells into the barrels.

He had figured that they must have covered close to two hundred miles so far, and things were going all right. Well, except for that fella Fender and now these five little girls on their hands. And there was Tom's sliced-up leg. Still, he felt confident that they were making good time and that luck was on their side.

A pair of doves flew up and then landed in a persimmon tree. He raised the gun and walked toward the tree. The doves took flight, and Print led them with the gun. He fired. One, then two. He retrieved the birds and stuck them in his left vest pocket.

Print continued along the bank, flushing another pair of doves and bagging one of them. He found the birds in some willows. He took his knife and pared green bark from the willow until he had two handfuls. He picked another handful of buds from the slender tips and he stuffed it into an empty sack of tobacco makings.

He walked out of the cover and turned to make a wide loop back to camp. Walking through knee-high grass, Print flushed a grouse and took it on his second shot. He found the bird easily as it wasn't dead and flopped about in the grass. He gave it a quick twist of the neck. Print broke down the shotgun and extracted the two empty shells and put them in a pocket. He cradled the gun in one arm and carried the grouse by the feet in the other. He backtracked to the willows and cut three long pieces as big around as his thumb, and then headed back to camp.

He returned to find the camp set up and a good bed of coals for cooking. "How's some bird meat for supper sound?"

Tom had been washing the wound and bloody pants with a pan of warm water and his cleaned kerchief. He straightened up at Print's approach. "Sounds good. There's not much in the way of food that I won't eat."

"Would that include deep-fried grasshoppers?"

"That I might pass on, thank you."

"Considered a delicacy when cooked in buffalo marrow."

"No, thanks. What did ya get?"

"Couple a birds an' a grouse. Got some stuff ta help with that leg," he said, pointing to the stained pant leg.

"I got it pretty well cleaned up."

"Now don't be doin' too much cleanin'. The body's got its own medicine for such things. I did get some willow ta make you a tea, though."

Print kneeled and took the empty coffeepot and ladled water into it from the water bucket beside the fire. He set the pot on the coals to heat and took the little sack out of his pocket. He unknotted his kerchief and spread it out on the ground. He sprinkled the contents of the tobacco sack on it and pushed the bark shavings and buds about with his finger. He tossed a handful into a tin cup and waited for the water to boil.

"What's been goin' on here?"

"Not much. Can't figure out how I can sit on a

horse all day with no problem but sit on the ground for an hour and my ass aches."

"One of the unanswered mysteries of life."

"Nothing in your book reading to shed some light on it?"

"Nope. How're the girls doin'?"

"They're keeping themselves busy. 'Cept for the one I brought back. She's in pretty rough shape, if ya ask me. He was forkin' the hell outta her when I came up on them. He must have knocked her around too."

"Maybe I'll give her some tea too," he said, reaching for the pot.

"She'll need more than roots and hot water."

"She come from the country of tea drinkers. Give 'er time. She'll sort it out."

He poured the water into the cup and swirled it around. He set the cup down and prepared another cup and did the same. "Here, drink this down, but don't toss out the dregs."

"This tastes awful," said Tom, taking a sip.

"So's blood poisonin' an' gangrene. Just drink 'er down."

Print rose and took a cup of the brew over to the wagon to where Number Four lay. He gently shook her foot and she jumped. He extended the cup to her. She looked at him. He nodded yes and reached closer. She took the cup and he backed off and walked over to Tom.

"That's good medicine yer drinkin' there, son. Cleans the blood, mends the flesh, an' eases the pain."

"When did you find time to fit in being a doctor al'ng with punchin' cows and book reading?"

"I learned it from your grandma. She knew all about the roots an' barks. Berries, nuts, an' thistles too. There was a time when that's all ya had. Not like today, with all the modern medicine ya got now. No, sir. She made teas an' salves, poultices an' syrups, balms an' pomades. Made 'em outta ever'thin' from bear grease ta beeswax."

Tom took another sip and grimaced. "Was that my ma's ma?"

"Yep. A fine ol' Huguenot gal. Her kin came over by way of Alsace, France."

"Ma told me they came from Pennsylvania."

"They did, once they got ta America. They was a long line of carpenters. Found there was calling for well-built barns. They built barns all over Pennsylvania. Then they drifted south, comin' down the Shenandoah. Couple of generations an' they'd worked their way down the valley."

Print gutted and dressed the birds as he talked. Feathers and down swirled in the light breeze. "Your grandad was working at a sawmill over by Piper's Gap. They sent him with a wagonload a timber ta where the Bouchees was puttin' up a barn. That's where he first saw Miss Juliett Bouchee. Well, that was all it took. Just the sight a her sunk the hook in Reuben Ritter, an' 'fore you know it, she had him buildin' a fine log house. His future brothers-in-law helped him. It was as right an' tight as any barn they ever built. Right in the shadow of Beamer's Nob, they started makin' a family. They was good at it too. They had ten children."

Print skewered the doves on the green willow sticks and ran two sticks through the grouse.

"Four of 'em died at birth or as infants. But four boys an' two girls made it. There was Nimrod, Levi, Mason, and me. On the girl's side, there was your ma, Julie Bouchee Ritter, and Haney Louise Ritter. Your ma was the baby of the family."

Print got up and planted the sticks into the ground, leaning over the fire. He added another stick and waved to the girls to come over. Number Three came to him and he handed her the bucket and motioned to the creek. She nodded and took the bucket.

Soon they were eating, although the girls still were shy about the food. They were careful when eating the doves. Print and Tom had no problem putting an end to the grouse, along with beans and biscuits.

"How did they meet?"

Print put his plate aside and brought out the whiskey bottle. "Medicine for you," he said, and then, lifting the bottle, "Medicine fer me."

"I'm not exactly sure how they met. Yer daddy was from over to Floyd County. But I believe his people were from somewheres on the New River. He may have been workin' for the brothers-in-law, buildin' barns. Same thing happened ta him as old Reuben. He saw your ma, and that was pretty much it. Those Bouchee women all made their fiancés build 'em a nest 'fore they walked down the aisle. It helped ta have relatives that was carpenters if you were plannin' to seriously court a Bouchee gal. Even one that was half Ritter. They was practical in all things."

Print drained his cup and rose. "Think ya can orchestrate gettin' the dishes done? I'm gonna check on the horses."

He walked among the horses until he found the flea-bitten gray. The one that Tom had already said he wanted to keep for himself. He checked her hobbles and that of the two other mares that were always near her. He walked slowly through the herd to the other side. The pace they had been going at was working out well. The horses were good and tired at the end of the day but were in good flesh, and other than a couple of gimpy ones, all were sound.

Print breathed in the night air, unbuttoned his

pants, and relieved himself. He walked on around the perimeter of the grazing herd. The moon hadn't come up yet and the night sky was brilliant with stars. The same sky he had been looking at for over sixty years, and still he never tired of watching it.

He saw a log that had once been a ponderosa that some west wind had long since pushed over. He sat down and took out his pipe and tobacco. He paused and softly whistled a few bars of "The Maid of Fife" to make sure the horses were aware it was him and then struck the match. He cupped it quickly and sucked on the pipe.

Print mused about his earlier conversation with Tom. He sometimes forgot how much family history he knew. There had been little call from anyone to repeat it. He had gone for what seemed like years without thinking about the family and his youth. It was sure a different world he came into than the one he would be leaving. Even now, this was so far away from the steps of the courthouse in Galax, where he and other country lads had volunteered when called. There were plenty of hot speeches, but not all were so ready to leave families behind and farms that would have to be tended to by women and younger children. Even in his family there had been arguments for and against.

The pipe had gone out and he relit it. He listened to a bobwhite and the peepers down by the creek. The same kind of sounds as back home, but this surely wasn't Carroll County, Virginia. He smoked the last of the pipe, then tamped it on the log. He ran his little finger around the bowl and tamped it again.

Chapter Fourteen

Print woke up the next morning to find that little Number Five sometime in the night had dragged her bedroll over and curled up next to him. He carefully slipped out of his bedroll. The morning light was just coming up as Tom limped over to the fire.

"Horses sure are falling into the routine."

"Sure they are, an' that's good now that we're back to two men. Probably should have taken on another hand back at the Malheur. Wasn't countin' on the extra company."

"Glad you brought it up. What are we going to do with them?" Tom said, nodding in the direction of the sleeping girls.

"I been thinkin' about it. We need to get them ta some proper authorities that are set up ta handle such things, 'cuz we sure ain't."

"Any idea where and when that might be?"

"We'll need to reprovision soon enough. Probably then, why?"

"Well, they sure are a drag on our goal to get this herd to Sheridan."

"Son, if they was five ladies from Canyon City, you an' me'd be about ready ta slit our own throats just ta get away from the gagglin' an' prattle that would be goin' on. No, sir, these little ones are pretty easy on the nerves."

"I'll feel better when we find a place to leave 'em and get back to the job at hand."

"Well, of course ya do. So do I. Until that time, it's no use in takin' it out on them."

"Sure," said Tom, tossing the dregs of his coffee.

"Here, put this on yer leg couple times a day, but don't mess wit' the wound too much. Just let nature an' yer grandma's medicine do their work."

Print handed Tom a tin cup. Tom sniffed the contents.

"Mostly bacon drippin's an' mashed-up willow buds."

They were on the move and the weather held. Good now, thought Print, but it could go dry on us and there was a lot of distance between the herd and Sheridan. Number Three took to the driving, and in little more than a week, Tom was back in the saddle, although he did spend the first few afternoons back in the wagon. Again the land was changing as they bumped along the country of southern Idaho, past the Sawtooth, and south of the Twin Falls.

The crossings were mostly creeks, which were easy enough, and the one river, the Clover, had been down, so it was easy too. All the time they kept edging slightly north, getting closer to the Oregon Trail, which Print had traveled west on so long ago. They forded Goose Creek and pushed on for the Raft. They arrived late in the afternoon and found their side of the crossing occupied by a large flock of sheep. There was a round sheepherders' wagon with a piece of stovepipe sticking out of the top. Several men walked along the edges of the flock.

Print gigged the red roan into a lope, heading him toward the sheep. He was giving Bob Tate more time off; as he felt the grind of the trip, he knew that the horse was too. He was the only horse that Print was really interested in riding anymore, and he tended to forget that the big chestnut could get just as bone weary as himself.

As he neared the flock, he brought the roan down to a trot and then to a walk. Hearing his approach, one of the shepherds turned and started walking toward Print. He walked with a staff and wore a sheepskin vest, woolly side out. A shapeless felt hat covered a face the color of a cured ham. A week's growth of silver stubble stood out against the darkened face.

"Afternoon," said Print as he brought the roan to a stop and made him stand still.

"And to you, too," replied the herder.

He grinned and showed a mouthful of very white teeth. Now that's what I like in a fella, thought Print. This here's a man that what's on his face, ya know is in his heart.

"You local boys or just passin' through?"

"Heading north," replied the shepherd, pointing with his staff.

"Comin' up from Old Mexico?"

The old man laughed and shook his head. "No, from Navarra."

Print cocked his head as if to think about the man's reply.

"Navarra. Navarra, Spain. We are Basque. Sheepmen."

He extended his hand up to Print, who leaned forward to grasp it.

"Valinten Ugalde."

"Print Ritter. Pleased ta meet ya, Mr. Valentine. How's the trail east ta here?" he said as he sat back in the saddle.

"We are heading north. We were told in Almo

that there is trouble with some Utes and Paiutes that have left the reservation. I cannot afford to lose my sheep. . . . I would not go farther east, especially with such fine-looking horses."

"Hard ta believe that there's still any around that want to start trouble."

The old man shrugged. "It is very dry to the south. Worse than dry. From Elko to Wells and almost all the way to here."

"Thanks for the advice. Say, Mr. Valentine, ya think ya might sell me one of them sheep? We're kinda played out on rabbit these days."

The old man smiled and pointed back to the flock. "Perhaps you would like lamb rather than mutton."

"Even better."

The old man pointed his finger at Print. "You buy the lamb and I will cook it for you. We are going to camp here for the night. And you?"

Print looked up, beyond the sheep, and then back at the old man.

"I was thinkin' the same thing. We'll move up a ways. The horses have been a breeze so far, but ya never know."

The old man nodded in agreement, and Print turned the roan and trotted back to Tom, who had stopped the herd and was waiting on Print.

"Basque. Come up from the south. Say there's problems with some Utes and Paiutes. Recommends we change course. Says it's parched an' pretty well blowed out all the way down ta Elko."

A big greenhead fly landed on the rump of Tom's horse. It swished its tail, but the fly didn't move.

"Tomorrow let's point 'em more ta the north and we'll tie in ta the south fork of the Oregon."

Tom nodded at the same time his horse put in a halfhearted buck to dislodge the fly. Tom kept his seat, ignored the buck, and reached behind him to swipe the fly away.

"I told the old man we'd put 'em up ta the left. Don't know about you, but I'm lookin' forward to some lamb."

They made their camp between the horses and the flock of sheep. Tom got the girls to haul water to replenish the water keg on the wagon while he tended to the horses and Print made a pot of beans. He noticed how covered with dust and tired the girls looked. Number Four seemed to be coming around a bit.

"Tom, tell those girls that this is a good place to bathe an' wash up. There's good water in the shallows."

"Uncle, how am I suppose to convey that thought to them?"

"Well, son, I had 'em named an' numbered in a snap. I am sure you can figger out how ta get yer point across."

Tom shook his head and picked up the wooden bucket. He felt self-conscious and just plain stupid calling them by their numbered names. But it didn't seem to bother his uncle or the girls.

"Hey, you. You, Number Three. Yeah, you. All of you," he said, gesturing with both of his arms. "Come and follow me. I'm gonna show you where to take a bath."

Number Two and Three looked at him. Little Number Five and Number One stood up. The littlest girl shuffled toward him with her tiny feet.

"Take a bar of that brown soap and som' of that muslin that I bought for Billy."

Tom retrieved the items from the wagon, which they were now using to stow their gear.

He turned to the girls, who were now standing. "Well, come on." He gestured and started to lead them to the water. He shortened his steps to allow them to keep up with him.

He walked upstream, out of sight of the camp. Twice he had to tell them to keep going, as they grew apprehensive and hung back. He found a spot that had a small sandbar and was set back from the faster moving water. Willows hung over the bank and made a natural screen. He walked out onto the sandbar.

He turned to the girls. "Come on. This is a good enough spot ta wash up."

Again he gestured to them. They stood all in a row, watching him. He pantomimed washing and scooping water up and drying off. He placed the bucket in the sand along with the soap and muslin.

He stepped over the two feet of water that separated the bank from the bar. He reached for Number Five, who pulled back.

"Now don't be like that. I ain't gonna hurt ya. Come here."

He picked her up, her eyes wide open, more from surprise than fear, and with one foot on the bank and the other on the sandbar, he turned and placed her down. He turned and offered a helping hand to Number Three. She waited a moment and then took it and stepped over. One, Two, and Four followed.

He stepped back on the bank and turned to face them. He talked and gestured at the same time. "You go on an' wash up. I'm gonna go back to the wagon. I'll come back an' fetch you."

He remembered Fender saying that they was "dumb as dirt at understanding English." Maybe they didn't understand English, but they wasn't dumb, and he felt that they did understand what he was trying to tell them. He started back for the camp. He turned back, and looking directly at the oldest one, said, "Now you have any problems or get scare't, you just holler."

He held his hands to his mouth, He turned and stepped through the willows and walked back to camp.

"Mai Ling, help me with her bandages," said Sun Foy to Number Two as she knelt to help Ghing Wa. She removed the special slippers from the little girl's feet.

The shepherd and Print were busy preparing dinner. Valinten had the lamb on a spit and was basting it. Print was working on a second round of biscuits to cover the additional guests and had a pot brimming with beans and a generous application of dried sliced apples. He had found a currant shrub not far from the water and had added several handfuls of golden currants.

"Nephew, we're goin' ta dine tonight. I have fallen in with a fellow disciple of gastronomy. Like me, he's one of the wanderin' kind."

The smiling Basque looked up from his basting of the lamb. "Do you share your uncle's taste for lamb?" asked the shepherd.

"Oh, I'll eat pert near anything," replied Tom.

"Now see there, Valentine, that's the work I got cut out for myself, to educate this lad's mind an' his palate 'fore we get to Sheridan."

Tom leaned in close on the lamb that the shepherd turned slowly. "You'd think all I ate was pinecone an' buffalo chips ta listen to him. I know what good food tastes like when I get it in my mouth."

"Well, yer gonna get yer chance tonight. Though ya might have stayed with the girls."

"They wasn't gonna do no bathing with me even in earshot of them."

"How 'bout a short snort, Mr. Valentine? An' the other sheep fellas too?" asked Print as he produced his bottle.

"Only if you let me return the money you paid for the lamb. I cannot accept such generosity and money," he said as he took the tin cup from Print.

"We'll talk about that after supper."

Print poured into all the men's cups. He lifted his to toast them. "Confusion to our enemies."

The men drank from their cups, the sheepherders not sure what to make of Print's toast.

Print recharged their cups as they settled down around the fire. "How's that lamb comin' along, Mr. Valentine?"

"Not yet, but soon."

"What ya slatherin' on it?"

"I use olive oil, garlic, paprika. What I have left-over I add: onions, dried peppers, and wild mush-rooms, and maybe I slice up some chorizo."

"There ya go, Nephew. This might be the best meal we'll get the entire trip. . . . Think you oughta check on the girls. I told Mr. Valentine the circum-stances of their bein' with us."

"I'm not going back there to pester them. I told them to holler if they needed help."

"Oh, you did, did you?"

"Yes, I did."

Tom stretched out his game leg and started to roll a smoke.

"That shit-bird Fender did say they was attached to the idea of cleanliness."

Tom struck a match and puffed. He offered the bag of makings to the sheepmen. One nodded and he tossed it over to him.

"Hygiene. Now there's a subject we haven't touched on yet."

"Is there that much to talk about?" asked Tom, flicking the match into the fire.

The sheepman tossed Tom's makings back to him.

"God, yes. Why I got a whole theory on hygiene."

Tom shook his head. "Maybe these sheep fellas won't be as interested in your theories as me and the Chinese gals have had to be, Uncle."

"What are you talking about? First time I saw Mr. Valentine here, I knew right off he was an inquisitive man, Curious 'bout the world around him."

Valinten carefully painted the roasting lamb. He held a tin plate under it to catch the drippings. He looked over at Print but said nothing.

"The history of cleanliness goes way back, farther than the Greeks. They had a god for cleanliness. Hygeia. Mighta been a goddess. Sounds more like a goddess name."

"It takes my uncle a while to get 'round to the point on some of these stories, Mr. Ugalde," interrupted Tom.

Print offered the bottle to the other men, who declined. He poured a short dram for himself.

"See, Mr. Valentine, I am trying to instill in my nephew if not a hunger, at least a passin' interest in that world beyond his horse's nose. On this subject of hygiene, I can tell ya that you can measure the success of a civilization based on the weight it puts on matters of hygiene."

Print stopped and looked up at the approach of the girls coming back to the camp. "Could I ask for a better example?"

The girls walked slowly over to the wagon, their hair damp and slicked back. Number Three hung the bucket by the water keg, and Number One took the strips of muslin and placed them over the scrub bushes behind the wagon. They sat down almost under the wagon and looked at the men, who were looking back at them.

"Like I was sayin', mosta the great civilizations had an enlightened way a thinkin' when it came to hygiene. Settin' here tonight reminded me when I first come west with the wagon trains. You could almost always tell when ya had a river crossin' comin' up, 'cuz you could smell it from three miles away."

"Ya mean like Billy?" asked Tom.

"Same ingredient. See, folks usually gathered up the night before they crossed, made camp, an' then attacked the crossin' the next day. Well, didn't take long for the area to start getting' ripe as it was used by thousands of people, an' mosta them all went cros't at the same place. . . . Mr. Valentine, you got any rice?"

"I am sorry, sir, but I do not. It is expensive and not always easy to get."

"That's all right. If ya did, I was gonna stock up on it for the girls. . . . Where was I? Oh yeah. Folks was only goin' ta be there a night, so they didn't care a fig 'bout the others comin' along after them. They was all travelers, so ya can't point the finger at 'em too much. But if ya let that kinda attitude prevail in a metropolis, pretty soon ya got cracks showin' in the foundation of society."

Print got to his knees and, using his kerchief, he pulled the Dutch oven away from the coals. He looked up at Valinten.

"Almost," said the shepherd.

Print sat back and took a sip. "Show me a critter in the wild that lives in his own shit."

"What about pigs?" asked Tom.

"Pigs? Pigs're fine animals. Smarter than most. Study a pig sometime, A pig 'ill never sleep where he shits. If possible. If he does, it's 'cuz people have forced him to. No, left on his own, a pig is a tidy fella."

"You got that out of a book?"

"Like I said, study a pig. The worst mistake you can make is to think you can get all yer knowledge from a book. You'd be better off never seein' a book than fall fer that trap of believin' that it all comes from books. No, sir."

"Guess I'll add pig studying to the list, along with birds."

"'Course, some things ya need the books for. The Romans was the best in the world at sewage an' civilization. Fer that ya need books. They brought water from the mountains right inta their town. Had sewers for bathin' and swampin' out the latrines. Even had a sponge on a string ta clean yer backsides when yer done doin' yer business. Course ya had ta rinse it out when yer through. Now that's the heart of civilization. People respectin' one another. Actin' civilized. Take that an' apply it in anything. Racin' wagons and horses down Main Street. Stealin' other folks' money outta banks. Pickin' up dead dogs lyin' in ditches."

Print picked up a smooth stone beside him and opened his pocketknife. He spit on the stone and stroked it with the blade's edge. He enjoyed playing the wag sometimes.

"Let things slide, though, let folks start tossin' chamber pots out the widows on their neighbors passin' by, an' ya know what ya got?"

Tom sighed and Valinten shook his head.

"Ya got the Dark Ages, Mr. Valentine. Let a few folks get away with it, an' pretty soon ever'one's slingin' piss pots out the window. Then ya got a whole continent wadin' around in shit. Next comes plague an' pestilence. They say almost half the people in the world died a disease. But that ain't the worst."

Tom struggled to his feet with his sore leg. He got himself a plate and a fork. "It ain't?"

"No, it ain't. The worst is the loss of knowledge.

Ya lose that an' ya lost ever'thing. And mankind almost did. That's why they called it the Dark Ages."

"I guess we're safe from that on this trip," said Tom. "We got a walkin', talkin' encyclopedia to keep us topped off with knowledge."

"Ya bet ya do," replied Print, folding up his knife and struggling to his feet.

"Mr. Valentine, if you don't start dishin' up some a that delicious-smellin' lamb, I'm gonna start actin' uncivilized."

He turned to the wagon. "Ladies, time ta eat. One, Two, Three, Four, an', come on, Five. Let's go."

He waved to them, and they stood up and came over to the fire. He handed out plates and forks. The shepherd sliced long strips of meat from the lamb's shank and placed them on everyone's plates. He cut off ribs.

"Better give the ribs ta the girls. We're kinda shy on knives. They can gnaw, though."

Print ladled beans and apples laced with currants onto the plates. The girls started back to the wagon.

"Hold on there. Hey, Three, come on back here."

The girl turned as Print motioned for them to come back and sit down. She spoke to the others and they all found a spot around the fire. Silence overtook the camp as the men devoured the food on their plates.

Print wiped his chin with the back of his hand and saw that the girls were picking at the food. He studied them as he finished his supper. He put his plate down and rose to his feet. He stretched and walked over to the wagon and rifled through the three-cent flour sacks. He dug out a jar of jam and walked back to the fire.

He tried to open the jar, but the lid wouldn't budge. He squatted and held it close to the fire. He tried it again and it opened. Next he took out his knife and cut a biscuit in half and spread a generous dollop of jam on one of the halves. He handed it over to Number Three. He did the same with the other half and handed it to Number Two. She took it, and he made another one and gave it to Number One.

"Go on, eat up."

He gestured to them, and they took a bite and then another. Print started cutting up more biscuits and slathering jam on them. He passed them to all the girls, who started eating.

"Look at that, Nephew, we was just fishin' with the wrong bait."

Print got them to use the biscuits to push beans on their forks. A forkful of beans and a bite of biscuit. A bite of meat and a mouthful of biscuit and jam.

"Just a matter of primin' the pump."

The girls looked at him as he spoke. Red jam smudged the corners of their mouths.

After supper the camp settled down. Print was fast asleep, snoring. Valinten and two of the shepherds could be seen inside their wagon, playing cards. The light from inside played their silhouettes on the canvas cover of the wagon. Tom was out among the horses on the north side of the camp, and another shepherd was tending to the flock on the south side.

The girls had taken to sleeping under the wagon, and this evening they lay on the blankets and bedroll looking out from under it. Out into the darkness. A big moon was rising. Like a slightly squashed pumpkin, a golden orange color. Except for the great North Star, Polaris, which shone in the constellation of the Little Bear, there was nothing else in the sky. The night was purple-black and devoid of all other stars. Even the Milky Way. The moon hung like a paper lantern. Slowly it floated up. It wasn't part of heaven and it wasn't part of Earth.

"Look, there she is," said Number Five.

The others looked into the darkness and then at her.

"What?" asked Number One. *"Nobody is out there."*

"Look, there she is. There," said the little girl, pointing into the night sky.

"What? The moon?" scoffed Number One.

"Yes. She comes over the fields of my family's village," replied the little girl.

"Don't be stupid. The moon is everywhere."

"Stop it, Ghee Moon," interrupted Number Three.

"It means we are close to my village. She is leading us home," said the little girl.

"Stupid."

"Be quiet, Ghee Moon. She is young, but Ghing Wa is right," snapped Number Three. *"Maybe the moon will show us the way home. But we must not fight with one another. We must help each other and be brave."*

"She is not always there, Many nights she is gone," replied Ghee Moon.

"She is like us. Sometimes she cannot reveal herself. We have to do the same. We must be as silent as the moon. Show little of ourselves to anyone but one another. She will guide us. We must believe this," said Number Three.

"Did the moon guide us to the man who defiled Ye Fung? Where was the moon when we nearly died on that boat? Was it she who led us to these men? These men who will defile us too and then kill us?"

"Do not talk that way! Your fear and bitterness will be our ruin. We must protect each other. We must," whispered Number Three.

"You may be the oldest, Sun Foy, but I do not have to take orders from you. I will make my own decisions."

Sun Foy reached across Number Two, Mai Ling, and little Ghing Wa and grabbed Ghee Moon and pulled her toward her. *"I am not going to die because of your stupidity. You are so arrogant!"* Sun Foy hissed at her. *"These men saved Ye Fung. They feed us. They want us to eat. To bathe. I do not know what is in their hearts, but I know that they have not touched us or harmed us."*

"Sun Foy is right," said Mai Ling. *"If we displease these men, it could be the end for all of us."*

"You should listen to what Mai Ling says," said Sun Foy. *"The old man talks much, but he is not stupid. If you act this way, he may tire of your arrogance and sell you to someone who will want to do more to you than give you food. We will be done with you and you will be on your own."*

Sun Foy released her grip on the girl, who rolled away from her. They were all silent. Mai Ling and Ghing Wa looked first at Sun Foy and then to Ghee Moon. Ye Fung said nothing. She lay on her stomach with her chin resting on her folded arms, looking at the rising moon. It was turning from orange to yellow the more it rose in the sky.

Before dawn Print woke and found that Number Five and Number Two were sleeping next to him.

Chapter Fifteen

They parted company with Valinten and the sheep. They crossed the Raft River and directed more to the north. A week of cold rain all but mired them down. Print kept the herd grazing more. One particularly bad morning he decided not to even break camp. Instead he and Tom went over the wagon, greasing axles, checking wheel pins, and mending a long tear in the canvas cover. The girls stayed in the wagon and Tom rigged a fly sheet for himself and Print, which managed to keep the wagon just cold and wet enough to be somewhere between uncomfortable and miserable. As Print repeated numerous times, "There ain't no such thing as a warm rain in this part of the country."

As much as Print disliked the damp and cold, he knew that the forage would continue to be good for a while. A front finally came through and warmed things up and put quite a shine on things. The pink prairie primrose was everywhere. Purple spikes of larkspur shot up, and Print's favorite, Indian paintbrush, made its appearance. He took the point on the herd simply so he could see all this before the herd obliterated it. He watched the meadowlarks and grasshoppers take flight as he flushed their cover. Tom was still lame, and Number Three had taken control of running the wagon. It had not gone unnoticed to the men how the girls seemed to be trying hard to lend a hand. He figured that they were over halfway across Cassia County, heading northeast to hook up with the old Oregon Trail.

The trail took more turns now as they had to zigzag around the last of the hills and mountains of several ranges that started up north, beyond the forty-ninth parallel, and petered out at the south end of the state. There was plenty of game and they ate well, as long as there was a town or camp to reprovision. So far they had only lost three horses, a fact that surprised and worried Print. He had calculated for much greater losses, and the fact that they were so low gave him pause. Not an overly superstitious man, a moderately long life had given him a grasp of basic statistics.

Late morning on a bright day with already four hours on the trail had the herd rounding the base of another small range. Up ahead they saw smoke from the chimneys of a small village. They walked the herd toward the town until they came up on a shallow pond fed by several rivulets that trickled down from the surrounding hills.

The horses waded into the water to drink. Tom rode over to Print, and the wagon drew up along the trail, which was taking on all the looks of a road the closer they got to the village.

"Looks like a good place to stock up. I'm gonna go in. Anything ya want?" asked Print.

Tom rose up in the saddle. He pulled back his shoulders and then settled back down. "If you can find a piece of rawhide, I wouldn't mind patching these chaps."

"Good idea, we oughta have some on hand anyway. That's it?"

Tom thought for a moment. "Ya might replenish your arthritis medicine."

"I intend to."

"Oh, how 'bout a big sack of peanuts?"

"I ain't goin' inta downtown Omaha. Peanuts? We'll see."

Print looked back at the wagon, then turned and trotted off toward the smoking chimneys. Tom dismounted and led his horse over to the pond for a drink.

The trail did become a road, a muddy track that split a dozen or so buildings. At the edge of town, he noticed an old wagon rotting away, its wheels buried past its axles. He slowed to a walk and parked Bob Tate in front of a store declaring itself to be Burstram's Dry Goods and Mercantile. A man in an apron was leaning a box of potatoes against the front of the store. Several other crates of vegetables were arranged the same way.

"Mornin'," said Print.

The grocer straightened up and turned to face him. "Good morning to you, sir," said the man, brushing his hands on his apron.

"Nice little town ya got here."

"More than nice. I've seen lots of them. You couldn't ask for anything better, if it suits your style."

"That makes all the difference in the world. Ya open for business?"

"I am a merchant, sir. I am always open for business," smiled the grocer.

Print eased Bob Tate sideways and stepped off so as to miss the mud and set foot on the planking. The grocer noticed his maneuver.

"Guess you saw it, just out of town."

Print looked at him, not knowing where he was going with the conversation.

"The wagon. The one that's permanently sunk in the ground. That's my wagon. Been there since the first day I arrived at this little dale."

Print looped his reins around the hitching post. He made a cursory inspection of the vegetables on display. "I did notice it. An interesting artifact."

"Oh, more than an artifact, mister. More like a monument. A testament."

Print turned from the crates to face the grocer. "Is that a fact? Seen lots a monuments but never a mired wagon before. Name's Print Ritter." He extended his hand.

The grocer reciprocated. "Andrew Burstram. I doubt if you ever will."

"What's it a testament to?" asked Print.

The grocer knew he had a new audience, and Print could tell that he was about to hear a story that Burstram set a lot of stock in and had told many times before.

"Step inside, Mr. Print Ritter. You look like you could use a cup of coffee," the grocer gestured with his arm.

Print looked back up the muddy track and then stepped inside the store. He was impressed at the depth of inventory that Burstram had to offer, considering that the size of the town didn't seem to warrant enough commerce for such supplies.

Burstram disappeared behind a curtain in the back and then appeared with a china cup of coffee. Print took a sip and took a seat on a nail keg. He could tell that the grocer was getting puffed up in preparation to unload more of a tale than Print had time for this morning. Burstram seated himself on a keg facing Print and placed his hands on his knees.

"Welcome to Albion."

Print tipped his cup in the grocer's direction.

"We were with a party that had started out from Indiana. All of us had our possessions freighted by rail. The intention was to go to Salt Lake City and from there use wagons to come to Idaho. Well, the man who was holding the money we'd paid out cut us short and the whole party of pilgrims were off-loaded with every stick of our goods, courtesy of the Central Pacific, at a watering stop just east of Rawlins."

Print shifted on the keg, which was already getting uncomfortable. He sipped the coffee and listened.

"We managed to pool enough money together to purchase wagons and oxen with the money that we hadn't given to the thief who had stranded us. Two families bought tickets to Davenport, and one unmarried man said he was going to find the agent who had left us in such a dire predicament. We all chipped in some money to help him in his endeavors. Never heard from him or the whereabouts of the thieving agent. How's the coffee? Another cup?"

"I'm fine, thank you. I do need to get some supplies, though."

"Of course you do. So we headed out. Wettest summer on record. Mud was our middle name. We came into this little valley late one evening in a driving rain. All of us had been soaked for a week. We were all too tired and cold to make much of a camp. Well, that night a Mrs. Thomas Hackett kind of went 'round the bend and commenced to stabbing her husband in his sleep. She stabbed the hell out of him with a good-sized kitchen knife, and he succumbed to her efforts. It rained all that night and kept on raining, even as we buried the victimized husband the next day. Buried him on the high ground just outside of town. Time we got through putting Mr. Thomas Hackett to rest, our wagon was sunk up to its axles, just like you saw it. I told Mrs.

Burstram 'It must be a sign 'cuz I am not digging that wagon out of the mud ever again.' Told those pilgrims we had seen the elephant and we weren't goin' any farther."

Print stood on the mistaken belief that the grocer's story was over.

"Here now, don't take off before you hear the rest of this little history."

Print rubbed his buttocks and sat back down.

"They pulled out of here with Mrs. Hackett tied fast for her own safety, and theirs too, I suspect. Headed for Glen's Ferry to give her over to the authorities. So there we were. Alone and sunk in the mud. Now my wife, Mrs. Burstram, is a well-read woman, and she said we should name this place Albion after a French king who was murdered by his wife, the queen. In honor of Mr. Thomas Hackett, our first permanent resident. We operated right out of that wagon until I got a cabin built, and then we put the store on the front of it."

The grocer patted his knees and smiled at Print, who didn't say a word, afraid that it might elicit another round of history.

"So, you in need of resupply?"

Print rose, rubbed his numbed backsides again, and proceeded to tick off his requirements. "Got any jam?" Print asked.

"No, sir. However, I do have clover honey."

"I'll take all ya got. We crossed the trail with some sheepherders that said it ain't safe to travel east."

"Hostiles off the reservation. Shoshone, I heard. Mostly stealing livestock,you got livestock?"

"Five hundred–plus horses."

"I'd say that qualifies as livestock. Family?"

"Five Chinese girls."

The grocer looked at Print in a whole new way.

"It's our plan ta hook up with the Bozeman and

move north ta Sheridan," said Print, placing the empty cup on the counter. The grocer slid his hands into his pants pockets, under the apron.

"I'd say that's a big plan, considering you got maybe seven hundred miles to travel with a herd of horses and a wagon full of women."

"Five girls," Print corrected him.

"Your best bet is to head north toward the American Falls. There's plenty of soldiers at Fort Hall, so I suspect the Shoshones will stay clear of that country. If you loop well north until you cross into Wyoming, you can drop south and pick up the Overland."

"Sounds outta our way," replied Print.

Burstram shrugged. "You're the one with the herd of horses and girls," said the grocer, stuffing supplies into the flour sacks.

"You charge for those sacks?"

The grocer looked at him. "I am a merchant, not a robber," replied Burstram.

"Nice town ya got here."

"Thank you."

Bob Tate picked his way through the muddy ruts back to Tom and the girls. They off-loaded the supplies into the wagon, bunched up the herd, and headed north. On a knoll outside of the village, they passed the grave of Thomas Hackett, the first permanent resident of Albion.

Chapter Sixteen

They pushed north and east toward American Falls and Fort Hall that lay beyond. The weather turned again, and more cold rain pelted them for three days. Finally Print called a halt, and they camped on the south bank of the western Snake River.

They had passed an Irish tinsmith leading a big dog that was pulling a goat cart with his tools and gear. He said that Fort Hall was only eight miles to the north, but that it wasn't a place where an honest tradesman could earn his keep. He said if he owned such a herd of fine horses, he wouldn't go near the fort, as the army was known to requisition livestock, cattle, and horses for its needs. Such transactions were done with papers or chits that were supposed to be backed by the U.S. Treasury. Finding an alchemist in the government bureaucracy who could actually convert those papers into gold, or anything close to it, was not always easy.

They shared their supper with the tinker, and then, declining an offer to stay the night, he led his dog and cart into the drizzling twilight.

"I have been thinking that the fort might be the

place to find some folks that can take proper care of these girls," said Print as the girls were cleaning the plates.

Tom was using an awl and a heavy leather palm pad to repair his chaps. "Maybe I should go up there. Leave the herd with you and the girls," replied Tom as he turned the chaps and punched a hole through the rawhide patch and into the stained chaps. "Don't like the idea of losing the herd to some major that will probably pocket half the money for himself."

"I was thinkin' right along those lines too. 'Cept I think I'll go. Don't want ya getting sidetracked by one a Miss Lucy Highsmith's cousins."

"Suit yerself. We could use some Prince Albert."

The rain came back and continued all night. Print was awake long before daylight but lay in his bedroll, putting off getting up and facing another wet morning. When he finally did get up, he saw that there were now three girls sleeping around him.

After a breakfast spent trying to stay out of the rain, he and Bob Tate headed north to Fort Hall. The ponderosas were taller and the land definitely had a big northwoods feel to it. He saw three mule deer in a thicket of spruce, hunkered down out of the weather. His approach was not enough to roust them into the cold rain.

He was trying to count how many days the girls had been with them. He knew they had been in his care long enough that he was not looking forward to parting company with them. The prospect of spending the rest of the journey with a stoic buckaroo nephew was as depressing as the rain that was seeping through his slicker. The girls were a big liability, though, and he had to be practical. Fort Hall was probably the place that could take care of them.

Halfway to the fort, the rain slackened and then ended. The sun didn't come out, but he could tell that the temperature was going up. He eased Bob Tate into a trot when he saw the stockade in the distance.

Fort Hall was like many of the forts the army had strung across the West. Originally it had been a trading post. It still was, with a Sutter's store and a garrison of soldiers. There were always a number of Indians in and around the fort. Mostly people who no longer had a band or tribe to be with, Many had fallen victim to the whisky traders. All were on a low-grade trail to oblivion. Outside the stockade was a collection of tents and shacks awash in deep mud. It was here that most of the frontier capitalists dwelled. The whisky traders, whores, and gamblers plied their trade. Then there were the teamsters, mule skinners, tinkers, and low-class travelers who were the recipients of that trade.

Little streams of mud and manure trickled away from the shantytown as Print pulled up the big chestnut. The break in the weather had most of the residents and visitors out of the tents. An approaching rider always managed to get a welcoming committee of the saddest women of the oldest trade. Two women clutching shawls around their shoulders waded out in the muck to meet Print. Other less-motivated gals called out to him from plank stoops in front of the shacks.

Print smiled and tipped his hat to the waders who were slip-sliding through the mire. They hung on to each other for balance and were still trying to keep a grip on their shawls. He pressed his right leg hard against the horse's side, and the chestnut made a lateral walk away from the women.

"Hey there, cowboy. Want ta ride the tiger?" one of the whores called out to him from her secure perch on the decking.

Again Print tipped his hat and turned his head at

the same time, hoping that would suffice for all the remaining doxy women. "Ladies."

This cesspool was built on ground that sloped away from the entrance to the stockade. It added to the feel that it was all about to slide down on itself. The sucking sound of Bob Tate's hooves filled Print's ears as he carefully navigated the slippery footing.

"Come on, you old billy goat, gimme a ride. Ya kin' do me all night if ya got the strength."

Print looked straight ahead, not wanting to make eye contact before he cleared the fort's gates. From the side of a shack, a young man stepped toward the horse and rider. He moved quickly and almost slipped.

"Mister. Hey, mister."

He placed himself almost directly in front of Bob Tate. Print pulled up, irritated and ready for trouble. The man placed the palm of his hand on the horse's shoulder. Print saw that he had a purple mouse under one eye and a swollen lower lip that was split and scabbed.

"Mister, I'm sorry to stop you here, but I need help and I could tell watching you coming in that you might consider lending aid to someone in trouble."

He stroked the horse as he talked, and Print took in everything without moving his eyes.

"Take yer hand off my horse, son."

The young man jerked his hand away as if it had been bitten. "Sorry, mister. Please listen. I'm not part of this riffraff. They're the reason I'm in this predicament. I don't want money. I just need help."

Print eased a little. He wiped the bottom of his moustache with the back of his forefinger. He was casual in his movement. He did it to make sure his arm was free and clear to draw the big Colt if needed.

He could tell that this lad was in trouble. He was in trouble and scared.

"Mister, if you could just help me get clear of this place, I'll do whatever is required to make it up to you."

I got no need ta add this fella's troubles to mine, Print thought. He sighed and moved his head as if to look up at the entrance to the stockade. But he kept his eyes wide to any and all movement around him.

"Young man, I've got business inside the fort. I doubt if I can be of any help ta you."

Bob Tate took a step forward, and the man placed his hand on the horse again.

"Son, I asked ya not ta put your hand on my horse."

This time he did not remove it. "I have been taking care of myself for a long time, sir. I am not the sort that goes around asking for help. But they have me treed here, sir."

"As I said, I've got business in there," said Print, nodding to the entrance. "When I leave, if yer still here, we'll talk."

The young man removed his hand from the horse. "My name's Henry Gilpin. You can call me Heck. Be careful in there, sir. There can be less law inside those walls than there is out here."

That stopped Print. He looked at the lad. "Son, I got over five hundr'd head a horses down the track. Is there somethin' I need ta know about 'fore I go in there?"

"I wouldn't go in there with five horse collars and a one-eyed dog, sir."

Print said nothing. He looked down at Henry "Heck" Gilpin.

Heck spoke. "There's a Major Bolen that's in charge of the garrison. He'll take your stock, your cock, and the gold from your teeth. I'd put as much distance between you and this place as possible, sir. I'm not saying this because I need help. It is the truth, mister."

Off behind Print, he could hear one of the whores yelling, "Hey there, old-timer, you don't look like the sort that favors boys. Com' on back here an' I'll show you what the Lord really intended that piece of lumber for."

Print looked from Heck to the stockade, then back to the desperate lad in the mud, and then turned in the saddle to see several working girls gathering and watching him and Heck. He looked down at Heck. "Get yer horse an' come on."

"Sir, I don't have boots, much less a horse and saddle." said Heck, lifting one leg to show a mud-caked foot.

"Shit. . . . Shit. Climb onboard."

Print offered the toe that protruded through the stirrup as a step and his hand to help Heck swing up behind him. Print pulled and sucked him out of the mud. Bob Tate took a step under the added weight. Print turned the horse slowly away from the fort.

He didn't look at them, but he saw them. The whores and several layabouts who had been watching the men.

Aw, come on, mister. That's a sacrilege. Let me show you the true way. Hell, I'll speak in tongues to that little tent pole of yours."

The crowd laughed and a chicken flew from atop one of the shacks and landed in front of Bob Tate, who was carefully making his way through the slippery footing. The chicken struggled to free itself from the mud and briefly took flight, only to land in more mud. It was all Print could do not to gig Bob Tate into a lope and put heels to this pustule smear of shacks.

Chapter Seventeen

On the ride back to the herd, Heck told Print how he had come to be in such a sorry state. He had gotten in a protracted card game with several soldiers and luck was with him all the way until the "blue boys" decided to amend the rules and took him out back and reversed his financial situation. They then beat the tar out of him. Took his horse and anything else they thought had value. They picked him clean and left him to the mud and the whores and whisky peddlers. He was from back East. He had been on the move for almost five years. He claimed he could turn his hand at almost anything, He said he was game and not afraid of hard work. He was from Pennsylvania. A damn Yankee, Print thought.

They drifted into the camp as Tom was trying to get supper ready. He and the girls watched silently as Heck swung down and cringed as one of his bare feet landed on a stone. Then Print dismounted. Bob Tate gave himself a good shake. Tom was looking at the unshod young man his uncle had brought in.

"Whatta we got here?" asked Tom.

Print followed his gaze to Heck's muddy feet. "Work of another boot stealer."

"Footwear must be at a premium in this part of the country."

"Heck Gilpin, meet Tom Harte, my nephew. He's the *segundo* of this outfit."

The men nodded to one another.

"Mr. Gilpin has asked if he could sign on to help us. Claims he's a hand. We'll see."

Tom kept staring at his feet. He turned and walked to the back of the wagon and leaned in. He pulled back and held a pair of worn-to-hell boots.

"If your feet ain't too big, you might fit into Capt'n Fender's boots," he said, handing them to Heck. Heck pulled a pair of gray woolen socks from his coat pocket.

"Thank you, Mr. Harte."

"Tom. There's only room for one mister in this outfit," Tom replied, looking over at Print, who was already making a plate for himself.

"I'll go wash up," said Heck, jerking his head in the direction of the riverbank. He gingerly walked away carrying the dead man's boots.

Tom turned to his uncle. "No horse, no gear, no boots?"

His back to Tom, Print didn't look up. "I know. I got a feeling 'bout him. He mighta saved this herd for us."

"He don't leak, does he?"

"No, not this one."

Heck returned in Fender's boots. He was looking at Print eating.

"Grab a plate," said Tom.

Heck hadn't lied. He could sit a horse. Uncle and nephew put him to work. He switched off riding flank on either side and drag. Print put him on the red roan and he showed that he could ride without showing off. Both men watched him and he passed muster.

Print liked that he took to the night work, and in the three days he had been with them, he never once asked about the girls. He must have come from a good Yankee family, thought Print.

Tom liked the idea that he was getting more sleep and that maybe Heck could take over as the recipient of his uncle's theories on the universe, cooking, and birds.

Print decided to end the idea of heading north. It was a land he was not that familiar with, and the prospects of possibly running into a few braves on a jaunt off the reservation was starting to bother him less than the chance that the authorities—and any other people of lighter pigmentation—might just be more of a threat to them. The problem was that the change in their trail required them to divert somewhat south to avoid the higher ranges that had little or no passes to get through. He was beginning to feel the clock starting to run against him.

His plan now was to aim for the Wyoming line near the Star Valley and then skirt the Salt River range and move directly on to Lander. Somewhere along the way, they could hope to find someone to take the girls.

The morning of the third day since picking up Heck, they started to move out, Print on point with the gray mare and her lieutenants on her tail. Heck and Tom rode flank, and the wagon with Number Three at the helm brought up the rear. They had barely cleared camp when Tom, turning in the saddle to look back at the wagon, saw a horse standing by itself. He wheeled and loped back to the lone horse. It had made no attempt to follow the herd and it wasn't grazing.

He dismounted, dropped his reins, and walked over to the gelding. It didn't seem to be favoring a leg and there was no blood to be seen. He carefully ran his hand down the legs. First the front and then the hind. As his hand stroked the left hind, the horse pulled the leg up and tried to step away. On the inside of the leg just below the spavin was a deep cut and there was dried blood. The hock was swollen and hot to the touch. Tom went back to his horse and removed his revolver, which was wrapped in an oily rag, an old La Mat .44 caliber from his saddlebag. Over his horse's rump, he saw that Number Three had stopped the wagon and the girls were watching him. He stuck the revolver in his belt and removed his rope and walked back to the injured horse.

He played out a small loop and slipped the rope over the horse's head. He made another loop for the nose, making a temporary halter. He stepped back and with his forefinger drew an "X" between the ears and the eyes, the center being in the middle of the animal's forehead. He pulled the La Mat from his belt. He placed the barrel on the imaginary spot of the intersecting lines. He fired, and the horse sat back on its haunches like a dog. Tom held the rope tight. It then keeled over on its side, legs stretched out. It shivered once and then went stiff. The girls had turned away at the sound of the shot, except for Number Four. She didn't flinch. She continued to look at the dead horse, even as Number Three started the wagon moving.

Tom rewrapped the revolver, first removing the spent cartridge and replacing it with a new load. He placed it back in his saddlebag and then retrieved his rope, coiling it up. He mounted up, secured his rope, and rode back to the herd, which had stopped at the sound of the gunshot. He rode up to Print. Heck watched him from the other side of the herd and turned to look back at the dead horse on the ground.

"Busted hock," said Tom.

Print listened, nodded, and then moved on.

* * *

Late that afternoon they stopped to let the horses graze on some good forage. There was no creek or watering hole, but the grass was too good to pass up. Besides, they had had nothing but water almost everywhere on the trail. Print was sure they would hit water in the morning.

The men were still mounted when Heck called out, "Mr. Ritter, we got company."

Walking toward Heck on the other side of the herd were three mounted braves. Print caught Tom's attention and motioned for him to ride around the herd. Print did the same from the other direction. He came up behind Heck, who had the red roan pointed toward the visitors. Print stopped a few paces behind Heck.

Tom took up a position farther away, off to the left. As he rode around the horses, he had removed the Remington from its scabbard. It now rested across the pommel of his saddle.

The visitors rode thin ponies rigged in war bridles. They were representative of their people. Coppery, oiled skin. Little of their clothing was native. Ill-fitting white men's pants and boots. A woolen coat. A broadcloth shirt. One wore a deerskin shirt, greasy and devoid of any decorations and embellishments. All wore their hair long. One had a red ribbon braided into his. Even with the blended clothing, you could tell they were different. You could see it at a hundred yards. They had a look. A way they carried themselves. So at ease, bareback on their ponies, with braided rawhide for their bridles. Their faces revealed nothing that they didn't want you to know.

"They look like Crow, Mr. Ritter," said Heck over his shoulder, not taking his eyes off them.

"Crow? You know Crow when ya see them?"

"I spent time at the agency in Laramie. Are you conversant in Crow, Mr. Ritter?"

"Hell no, Are you?" asked Print, carefully removing his gloves.

"I can sign and muddle my way through a little."

"Well then, muddle on, and let's find out what these sunburned children of misfortune want."

Heck eased his horse forward, He started to sign and talk at the same time to the three mounted men. The one with the yellow neckerchief talked. He barked at Heck. Short bursts. Very declarative.

Heck turned his head to the left and spoke over his shoulder. "He says we are crossing their land and that you must pay to do so."

"Are we in Crow country?" asked Print.

"No. Not really."

Print carefully folded his gloves and tucked them into the fork of his saddle, beneath the pommel. "You figger they got any legitimate claim?"

"No, not really."

"An' that would include the ground we're standin' on right now, I suppose."

"You can be sure of that, Mr. Ritter."

"So, what's the tariff?"

Heck talked and signed some more. "He says it is going to cost you two horses to cross their ancient hunting ground."

"This feels like a shakedown ta me," said Print. "Tell 'em they can have one horse. Their pick."

Again Heck talked. Tom looked back at the wagon and noticed that the girls were nowhere to be seen.

"They say two, Mr. Ritter."

"Bullshit," snapped Tom as he lifted his rifle from where it rested on the pommel and held it in both hands.

Once more Heck addressed Print over his left shoulder, never taking his eyes off the three braves.

"It's your call, Mr. Ritter, but from where I sit, they do have the look and smell of wildness about them."

Print said nothing for a long moment.

"Mr. Ritter?" asked Heck.

"You tell 'em I said I'm an old man. Tell 'em I'm sick. Tell 'em sick an' dyin'. Tell 'em I don't give a shit if I die today or tomorrow. One horse."

Heck talked and then there was silence. After several long moments, Print squeezed Bob Tate and eased him up past Heck and right up alongside the fellow who was doing all the talking. His left boot touched the shoulder of the Indian pony. The pony took a step backward. Print had a thin smile on his face and never took his eyes off the brave.

He could see the grime on the faded yellow scarf. The brave's face revealed nothing. He was completely self-contained and yet serenely confident at the same time. He looks like he don't give a shit if he dies or not, either, thought Print.

Keeping locked in on this warrior's eyes, Print ever so slowly reached into his vest pocket and removed the little wooden figurine of a horse he had been whittling. He raised up in the saddle and reached over to offer it to the brave, who broke eye contact for a moment to look at what was in Print's hand and then looked right back to Print's eyes.

Print never stopped looking at him, even as he nodded a silent yes at the shiny face that was the color of brick. He felt the wooden horse leave his grasp, and he sat back slowly. He raised his hand, holding up two fingers. Then he picked up the reins and backed Bob Tate until he was abreast of Heck.

"Tell him to go pick out the other one."

Heck said nothing, but from the corner of his eye, Print could see him gesture with his hands. They all just stared at one another. One of the Indian ponies stomped at a fly. Print slowly turned to look over at Tom, who had his cut-down Remington resting in the crook of his left arm. He brought his gaze back to the brave.

As if on cue, all three ponies backed up and kept going backward for a good twenty feet, Then their leader barked like a dog, and they turned right and leapt forward to skirt the herd. Print, Tom, and Heck turned their mounts to keep facing the departing braves, who went about cutting out a dandy blood bay. From nowhere, one of them slipped a braided rawhide line over the horse's neck. The bay, frightened, started to back up and toss its head in resistance. Instantly another rider swatted it across its rump with the carbine he was carrying and the blood bay jumped forward. They barked and whooped and turned heels to the herd and were gone.

Print and company watched in silence. Tom spat.

"He knows horses," said Tom, wiping spittle from his chin as he saw the last of one of their better horses disappear.

"Yer right, Hank, there is a look an' smell of wildness about 'em. Even young bucks off the reservation."

Print turned for the wagon and saw Number Three leading the other girls from a thicket of hackberry bushes. "We gotta find a place for these gals 'fore we lose the herd, our scalps, an' them," muttered Print to no one in particular.

Late that night Sun Foy got up and went off to the bushes to pee. As she was squatting, she looked off to her left and was sure she saw a brave looking at her in the dark. She rose and hiked up her pants and ran back to the wagon. She snatched her blanket and joined Ghing Wa and Mai Ling next to Print.

Chapter Eighteen

On top of a rock outcropping up in the timberline, a Cooper's hawk held a chickaree in its talons. With its yellow beak, it ripped meat and entrails from the dead squirrel. Far below, the herd of horses moved in a long line followed by the wagon.

Print had explained to Heck the story of the girls and why it was now so important to find a place for them. Heck told him that the next town of any consequence was Cariboo, a mining camp down the track. After that there was Soda Springs. Then nothing that he knew of until long after the Wyoming line.

"I'm not sure it is what you are looking for, Mr. Ritter. Like most of these camps, it's as rough as a cob. But then you don't have a lot of choices out here."

"Ya got that right, Hank."

"Actually it's 'Heck,' Mr. Ritter,"

"'Course it is, Hank."

It was a Rocky Mountain summer day. Hotter than it felt and brighter than a young man's possibilities. The land was thicker with spruce and ponderosa, but the meadows were carpeted in buttercups and wild violets. You could smell the pine sap in the air.

From way above them, the Cooper's hawk uttered a deep-throated cackle followed by a long, high-pitched whistle. "Swee-hee." Print breathed in the smell of the evergreens, the horse sweat of the herd, and the crushed plants they trampled underfoot. He was going to miss these little girls.

By afternoon they could see smoke rising from a small vale in the distance. Heck said it was probably Cariboo and Print called a halt to the day. He said they'd give the horses more grazing. They made camp and Print announced that he was off to look for supper. With the side-by-side resting against his shoulder and a pocketful of shells, he trekked into the timber. It was easy pickings as he shot a dozen quail and two partridge. Print dropped them into a flour sack he had brought along. He came to a stream and knelt and then lay on his stomach and drank. He splashed his face and cupped cold water over his hair. He sat beneath a big hemlock, his back to the rough bark, laid the shotgun beside him, and closed his eyes.

Print had dreamed last night about the little girl with the button-up shoes. Her crinoline dress. Her brown eyes. He could not remember where the dream was. There was no zebra pony this time, but the girl's mother, Ann, was there. She led the child away, but the little girl returned. The dream woke him and he propped himself up and looked around the darkened camp. The Chinese girls were sleeping around him. He lay back and drifted back to sleep.

The more he thought about his dream, the sleepier he got. He felt the warm sun and heard a meadowlark in the field behind him. Soon he dozed off. He dreamed of the Chinese girls dressed in white dresses and riding horses on a merry-go-round. But the horses were real and leapt from the spinning wheel with the girls on them. He stood on the turning platform, hanging on to a pole. He watched the girls on the horses disappear. From deep in the sleep of the dream, he heard a sound near him and snapped his head up. He grabbed for the gun and saw the girls approaching him.

They stopped when they saw him reach for the shotgun. He was still half asleep and unfocused. When he realized that he was awake, he took his hand from the gun on the ground. The girls stood in their tracks.

"Come on over here," he called, "Ya caught me nappin'. I was dreamin' all about you gals."

Sun Foy, the eldest, stepped forward. Print got to his feet. Picked up the shotgun and the flour sack. He handed the sack to Number Two to carry.

"Did Tom send ya to fetch me?"

"Tham," Number Five repeated to no one.

They walked back toward camp. Insects hovered over the wildflowers and grass. Swallows dove and turned and banked and dove again at the insects flitting in the afternoon sun.

"Remind me to tell y'all about swallows and how far they come just ta eat our bugs up here. Fascinatin' story."

They flushed a grouse and Print swung the gun up and dropped it with one shot. The girls stood wide-eyed at the sound of gun. Number One ran ahead to where the bird had fallen. She held it up for the others to see.

Print took the bird from her and examined it. "Thought it was a grouse," he said. "But this ain't no grouse. Least not one I ever seen."

He held the bird at arm's length and turned it over. "Maybe a ptarmigan. Well, we'll see if it tastes like a grouse," handing it back to Ghee Moon.

They got back to the wagon and he showed them how to pluck and dress the birds. He then went and saddled up Bob Tate and walked him over to the girls. He tapped Number Five on the shoulder and motioned for her to come with him. Ghing Wa looked to Sun Foy to tell her what to do. She nodded and told her to go on.

Standing next to the horse, Print reached down and lifted the little girl up on the saddle. He set her sideways and hooked her right leg over the horn as if it were a sidesaddle. He placed her hands on the saddle horn and patted her knee. Ghing Wa looked to the other girls and Sun Foy nodded her reassurance.

Print removed his lariat and slipped a loop over Bob Tate's head and stepped back. The little girl reached for him. He grabbed her hand and replaced it on the horn and stepped back again. Print winked at her and told her not to be afraid. He flipped the lariat, and Bob Tate started to walk. He walked slowly in a circle around Print, walking in time to the clucking sound Print made.

Ghing Wa was terrified, but she held on. Print smiled at her and said she was doing just fine. The girl and the horse made three trips around Print and then he clucked louder and flipped the rope again and the big chestnut broke into a slow trot. Ghing Wa squealed. The girls called out to her and in their own tongue told her she was doing just fine.

"Easy. Easy does it. Relax. Yer doin' fine."

When it came to her that she was not going to fall off and die, she almost smiled and breathed. Print lightly tugged the rope and the horse transitioned back to a walk. Then the girl really did smile.

Beyond the girls stood Heck and Tom, watching. Print tugged again and Bob Tate planted himself. Print walked toward the horse and rider, coiling the line. He laid his hand on her tiny, slippered foot and gave it a pat. He told her she was brave and that she was a natural at riding horses. He told her he knew that the first time he laid eyes on her. Her face was flush and she smiled at him the way he dreamed the girl in the button-up shoes did. He knew she wanted to go again, so he walked to the other side of the horse, played out the line, and sent them into a circle. Around they went. She called out to the girls and they back to her and she laughed. Print made a soft popping sound with his lips and let out more line and Bob Tate eased into a soft, rocking-chair lope and again she squealed, and the girls watching her did too. And for just a moment, he thought of his dream and the merry-go-round. He brought them back to a trot, and then a walk, and finally they stopped.

He helped her remove her legs from the saddle horn and held her under her arms and lifted her down. She steadied herself against him to get her balance and he took her hand and walked her back to the girls. A tiny, crippled girl about as far away from home as she could be, shuffling beside a bowed and bandy-legged old cowboy.

Supper was spent mostly with the men watching and listening to the girls talk to one another. They were more animated this night than any time since Tom and Print first met Fender. Print hadn't felt much like cooking tonight, so he let Heck do the duty. He found a comfortable spot by the fire and smoked and whittled on a new piece of wood and sipped a little whisky for his arthritis.

"Hank, if ya don't mind, I think I'll let you watch things here in the mornin' and Tom an' I'll take the girls inta town an' see if we can find the right people ta take care of 'em."

"Whatever you say, Mr. Ritter. Easy enough for me. Hope it isn't a disappointment for you. The town, I mean."

"So do I, Hank. So do I."

That night he dreamed. But not of little girls or zebra ponies or merry-go-rounds. It was mostly about Virginia and the boys from Carroll County and things he hadn't thought of in many years. He tossed, woke himself up several times with his own snoring, and once he looked about and saw that all the girls had dragged their pallets over and were sleeping around him. He fell asleep thinking of little Number Five going 'round and 'round on old Bob Tate.

Tom had stayed up with the herd and not wakened his uncle, so Print was confused when he woke up and saw that light was breaking in the east. He gingerly got up without waking any of the girls and walked off to pee. Tom came in as Print hobbled back in his stocking feet and slipped on his boots.

"What happened?" asked Print.

"I wasn't tired. It was a pretty night, so I thought I'd let you sleep."

"Can't believe I slept through the night."

"Must have needed it. What are your plans for today?" asked Tom, nodding in the direction of the girls, who were getting up and rolling up their blankets and bedrolls.

"Gotta do it. Gotta take 'em inta that town and see what we can do. Ain't fair to them nor us ta keep 'em on the trail. We don't put an end ta this, we'll lose the herd and God only knows what'll happen to them. No, you an' I'll take 'em in after breakfast."

Tom looked off into the distance and saw the rising smoke from the mining camp. "Any thoughts on how you're going to explain it to them?"

"Nope. I'm just gonna take 'em in. They ain't got a say in it."

"I'll be ready to go when you are. Coffee'll do me for breakfast."

"Nice sewin' job," said Print, pointing to Tom's pocket.

"Thanks."

Tom walked back to the herd while Print slipped on his boots, tucked in his shirt, and slid his suspenders over his shoulders.

Sun Foy was always attuned to the subtleties of disposition between Tom and Print. The tone and modulation of their voices told her all she needed to know. Not what they were saying, but if they were cross with one another or if something was troubling one but not the other. She knew that how they felt had everything to do with her and the girls' future.

This morning she heard them talk. Not angry, but low. The old man had the new one cook breakfast as he went off for a walk. And Tahm didn't eat but instead stayed with the horses.

When Honke Pren returned and hooked up the mules but made no to attempt to secure the camp for travel, she knew that something was very wrong. They way the men averted her eyes when she looked at them. Especially the new man. The old man brought his horse up and Tahm climbed into the wagon and took the reins. Honkle Pren called to her and the others and motioned for them to join Tahm in the wagon.

"This is not right. I think it is not good, but be quiet. Here, take this," she said to Ghee Moon as she slipped her a fork she had taken when they packed the wagon.

Number One took the utensil and hid it in her sleeve.

"Hank, this shouldn't take all day, but if it does, don't leave the herd. No matter how much ya might want to. You stay here."

"Yes, sir. I'll have supper ready"

Print turned his horse away from camp, passing the wagon. Tom slapped the reins and the wagon lurched forward.

"Let's get 'er done nephew."

Tom didn't know Chinese, but he could tell that the girls were pretty upset. Number Three would cut them off when they started talking among themselves. Print rode out in front of the wagon and didn't look back to check on them.

As they drew close to the camp, they could see tents and shacks in a gap between two short mountains. It had steep sides and gave the impression that they were all piled on top of one another. Less than a quarter of a mile from the tent town, they came upon a man with a bucket in one hand and a wide brush in the other. He turned at the sound of their approach. He held his hand with the brush high to block out the sun from his eyes. There was an assortment of signs in various sizes pointing in all directions. One said Soda Springs. Another said Christian Cemetery. Beside it, pointing the opposite way, a sign read Catholic Cemetery. One simply said Diggings and seemed to point to nowhere. Next to the man with the bucket and brush was a sign that was getting redone. It read, CARIB—.

"Morning," said the man with the brush, moving the brush so he could see who he was talking to.

"Morning," replied Print. "New town?"

"No. Just a new name. Use to be called Porcupine. Then we became Broken Nose, but now folks thinks that's too rough and common so we're goin' with Cariboo. That's for Caribbo Jack. Heard of him?"

Tom and Print shook their heads.

"Real name's Jesse Farichild. But somehow he got the handle Cariboo Jack."

"Is he the authority in town?" asked Print.

"Well, to hear him tell it, he was the authority on everything. Sort of a windbag, but he was the real deal. He's the first one to hit gold here."

"Where might we find Mr. Cariboo?"

The painter lifted the arm with the paint bucket and pointed to the sign, "Christian Cemetery." "Just follow the sign."

Print looked at the sign and beyond and then back to the painter. The mules shifted their legs and the harness creaked and jingled.

"Ya missed him by about a month."

Uncle and nephew said nothing.

"Prospector come into the High Dollar carrying on about a wounded grizzly cavorting down by Bear River. Jack starts blowing about what he would do to that griz' and someone took him up on it."

The painter set the bucket on the ground and placed the brush across the top.

"So they set out well fortified with whisky and shot. Jack come up on the bear an' tore into the brush, shootin' to beat hell. Trouble was, he was so drunk he couldn't put a ball in the beast."

The painter took a rag from his pocket and wiped his brow. "Forgot my hat. Well, the bear started to work on Jack and finally Jim Havard shot the griz' dead. 'Course by that time, Jack was looking pretty used up. They hauled the doctor up from Malad to tend to him and then they brought him back here."

The painter wiped his forehead again and patted his shirt pockets.

"Didn't work out?" asked Print.

The painter kept patting himself, looking for something. He looked up. "No, it didn't. Doctor did a swell job of sewing him together, 'cept he didn't leave no openings to drain. Blood poisoning took hold and he passed on."

"White of you to name the town after him."

"Had to. Folks over at Soda Springs wanted to lay claim to him. Wanted to bury him there being he's such a big deal in these parts."

The painter gave up on trying to find what he didn't have. "You fellas got a smoke?"

Tom reached in his pocket and tossed his makings to the painter.

They sat in silence as he took a paper and laid it on the tops of two fingers, sprinkled cut tobacco on it, carefully twisted the paper's ends, inserted it in his mouth.

"Yes, the folks in Soda Springs got exercised when they learned we had him deep in the ground."

He lit the smoke and drew deeply. From the back of the wagon, Tom heard the girls whispering and the big one shut them off.

"That wasn't going to stop those hardheaded Mormons. So we figgered we'd take the high ground by naming the town after him."

"Got a hotel?" asked Print.

"How long you planning on staying?"

"Long enough for a bath an' a shave an' maybe a beefsteak dinner."

The painter tossed the makings back to Tom. "Thanks. Then that would be the Queen of the Rockies. Everything else rents by the hour. You here to do business with those girls?"

"Maybe."

"Then you ought to talk to Miss Becker. Ask for Big Rump Kate. That's her working name. She's always looking for new gals to work the line. She's got the money too. Worth more than all the panners in town put together. She'll do right by you."

"Queen of the Rockies Hotel?"

"Yep. Thanks for the smoke."

Print moved out and the wagon followed.

"You'll know her when you see her," called out the painter to the departing wagon.

Chapter Nineteen

They proceeded toward the town wedged between the two high hills. The trail turned into deep muddy goo the closer they got to town. There were horses tethered, mired up to their hocks. The camp smelled of greasy smoke and overflowing privies. The sounds of men shouting and a cockfight came from behind one of the two rows of tents and buildings that lined the road. Paths of planking went in all directions, spanning churned-up mud and manure.

There was little activity visible. Print assumed that the men were in the mines and the whores were resting up from the night before. Everyone else was probably betting on the Shanghai rooster. The main street, the only street, was literally the point where the two hills came together. Everything on either side was sliding toward the street. A second tier of small tents and tents on top of log-walled sides clung to the hills above the front street dwellings.

Farther down it flattened out some and there were pens and corrals in the back. A red-and-white sign read "Seabolt Livery." Beyond that was the biggest building, labeled Queen of the Rockies. It was two stories and had a planked deck that ran the length of the front of the hotel. All the other shacks had stoops or just some boards tossed on top of the mud.

Print stopped in front of the hotel. He heard a roar from the unseen men at the edge of town and then the crowing of a cock and then cursing. He turned in the saddle and, leaning on the cantle with his right hand, said to Tom, "Better sit tight 'til I get this sorted out."

"Uncle?"

"Why don't ya let me see what's what 'fore we talk too much."

Tom wrapped the reins around the hand brake and started to roll a smoke. He turned to face the girls, who all had the look of impending betrayal on their faces. Number Three held a hard gaze on him, and he turned back around to finish rolling the smoke. The girls talked in whispers behind his back.

Print dismounted and his boots sank up past his spurs into the muck. He tied Bob Tate to the back of the wagon and struggled in the mud to the steps. He wiped the excess mud on the planks and ascended to the porch and into the hotel. He was concerned about all the mud he was tracking in and went back to the door to scrape off some more. He looked down on the wagon and saw the girls looking up at him.

He walked back to a small counter behind which a man was paring his fingernails with a pocketknife. The clerk put away the knife at Print's approach and stood to greet him.

"Needing a room?" asked the clerk.

"Two. Just for the evenin'. You stable my horse an' mules?"

"We don't, sir. Seabolt's next door does. Two rooms, two dollars each."

Print paid the clerk, who handed him two skeleton keys, each attached to a brass disk with numbers pounded into them.

"Is there a mayor in this town?"

"Not hardly."

"How 'bout a town council?"

"Nope."

"Sheriff?"

"No, sir. Not anymore. Mister, this town's as rough as a cob. It's hard on lawmen. Hard enough to put two in the ground in a year. Nobody's signing up for mayor, town council, or sheriff."

"So, who's in charge?"

"Well, the town sorta operates on a 'live an' let live' policy with some 'every man for himself' thrown in, This ain't one of those places where you check your firearms when ya get to town."

Print stood with his hands on top of the counter, palms down. He lightly rocked on the heels of his boots, looking at the clerk. He looked down at the counter and tapped his fingers and then looked back up at the clerk.

"Kate Becker is the big operator here. She and Avery Blanders. He freights in heavy equipment for the mines, but he stays over ta Soda Springs most of the time. You thinkin' of running for office?"

The clerk incorrectly assumed that sufficient time had passed since Print first walked in such that he could attempt some personal humor with the newest clientele. A disingenuous grin accompanied the last remark he made, but it quickly disappeared when he saw the lack of response on Print's face.

"How 'bout a bath? Can I get a bath here?"

"Yes, sir. Right out back. There's an old Chinaman. He'll set you up with soap and towels and all the hot water you can stand. He'll give you a shave, too, if you don't mind the idea of a Mongolian holding a razor that close to your gizzard. But no barberin'. He ain't worth a shit at cuttin' hair."

Print headed for the front door. Halfway, he stopped and turned to ask the clerk, "The Chinaman, does he speak English?"

The clerk, who had revised his opinion of Print based on his apparent lack of any humor, spit into a can behind the counter. "He knows 'soap,' 'water,' 'hot,' 'cold.' Things like that, I guess. I ain't in the habit of conversing with Chinks."

Print walked out the door. He walked down the hotel steps to the last board before the mud. "I got us two rooms for the night. You can park the rig next door. I'll take the girls inside."

"So, what's the deal? Did you find somebody to take 'em?"

Print motioned to the watching girls to get off the wagon. "Not yet. It doesn't sound promisin'. I at least want a bath and ta sleep in a bed for a while."

"What about the herd?"

"Maybe you can ride out after we get dinner."

Print took one step off the planking to lift Number Five off the wagon. His boot sank into the mud. Again he scraped his muddy boot on the steps. "I'm goin' to get them settled into a room an' then I'm taking a bath out back."

"Well, don't leave them up there. I'll be up in a minute."

Print held the arm of Number Five as she navigated the steps. On the porch, Number Three and Print looked back to see Tom steer the wagon around the side of the hotel. Print held the door for the girls. Once inside he led them toward the staircase at the end of the room.

"Hold on there, mister."

Print turned to face the clerk, who had returned to manicuring his fingernails.

"Mister, those rooms are for sleeping in, not cooching. You want to work those girls, you go talk to Big Rump Kate. This here's a real hotel."

Print gave a long pause before answering the spivvy character behind the counter.

"That's good 'cuz we want a bath, a good steak, and some sleep. You got a problem with that?"

The clerk couldn't hold Print's gaze. He swept his hand across the counter as if to remove some speck of dust. With the other, he waved. "Have at it."

He spit into the can behind the counter and took a seat as if to imply that he had gotten his point across. Print led the girls up the steps to the second floor and down the hallway to the last room. He motioned for the girls to go in and he followed, closing the door. He took a seat in a ladder-back chair by the window and faced the silent girls.

"Ya probably think yer about ta be played badly. Well, it just ain't so. I'm tryin' my level best ta make things right by you."

Footsteps down the hall and the door opening interrupted him. Tom walked in with saddlebags over his shoulder.

"Did you find a sheriff?" asked Tom.

"No. No sheriff. No mayor. No nothin'."

"What does that mean?"

"It means these little cherry blossoms ain't goin' nowhere, least not tonight, Nephew. You stay here with them. I'm goin' ta get a bath and talk to a Chinaman out back. When I get back, I'll sit with them an' you can clean up."

Print opened one of the saddlebags and pulled out a pair of long underwear. He draped them over his shoulder and left.

Out the back of the hotel, a catwalk of planking

led to a bathhouse that doubled as a laundry. Inside a Chinaman was stirring a large tub atop a woodstove with a stick stripped of its bark. Lines strung across the room held drying clothes and bedding. Three bathtubs were lined up in the center of the room. They were shaped like caskets.

"I come ta get a bath."

The Chinaman made a gesture that was somewhere between a nod and a kowtow, He motioned to the tubs. Print pulled over a stool and started taking off his boots and then stood to remove his shirt, pants, and underwear. He sat back down to remove his socks and, upon examination, realized the one was in need of repair and the other beyond repair. The Chinaman was filling the tub with hot water, and steam filled the room. Except for his hands and face and neck, Print was pasty white. He gingerly stepped into the tub, pulled back his foot, and waited as the Chinaman poured a bucket of cooler water. He got in, closed his eyes, and sank down. For several minutes, he said nothing. He savored the feel of the hot water as its warmth made its way through his body and into joints, sockets, and ligaments. He took a washcloth and draped it over his forehead and face.

When he removed it, he saw the Chinaman across the room sitting on a bench, his back to the wall, looking at him. The Chinaman rose and approached him with a bar of brown soap and a long-handled scrub brush. Print took them from him and the man returned to the bench. Print soaped up the bristles of the brush and commenced to scrub his back. Again he was momentarily transfixed by the sensation. The Chinaman got up and took a bucket of water off the stove and carefully poured some into the foot of the tub.

"You speak English?" asked Print.

"Yes. Yes," said the Chinaman as he returned the bucket to the stove.

"Well, maybe you can help me. I'll pay you. Ya see, I got these five Chinese girls . . ."

The Chinaman looked confused and then nervous. He returned to his seat and looked away from Print.

"Let's start over. My name's Print Ritter. What's yours?"

The Chinaman turned to face Print.

"Your name. What's your name?"

"My name is Lung Hay."

"Well, Mr. Lung Hay, through a series of circumstances, fate has placed five Chinese girls in my care. Now I ain't in the girl business, and I sure as hell ain't in the Chinese girl business."

Print paused, and the Chinaman, who was looking away, turned to face him.

"I'm in the horse business. I'm headin' ta Wyoming and I got stuck with these little girls an' one's half crippled. I can't converse with them nor they with me. You sabe?"

Lung Hay nodded yes.

"I want ta help 'em. I want to find some authority that can take care of 'em and be reasonably assured that no harm'll come to 'em. Know what I mean?"

Again Lung Hay nodded yes.

"So far ever' place we run up on has been such a shit hole I wouldn't leave a dead dog there."

Print grabbed his ankle and drew up his foot to soap it. "I'll pay you to help me talk to the girls an' get this sorted out. I know they ain't got the slightest idea what's goin' on and spend mosta the time in mortified fear. Ya think ya could help me with this?"

"Yes," said the Chinaman

"Can ya wash out those clothes?" Print asked,

pointing with the bar of soap to the pile he left on the floor.

"Yes," said the Chinaman.

"Good deal," said Print, sinking back into the tub.

Print walked down the hallway in his long underwear and boots, a damp towel over his shoulder. He entered the room to see Tom at the chair by the window and the girls sitting on the edge of the bed. He changed into a pair of pants as Lung Hay knocked at the door. Print opened the door and welcomed the Chinaman in.

At the sight of Lung Hay, the girls froze. Print was taken aback when he turned to introduce them.

"Tom, this is Lung Hay, an he's gonna help us get this all figgered out. Girls, I want ya ta meet Mr. Lung Hay."

Lung Hay made a slight bow, and the girls whispered to one another frantically.

"Tell 'em I have hired you ta help me talk ta them."

Lung Hay first asked if they all understood Mandarin. They said they did. He then repeated what Print had asked of him. The girls looked to Print and then back to Lung Hay.

"Tell 'em we are sorry for what's happened ta them and that we mean ta make sure that they have a good place ta stay an' are treated well."

Lung Hay repeated Print's words and the reaction from the girls was immediate. They all started talking urgently to the Chinaman. Lung Hay turned to Print.

"They say that they want to stay with you and your son. Please to be good as not to leave them."

Print looked at Tom. "My son?"

"No son?"

"No. No son. My nephew. Tell 'em they can't live

out on the trail with us. They need a proper place to live. A regular place and such."

Lung Hay relayed Print's message, and the girls got quiet. Little Number Five started to cry.

"Tell 'em they will be all right. They have my word on it."

The Chinaman did not translate. Instead he looked directly at Print.

"Go on, tell 'em."

"This is an old story," said Lung Hay. "There is no place safe for them. Nowhere. They will be like meat before hungry dogs. They will be eaten."

"I just gave them my word. You doubtin' that, Chinaman?"

Lung Hay continued to face Print. "No. I no doubt your word, maybe your wisdom."

Print's eyes flared. First at Lung Hay and then at Tom. Tom shrugged.

"I think maybe you speak better English than you let on, Mr. Chinaman," said Tom,

"I mean not to argue. I believe you want them only good. I have spent many years in your country and I have learned your language. I also learn your ways. Not to make you mad, but it would be a kindness to cut their throats than to leave them here."

Print turned red and shouted. "I said no harm is goin' ta come ta them! Now we got horses ta get to Sheridan before fall. And there ain't no way around that. Maybe this ain't the place for them, but I tell you, Mr. Lung Hay Chinaman, this whole country ain't all shit, piss, an' corruption. No, sir."

Lung Hay continued to face Print but said nothing. Several of the girls were crying.

"Ah, hell. Tell 'em not ta get upset. They're gonna stay with us for the time bein'. At least until we get it all figgered out. Go on, tell 'em."

As Lung Hay translated, Tom stood up and looked out the window.

"You sure are a hard case. They're going to be stuck to us like jackass burrs."

Print ignored his nephew.

"Lung Hay, can ya watch them while we go get somethin' ta eat? Maybe you could cook somma y'all's food. Bet they'd like that."

"Yes, I can do that."

Print put on a clean shirt and slipped his suspenders over his shoulders. He buckled his holster on. "Better stay heeled while we're in this burg."

Chapter Twenty

Print and Tom walked into the Highgrade Emporium just before dusk. The crowd was starting to build as miners and camp followers came looking for some gaiety. They made straight for the bar. The first thing Print noticed was that it was wider than most of the saloons he had frequented. It was at least twice as wide as others that conformed to the long, narrow, and dark shotgun style. The lighting was better than most, too.

It had the rough perfume of cigars, spittoons of tobacco juice, stale beer, and sweat. The bartender approached. A tall and unattractive fellow who looked as if he was deep in thought or maybe lacked the wherewithal to formulate even shallow thought.

"Gentlemen."

"Some good brown liquor, if you please," said Print, running the back of his forefinger along the bottom of his moustache.

"Glass or bottle?"

"Two glasses."

The bartender expertly filled two tumblers to the rim. Tom looked around the room and then he and Print carefully lifted the glasses and drank slowly and quietly. They replaced the tumblers on the bar top half empty and pondered the taste and burn on the whisky. They lifted them again and drained them. The bartender watched them and held up the bottle to see if they wanted another shot. Print opened his eyes and nodded. "Oh, yes."

He recharged their glasses and this time they sipped slower.

"Where's a good place ta get a beefsteak dinner 'round here?" asked Print.

"We can fix you up. Got a kitchen out back. Good as any in town."

"What's your name, sir?"

"Vincent."

"Well, Vincent, how 'bout you take that bottle and lead us to a table where we can have a couple of yer best beefsteak dinners."

The bartender gave a vacant smile that confirmed the shallow-brain theory. The men followed Vincent to a table close to the window. He placed the bottle on the table and then the glasses with his fingers on the inside. Tom took his kerchief and wiped out both glasses and poured two shots. More miners came in. Some from the front of the saloon and some from the back, escorted by tired-looking prairie flowers working the dinner shift.

"We seem to have gotten off the trail ta gettin' these horses ta the Moncrieffe brothers," said Print as he ran his finger around the rim of his glass.

Tom poured more whisky into his uncle's glass and then his own. "I ain't as cold feeling toward them as you might think I am. I'm not for dumping them off. We'll get the herd delivered," replied Tom.

Print looked up and nodded in agreement as two plates heaped with meat and potatoes arrived. "This almost makes the visit worthwhile. Too bad young Heck is gonna miss out on this supper."

A nasty little creature from the kitchen brought them a plate of green beans and a big stack of biscuits.

"Speaking of Heck," said Tom. "I think we oughta skin outta here when we finish."

"Much as I was lookin' forward ta a night in a bed, I think ya may be right."

The men sat and watched the saloon fill with hard-rock men. By Print's count, the men coming in the front were almost equal to the more relaxed ones returning from the rear. Tom noticed one lad who was making his third trip to the "delights" out back with a lady that Tom thought had the general contours of a turkey. It was obvious that the young colt intended to pass judgment on as much of the female talent as he could until his purse was empty.

A large woman in a bright blue satin dress came over to their table as they were nearing the finish line on the dinner.

"Evening, gentlemen. I'm Kate Becker. Big Rump Kate," she said, slapping her haunch to drive the point home. "I'm the owner here. Enjoying your dinner?"

Tom had never seen hair on a woman the color of Big Rump Kate's. He hadn't seen that color on anybody before. It was susceptible to change when she moved. It was a henna–champagne pink combination that could only be replicated just before sunset out on the range.

"We are, thank you. Nothin' like a bath, clean britches, and a little whisky ta make a man feel almost human again."

Big Rump Kate laughed. And when she did, there was a lot of independent motion going on in that blue satin dress. The cuffs and the bodice were trimmed in a white ruffle. The front was cut down to reveal two magnificent breasts that were trying to escape their restraints. Tom figured that, conservatively, each one was bigger than his head. He poured himself another shot and continued on that train of thought.

"That ain't all a man needs to feel human. How about topping off the evening with some high-grade sporting gals?"

Print pushed a big chunk of steak around his plate with a fork, collecting the last of the mashed potatoes, and put it in his mouth. He sat back and chewed, looking at the big operator of Cariboo. Tom was wondering if he was contemplating the steak or the proposition. He swallowed and took a sip of whisky.

"A fella can only handle so much humanity at one time."

"Come on, now. Don't be shy with me. I know you boys want to get under the sheets and talk to the boss. I bet you do."

Print pushed his empty plate away and took another sip.

"Maybe a matinee tomorrow?" Big Rump Kate turned to Tom with her offer. "Come on, lad, take your pick. I got a quadroon from New Awleens, brown as a berry and twice as sweet."

Tom said nothing. The whisky was slowing down his calculations on exactly how big each one of Big Rump Kate's breasts were.

"Not up for the sable gals? Hey, Rose. Rose, come here," she said, waving a big flabby arm in the air. "I call her my English Rose. Newest girl to work the line for me."

A big blonde girl lumbered over to the table. She was every bit as big as Big Rump Kate but without the appearance of amplitude. A different kind of density. Nothing bouncy there, thought Tom. She looked like she could milk a lot of cows, and probably had back home. Until she discovered she could make more money milking the miners and cowhands. To her there was little difference in getting knocked around out back and getting cow-kicked in the barn three hours before sunrise.

"Rose, we got a strong lad here that needs to have the knots worked outta him. I told him you're just the one to do it."

The blonde towered over the men and smiled at Tom with teeth that were in dire need of some attention. Tom leaned back as she leaned in. He looked over at his uncle and then back at the yellow-haired giant.

"I'll work out the knots, straighten your spine, and when I get through, you won't remember your mama's Christian name."

"A tempting offer, Miss Rose, but I was just about to leave, as I have an engagement down the track."

Big Rump Kate's face, caked with heavy makeup, hardened. She stepped closer, placing her hands on the table and leaning closer to the men. Both men stared at her magnificent orbs, which seemed twice as big at close range. Tom could not imagine what kind of rigging she wore that could possibly keep them from bursting forth and filling the empty dinner plates on the table.

"Maybe you prefer gettin' some trim from those Celestials you brung into town.You thinking of setting up shop here? Couple of cowpunchers goin' irita the skin trade?"

Uncle and nephew were listening, but they remained transfixed on the heaving mountains, framed in blue satin. She slammed her hand down on the table. The plates clattered and whisky jumped in the tumblers. Suddenly all the folks in that end of the saloon were watching her, including Print and Tom.

"Let me set you boys straight. The gold I mine from this burg I don't get from digging. There ain't a shot of whisky, a hand of poker, or any fella that wants to dip his pecker in some poontang that I don't get a cut of."

"Easy there, Miss Becker. My nephew and I are just passin' through."

Droplets of sweat were making their way down Big Rump Kate's breasts, disappearing into cleavage that still held Tom's attention, despite her table thumping.

"Then what you got those Chink girls stashed up in your hotel room for? You planning on opening a laundry here?"

Print wrinkled his nose and chewed his moustache. He said nothing. He stared at the plastered face of the woman. "That ain't none of your business, lady. By that I mean we got no designs on stickin' our finger in your pie. We're movin' on, an' that's all you need ta know, madame."

Big Rump Kate backed off a bit. "A woman's got to protect her ground. Tell you what, I'll buy them gals from you. I'll pay you top dollar."

Again Print waited. "We didn't come here to get laid or sell women. We wanted a bath, a drink, and dinner. That's all."

"Come on, old whiskers. Everything has a price," Big Rump Kate sneered at him.

Out of the side of his vision, Print could see Tom slightly change his body position. The timbre of Print's voice changed. "No, ma'am, it don't. Not ever'thing."

Big Rump Kate straightened herself. "Well, it's a stupid sack of shit that believes he can waltz all over this country with a wagonload of women and thinks he ain't in for trouble."

"You kiss your mama with that mouth?" asked Tom.

The contempt deepened on the big woman's face. "Come on, Rose," she said and walked away.

Both men watched the Teutonic women leave.

"English Rose, my ass," said Tom.

"Looks more like a Dutch elm to me," replied his uncle.

"I'll get the girls and meet ya out front," muttered Print as he worked a toothpick on some morsel of the dinner.

Just then they heard screams from the hotel. They bolted from the bar. Tom sprinted ahead of his uncle and was up the stairs by the time Print had cleared the lobby. Tom took out the door and most of the framing it hung on. What he saw was the back of a man with his pants down at the foot of the bed. Number Four, Ye Fung, was under him. Another man was on the bed on all fours, holding the girl's arms and pinning her down. A blonde woman was beating her fists on the man at the edge of the bed. Lung Hay lay motionless on the floor, his head covered in blood.

The man with his pants at his ankles swung his elbow at the interfering woman and clocked her right in the nose. She staggered backward and tripped over Lung Hay. The other girls were in the corner, screaming. The man returned his attention to the thrashing, screaming girl. He never saw Tom, who drew the heavy .44 Colt from his holster and calmly walked toward the man. He grabbed a handful of oily hair and brought the big hog leg down on the man's skull. Even with all the screaming in the room, Print, who was stepping through the doorless opening, could hear the quiet sound the man made as he slumped to the floor.

The man slid off Tom's right side. The other

man, still pinning the girl down, looked up in amazement to see Tom shove the barrel of his gun deep into the man's eye socket. The sensation that traveled down the steel barrel into his palm told Tom he had popped out the man's eye. By the force of the blow and the pain, he raised up on his knees, clawing at his face. Blood poured between his fingers.

Print was at the side of the bed. He grabbed the cyclops by his collar and dragged him off the girl and onto the floor. Tom and Print worked with a calmness and surety of motion that one might see in two men unloading a freight wagon. The one-eyed man struggled to his feet as Print cracked his head with the butt of his pistol. The man buckled at the knees. Print placed his boot in the small of his back and shoved him into the wall, where he slowly sank, leaving a bloody smear down the wallpaper.

Tom stood over the other man splayed out on the floor, facedown. He placed his boot on the unconscious man's wrist and took careful aim. The big Colt roared and filled the room with the smoke of spent powder. The body jerked as one of its thumbs was blown off. The report silenced the room. Tom stepped over to the other side of the body and placed his boot of the other wrist. He fired but missed, and Print stepped forward and helped by steadying the arm with the application of his boot at the elbow. Tom fired again, this time with better results.

For the first time, Print noticed the woman with the smashed nose sitting on the floor, her hand to her bloody face. He turned and looked out the window to the street below. The shots had brought out the curious and the bored.

"Better get down to the livery and get the wagon while you can."

"Not yet."

Tom stripped a sheet from the bed and dragged the thumbless miner over to the window. He tied an end to the man's ankle and the other to the metal frame of the bed. He lifted the man by the collar and his belt and slid him out the window. The falling man made the bed lurch across the room to slam against the sill. He grabbed the other man off the floor and tossed him like a bale of hay through the room's other window. He turned and looked at his uncle. Mitigated fury, Print thought.

"Get the wagon up. I'll meet you out front."

Tom dashed down the hall as Print got the Chinaman to his feet.

"Tell 'em to help their sister. We gotta get down ta the wagon. Can you walk, old man?"

Lung Hay nodded that he could but hung on to Print to steady himself.

Print turned to the woman with the smashed face. "Ma'am, could you help this fella? I got to carry the little girl."

The woman said nothing but went to the Chinaman's side. One and Three were helping Four off the bed. Print scooped little Five up in his arm and led the way down the hall.

At the landing, the hotel clerk and two other men met Print. The clerk was carrying a shotgun. Print set Number Five down and drew his Colt Peacemaker. He sighted it on the face of the clerk.

"Just lean that against the wall and back off!"

The clerk complied and turned, pushing his way past the other men. They stumbled and fell over one another all the way to the lobby. Print holstered the Colt and picked up the shotgun and Number Five as he made his way down the stairs. The lobby was empty as they crossed to the front door. He peered outside in both directions. Tom was bringing up the wagon. Bob Tate was tied to the back with just a halter and no saddle. Print ushered the group out onto the porch and down the steps. Broken glass crunched under his boots, and to his right, one of the miners lay in a heap.

Tom was out of the wagon to lend a hand. First Number Five, then the other girls, followed by Lung Hay and the woman, who helped shove him into the wagon bed and fell in after him. The crowd was growing and sounding ugly. Print snatched Bob Tate's lead rope from the wagon. He turned to Tom.

"Nephew."

Tom took the shotgun and held the rope as Print tried to jump up on the horse's back. Between the mud, the height of the horse, and his age, he couldn't do it. Tom leaned the gun against the wagon wheel and helped give Print a leg up. He handed the rope to Print, then tossed the shotgun to him. The winded Print settled his legs around the horse's sides and wheeled him to face the crowd. Catcalls and brave talk were shouted from the back of the crowd as it carefully slogged closer to the horse and rider. Print steadied Bob Tate and leveled the shotgun on the advancing mob.

"First one lays a hand on us, I'll open 'em up like a Christmas goose!"

Big Rump Kate waddled down the planking, yelling to the men in the muddy street. Print noticed the other miner hanging out the window. Blood ran down the paint of the hotel. No one seemed interested in helping him.

"I'll pay five hundred dollars for every one of the girls you bring back to the Highgrade!" she hollered.

Print swung the gun in her direction. He aimed from the hip, high and wide. And fired. The pellets broke window glass and sent chips of wood and flecks of paint flying. Big Rump ducked at the shot as debris rained down on her and the men behind her.

"You skinny old bastard!" she roared. "Somebody give me a gun!"

She turned to the man on her right, but he was unarmed. Then to the one on her left. She snatched an old heavy Colt Dragoon revolver from his side. Pointing it at the ground in front of her, she struggled to pull against the slow action of the hammer. Everyone in the street was watching her. Tom started up the mules, who leaned into the weight of the wagon, deep in mud.

Big Rump Kate cocked the gun, but before she could aim, it discharged. It bowled her backward into the cadre of miners huddled behind her. They all put their shoulders into it to keep her upright. Print responded by firing the second barrel even closer into the front of the hotel. More chips and paint flew and the flying buttress brigade behind Big Rump Kate melted away. The lack of support made her stumble backward, and she dropped the old pistol in the mud before she recovered her balance. Print held on to the empty shotgun and the lead rope in the same hand as he drew his pistol.

"I want those girls!" she screamed to no one in particular.

"No sale, lady," replied Print as he reined back his horse with only the lead rope.

"I want those girls!" she repeated.

"Not today. That's the price a bein' a capitalist, lady."

The mules pulled hard, and the wagon moved forward. Bob Tate kept stepping backward, allowing Print to cover the wagon's retreat. Big Rump Kate was now down in the muddy street, her blue dress held high.

"Just remember, you old goat, it's money that greases the wheels of this world."

"Maybe," Print called back. "But not tonight."

"Somebody shoot that son of a bitch!"

To make sure the mob was listening to him and not Big Rump Kate, Print fired a round into the deep mud at their feet. The slug slammed into the muck and splattered the crowd, especially the blue satin dress of Big Rump Kate.

"Will somebody please shoot him?" she screamed, turning to face the crowd. The veins stood out on her neck and temple.

Print fired another slug into the mud, which left an interesting pattern up the back of her dress. She spun around.

"Gimme a gun, I'll kill him!"

She turned back to the miners. "You titless old women!"

Print slipped a look over his shoulder to see that Tom had the wagon on its way. He held the crowd at bay but could see that several were getting bold and creeping along the sides of the buildings and tents. Big Rump Kate squatted in the road and scooped up handfuls of mud and started flinging them at Print in frustration. Bob Tate backed out of her range. She turned to a hapless fellow standing behind her. She hit him in the chest with both of her open palms. A Missouri mule could not have done a better job. With two muddy handprints on his shirt, he flew back into the audience, taking several to the ground with him.

"What are you looking at?" Big Rump Kate screamed to the onlookers.

The crowd momentarily distracted by Big Rump Kate, Print wheeled Bob Tate to catch up with the wagon.

Once the wagon hit some solid ground,

Tom picked up the pace until he heard his uncle hollering at him. He pulled the mules up and turned as Print came alongside.

"Nephew, my days a bareback ridin' are long gone."

They were well clear of Cariboo, and it didn't look like anyone was anxious to take a chance on Big Rump Kate's offer. Print tossed the shotgun to Tom, who stowed it behind him. Print holstered the Peacemaker, bent forward, and then slid off the horse. His legs went rubbery on him. He walked to the back of the wagon to tie Bob Tate.

"I tossed your saddle an' bridle in the back."

He looked into the wagon bed and saw Lung Hay stretched out. The girls and the woman were crammed in there too.

"I'll ride up front 'til we get to camp."

He walked forward, steadying himself on the wagon's side. He pulled himself up and saw that Number Three was sitting next to Tom. She moved over to make room. Shoulder to shoulder they sat, and the wagon moved out. Tom felt the warmth of the girl's thigh through his pant leg and that got him to thinking about the colossal prow on a certain blue satin prairie schooner.

The three up front rode in silence until they could make out the light of Heck's campfire. Print tapped Sun Foy's knee and pointed to the fire. "There ya go, Number Three. We're gonna make it. Ever'thin's goin' to be okay."

She looked in the direction he was pointing and then back to him as he talked. He patted her knee. "Ever'thin's gonna work out."

Tom slowed the wagon as they got close to camp so as not to spook the herd. Heck was waiting for them when the wagon rolled to a stop. Tom handed the reins to Sun Foy and jumped down. Print was slower getting off.

"Heck, we gotta roll. I'll turn the hobbles on the mares. Help my uncle break down the camp. Toss everything in the wagon!" yelled Tom.

"I'll saddle the horses," said Print.

"I should assume things didn't go well."

"No, they didn't," replied Print. "We'll be on the move all night, I suspect."

Soon Tom was leading the herd out into the darkness, with Print and Heck flanking and Number Three driving the wagon. The ground had lots of rock outcropping, so the going was slow. Sun Foy soon figured out that by watching the way the herd parted, she could steer clear of most of the obstacles. She still hit the smaller ones, which made the wagon roll and lurch violently.

The flea-bitten gray mare stayed right on Tom's tail, and he led them through the night. They rode the moon out of the sky, in and out of blankets of low-lying fog. When all that was left in the sky were the morning stars, Tom brought the herd to a stop. They milled about on the banks of a river as Tom paused for a smoke. The struck match shone on his face in the dark as Print rode up.

"Want to wait 'til it's light?" asked Tom.

They studied the river as best they could. They could make out the sound of rippling water, which usually meant shallows.

"Let's put this behind us."

Heck rode up and joined in the inspection. "What do you think?" he asked.

"I think we're swimmin' the Hellespont tonight, Hank," Print replied.

"Come on, boys. Come on," Tom called to the herd in a soft voice.

He eased down the bank and into the water. Print

and Heck peeled off and returned to the herd's flanks to keep them going in. Although the gray mare wanted to move faster, she allowed Tom to pick his way. Some of the horses got balky but Print and Heck turned them in and stayed on the bank until the last of the stragglers were in.

"I'll bring the wagon over. You follow them ta the other side an' give Tom a hand."

Across the water they could hear Tom calling to the horses. Heck waded in behind the last of them. Print joined the wagon at the bank's edge. He dismounted and stripped the saddle and bridle from Bob Tate. He tossed them in the back of the wagon and climbed up on the front seat. He took the reins from Sun Foy.

"I'll take it from here. Ya done a great job drivin' tonight. An' if Mr. Lung Hay survives his smashed head, I'm gonna make sure he tells ya so."

Print gathered the reins in one hand and kept the other on the hand brake as he nudged the mules forward. The wagon swayed violently as it slid down the bank. Sun Foy held on, looking at Print and then over her shoulder to the others in the wagon bed. Once Print heard the Chinaman moan. The wagon straightened as the mules edged into the water. The mules were now telling Print what they were going to do, and he didn't argue. They were sure-footed and smart enough to go slowly. Water reached the wagon bed but didn't breach the top, and by taking it easy, they made it to the other side. There wasn't much of a bank, and Print drove the wagon forward into the back of the herd.

He stood and looked back to see Bob Tate climbing out of the water and shaking himself. Light was now in the east and he could see that they had arrived on a bend in the river and that it formed a meadow that was ringed by large evergreens. The meadow looked to have grass and was high enough not to allow the river to jump its banks. The hemlocks and ponderosas formed a natural corral.

"This'll do just fine. Let's get the mule undone an' call it quits."

Heck rode up beside the wagon. "Why don't I cross back over just in case they tried to follow us?"

"Suit yourself, son. I doubt those miners are goin' ta take up that lady's offer. Tom's got another pistol he keeps in his saddlebag. You take that with ya, an' don't be shy about usin' it ta let us know if ya need help."

Heck trotted off to find Tom, and Print got down and started unhitching the mules. The morning stars were gone by the time the Print-Harte party fell asleep.

Chapter Twenty-one

The sun was overhead when Print woke. The girls were asleep, but Tom and Heck were sitting by the fire, drinking coffee. He got up stiff and sore, slipped on his boots, and went in search of a tree to stand behind while he relieved himself. Upon returning he finished dressing, ran his fingers through his hair, and put his hat on. Tom poured a cup and handed it to him.

"Thank ya, son." Print sipped and then stretched his back and shoulders

"Didn't start breakfast. Wasn't sure if we were staying long enough."

"Did ya see anything back there, Hank?"

"No, sir. I came over about an hour ago. I don't believe anyone's coming."

"Me neither. Guess we better take a look at the damage."

The woman with the smashed nose was out of the wagon and sitting in its shade. Print approached with a bucket and knelt beside her. He placed his hand on her shoulder.

"Mind if I take a look at that, ma'am? I just need

ta get this cleaned up. I know it's sore, but it'll feel a lot worse if an infection takes holt."

He cradled her neck in one hand and wiped away the dried blood with a piece of muslin. He squeezed the cloth and let the water run down her face.

"It hurts a whole lot worse than it looks," he said reassuringly.

Tom and Heck helped Lung Hay out of the back of the wagon and walked him over by the fire. Number Three was up and carried an armful of wood to set beside the fire.

"Ma'am, if you'll just hold this on your face 'til I can wipe somma that dried blood off. I'm gonna help them with the Chinaman, but I'll be right over there, and when I'm done I'll be back. Okay?"

She held the wet cloth to her face and nodded yes. Print got up and walked over to the others.

"This old boy's taken a pretty good whack to his brain pan," said Heck as he and Tom were bent over, inspecting Lung Hay's head.

"Now Hank, that's Mr. Lung Hay you're workin' on. You any good at sewin'?"

"Not on the hide of something's that's still alive, Mr. Ritter."

"Guess you're the one then, Tom. If ya can make as good a job of it as that fancy pocket yer wearin', I think Lung Hay won't complain too much, will ya now?"

Lung Hay shook his head as Tom poured hot water from the kettle into a saucepan. Print retrieved a small kit from his saddlebag and tossed it to Heck. "Got that from a saddler in Klamath. Great for workin' on leather and not too bad on scalps, either. Three. Three, come on over here."

Print pointed to Sun Foy and motioned for her to join him. He gave her the saucepan to hold as he washed the Chinaman's head.

"I could whipstitch it," said Tom.

Tom and Heck leaned closer as Sun Foy dutifully held the pan of water.

"I don't know, Nephew. One thing 'bout these Chinese fellas is that they seem to set a lot of stock in their head's appearance. Don't think Lung Hay here wants an ugly scar across the top of his pate. If I was you, I'd go with a tight little chain stitch. Kinda like the way that fancy pocket a yours is done. This is your lucky day, Lung Hay. You are fortunate enough to have two barbarians who have considerable experience at repairin' top notches."

Tom took one of the large, curved needles and threaded it. Print poured whisky into a tin cup and held it out to Tom.

"Sock 'er in there, son."

Tom dropped the needle and thread into the whisky and then retrieved it.

Print offered the cup to Lung Hay. "Ya look ta be a tough old bird, Mr. Lung Hay, but ya might want a jolt 'fore my nephew starts ta work on you."

Lung Hay sniffed the cup and rejected it.

"In that case," said Print as he took a drink and splashed the remainder on the Chinaman's wound, "let 'er rip, doc."

Tom sat himself down on an empty nail keg they used for storing gear. He placed Lung Hay's head between his thighs and clapped the sides of the Chinaman's head with his knees. Print took hold of Lung Hay's hands. He looked over at Sun Foy. She was intently watching as Tom prepared to poke the needle through the man's scalp. She saw Print watching her. He winked and gave her a nod.

Tom punched through the Chinaman's scalp and Lung Hay went stiff from the pain, but he didn't make a sound. Tom did the same to the skin on the other side of the wound. He drew the thread up, made a knot, and waited for Print to cut the remainder with his pocketknife. He repeated the process.

"Ya got one hell of a grip there, Chinaman," said Print.

Tom stitched and Print snipped until the wound was closed. When they were finished, Print indicated to Sun Foy to wash the wound. He struggled to his feet and went over to the wagon and bent down. He reached under and came up with a glob of axle grease on his fingers. He walked back and proceeded to smear it over the wound.

"Now usually I'd make that lard, but this'll do just as well an' keep the bugs off, too."

He took a closer look. "Not bad. Not bad at all."

"A man among men at stitching up scalps," said Heck.

They helped Lung Hay to his feet, and Print held on to him as they walked over to the shade of the wagon. He eased the Chinaman down and went back to the fire to pour a cup of coffee. He took it to the woman with the bad nose. He offered her the cup. She placed the bloody cloth beside her and took the cup and sipped.

"Not ta worry, ma'am, I won't turn them loose on you. Name's Prentice Ritter, an' that's Heck Gilpin, an' my nephew, Tom Harte. The ladies are One, Two, Three, Four, an' Five."

She looked at the girls.

"Well I had ta call 'em somethin'. More for convenience sake. Your nose might be broken, but it's too swollen ta tell right now. Why don't ya find a cool spot ta lie down an' we'll talk later."

Print left her and walked back to get a cup of coffee for himself. He poured for Heck and Tom. He looked at their surroundings.

"It might do us some good to rest for a few days. Couldn't pick a better spot. We go slower, we might get there quicker. We're bound ta have a few sore-footed ones after last night. Let's picket 'em in the river mud for a day. Cool them hooves out."

"We're burning time, Uncle."

"Way I see it, this deal is gettin' more interestin' every day."

"Seems to be getting less profitable every day to me."

Print looked at his nephew for a long time. "Never use money ta measure wealth, son. Let's get them sore-footed cavvys in the water."

Print and Heck went about running picket lines in the shallows as Tom found lame horses and walked them down to stand in the cool water. The girls busied themselves setting up the camp, and the woman and Lung Hay slept.

Tom brought the last of the horses down and tied them along the line. Heck walked back to the wagon, and Print helped Tom with the horses.

"You know, Tom, back there in John Day, when I said I didn't know what went on between you an' your ma, I meant it. I know my sister could be a difficult woman. Hell, they all can. Her bein' German Huguenot and Appalachian stock. That can make for tough stock. It also makes for the kinda people that could up and leave a place like Galax and ride an' walk across this country to find a new life."

Tom stopped tying horses to look at his uncle.

"It can also make for pretty starchy people ta have ta live with."

Tom went back to securing the horses.

"Now your pa was a regular hand. He was definitely the best thing that ever happened ta my sister. If she was here right now, I believe she'd agree with me. No matter how knotted up she might get, she couldn't put a dent in him. He was as serene as a Sunday afternoon."

"For all the hard praying she did, deep down I think she felt she got out here on her own steam," interrupted Tom.

"Ain't no one made it out here without some divine intervention attached, What I'm tryin' ta tell you is that was a man-sized thing ya done back there with that shit-bird Fender. And it was appropriate for what he done. Ya didn't blink an' that's good. We didn't go lookin' to save no Orientals an' a broken-nosed whore. It just happened. Sometimes ya just gotta roll with what's thrown at ya."

Print bent down and picked up a small stone and skimmed it across the water. It hopped a half a dozen times. He straightened and looked at his nephew. "I'd like ta see some more of your father in ya sometimes."

Print walked back to the wagon, leaving Tom to tend to the remaining horses.

The woman was lying on a blanket in the shade of some junipers. She sat up at the sound of Print's footsteps.

"How's the nose doin', ma'am?"

The woman raised her hand to hide her face.

"I didn't mean it that way, ma'am. It's bruised and swollen, but that'll be gone soon enough. We're gonna stay here a few days. Let the horses rest. We're takin' them ta Sheridan, Wyoming. We've been on the move from Oregon. You're welcome ta join us until we reach a place of your choosing."

The woman kept her hand over her face and extended the other. "My name's Nola. Nola Johns. Thank you."

"Well, thank you. I don't know what happened back there. You seemed ta be doin' your best ta help these girls. Would ya like a cup of coffee? A little whisky might buck up your spirits."

Nola shook her head.

"We eat simple on the trail. Mostly cowboy chuck, but I'll see if Tom can bring in some fresh game. If you're up ta it, you could join us for supper."

"Thank you."

Print walked over to Lung Hay, who was talking to the girls. "How ya feelin', Lung Hay?" asked Print. He tapped his forehead with his finger. "How's the noggin feelin'? Maybe ya could tell the girls that we're goin' ta stay here for a few days to rest the horses. So we can all relax an' rest up for the trail."

Tom was riding less than a mile from the wagon when he saw five pronghorns grazing. He dismounted and removed the rifle from the scabbard. He ground-tied the gelding and moved forward a half dozen steps. He knelt and took a pinch of grass and let it fall to test the wind. He raised the Remington and steadied it and fired.

That evening by the river the campfire was burning bright. An antelope was on a makeshift spit, and everyone but the woman was watching Print grind the pepper mill over it and sprinkle salt. They all looked up at Nola's approach. Tom, Print, and Heck stood and removed their hats.

"Evening, Miss Johns," said Heck. "Glad you could join us."

"We got biscuits, beans, an' fresh antelope," added Print.

Tom offered her the nail keg for a seat, and Heck handed her a plate prepared by Print. Print noticed that her face was a mess. Wine-colored bruises covered a good part of it.

"Lung Hay, I'm gonna let you talk ta the girls about whatever the rest of us are sayin'. You tell 'em as much or as little as ya see fit, it that's all right with you."

Lung Hay agreed, and Print proceeded to tell Nola the circumstances of their journey. She sat in silence with the plate balanced on her knee, eating and listening about Billy Via and Captain Fender and the sheepmen and Fort Hall. When he was through, he offered her more food and was surprised as she polished off a second plateful. There was the muted voice of Lung Hay in the background, much like the sound of the river. Once in a while the girls would turn their heads from watching the Chinaman to look at the men, as if they didn't remember the events that way.

Print finished the story about the same time the last of the food gave out. Everyone lent a hand to cleaning up. Heck stoked the fire, and Tom checked on the horses.

"The boys made a place for you an' the girls ta sleep. It's hard ta maintain much privacy on the trail, but we'll do our best ta give ya room."

Tom and Heck had rigged a fly sheet that stretched off the side of the wagon and put blankets and bedrolls under it. The increase in the members of the party was putting a strain on the bedding supply. The men opted to sleep on their horse blankets and cover up with slickers. Heck, who had come to them missing boots, much less a duster or slicker, said that he was just fine and laid his horse blanket close to the fire. Lung Hay preferred to sleep in the bed of the wagon. Tom felt sure the horses weren't going anywhere but promised to get up and check on them. Soon the camp was silent, save the sound of the water and the peepers.

Print was deep in sleep, having dreams about Lung Hay's head and Nola's smashed nose, and at some point, he dreamed about the Chimborazo hospital high on a bluff above the James River. He was sitting in the grass and it was evening and the boys were all joking and swapping stories. A soldier would say something about home, or the pretty girl back home, or the thought of a mother doing all the fieldwork back home, and the men would get silent. They would look over at the lights of Richmond, the biggest city most of them had ever seen. Then someone would start up about a fellow who had shit in his pants the first time he heard a twenty-gun battery unload. They would all laugh and then go on to another story. At one point the Chinaman was sitting with them, and he saw Nola pass by dressed as a nurse.

He woke and got up to relieve himself. He saw that Tom was gone and looked into the night to see if he was with the horses. He walked back and added wood to the embers. He could hear Nola snoring loudly. Considering the damage done to her nose, it was not surprising. He lay down and went to sleep and dreamed no more, or if he did, he didn't remember in the morning.

The morning was busy cooking and getting the horses out of the river mud and back to the rest of the herd. Except for a couple of young horses, the herd was in good flesh, according to Tom's assessment. The girls were anxious to walk with Lung Hay as he told them what he knew of this country they had been brought to. He told them what he thought of the uncle and his nephew and Sun Foy told him her thoughts.

Heck tended to Nola's face, cleaning the last of the dried blood. Tom left to hunt more game, and Print took a hatchet that they had found among the gear in the wagon and set about lopping branches from the spruce and junipers and dragging them back to the wagon.

When the girls returned, Lung Hay was carrying plants that had been pulled up from their roots, which he obliquely referred to as medicine. Print felt a momentary twinge of resentment, but it passed. Always be open to knowledge, he thought. He had the girls set about pulling the sprigs of evergreen from the larger boughs and had them start a pile under the fly sheet. Then he started to spread the pile and indicated that it would serve as a bed.

"An' it'll have a nice smell, too."

Later Nola took the girls upriver to bathe. Print warned them not to go too far and to yell loud if there was a problem. Armed with bucket, brush, and soap, they departed.

Tom returned with a saddlebag full of partridge and doves. Tied to the saddle horn was a brace of grouse. He was letting his horse set his own pace as they followed the river line. He passed a stand of stunted chokecherry trees. Below, he saw the woman and the girls bathing. Nola was cradling little Number Five in her arms as Number Two poured water from the bucket over the little girl's head. Their backs were to him except for Number Three. He tugged lightly on the reins, and the horse was content to stop. He moved his head from side to side as the breeze moved the branches.

Sun Foy looked up and saw him beyond the riverbank, looking down. He froze, hoping she could not see him. But she had. She was in water up to her waist but made no move to cover herself. She looked past Nola and the girls and up at him. Finally she broke the moment, as she didn't want the others to know he was there, spying on them. She helped Nola with Ghing Wa, and when Tom felt they were sufficiently preoccupied, he moved the horse along and out of sight. Sun Foy looked up again and saw that he was gone.

Print made a big deal out of supper that night and everyone ate well. Lung Hay translated the dinner conversation. The girls and Nola retired to the bed of evergreen sprigs and the men settled in around the fire and sipped some bug juice. Print whittled, Tom smoked, Lung Hay rebraided his long pigtail, and Heck kept the cups supplied, although the Chinaman was not a drinker of the spirits.

"Nothing like a couple of hot meals and some extra sleep to put a shine on things," said Tom.

Heck lifted his cup. "Relax, ruminate, and reflect."

Uncle and nephew joined in hoisting their cups.

"Ta be wild, woolly, an' hard ta curry," added Print.

Again they lifted their cups and drank. Print lay aside his knife and a piece of wood to take out his pipe. He packed the bowl with burly cut.

"What brought you out here, Hank?"

Heck still got thrown occasionally by the way Print interchanged his name. He swirled the whisky in his tin cup, then looked at Print. "Ever been to Philadelphia?"

Toni and Print shook their heads.

"It was all a little too neat back there. Too many people. Like all the air had been used up. I got a good education and all it did was make me want to travel. I knew there was more to life than Sunday strolls along the Schuylkill River. So I cashed out. Broke my parents' hearts, but I didn't look back.

"What about you, Mr. Ritter? What's in this for you?"

Print puffed his pipe, then took a sip and looked into the fire. "Well, ya see, Hank, I've spent mosta my life on the hurricane deck of a cow pony. An' more than a few evenings, I listened ta them cows settlin' down for the night an' asked my maker that very question."

"So what did he say?"

"Well, he didn't send me no telegram. Ya know, I've had ice water down my back, dust up my nose, an' boils on my butt. I've been rolled on, busted my ribs, a foot, an' my nose," he said, pointing to the parts of his body with the pipe stem.

"Had my heart stomped more 'n once. Truth be told, I spent a good deal of my life never bein' worth more 'n a hundr'd dollars. Boil all that down an' I don't believe there's been too many days I ain't felt that life was grand, that I've been a lucky fella to watch it."

Print clamped his pipe between his teeth and relit it.

"What about women?" Heck asked.

"Women? There's been a few. One I even set up house with. Black-haired an' green-eyed. We was bedded but not churched, ya might say. She did make me get baptized. Even held me under water. Guess they shoulda used som' soap 'cuz it just didn't take. In the end I think she wished they'd held me under for about ten minutes."

"You're just a pushover for the ladies, Uncle."

Print snorted and took another puff. "Nephew, there ain't a man alive that can stand up ta the power of that little cooter. The holt it has on a man is unbreakable. It'll bring a strong man ta his knees. Read your history. Look at the kings an' kingdoms that have fallen ta that little split tail."

Print looked from one to the other to make sure they understood him. "A road agent 'ill demand your money or your life. A woman requires both."

The men chuckled, and Lung Hay nodded with a sagacious smile.

"The mysteries of women are like the Egyptian hieroglyphics, an' I sure ain't found the Rosetta stone yet. Truth is, I never really understood their language."

"I think I'll stick to horses," said Tom, rolling another smoke.

"Don't let my lack of success put ya off. There's a lot ta be said for the companionship of a woman. Ain't that right, Heck?"

"I'm not sure I can shed much light on the subject. Other than the most shallow of dalliances with the ladies, I tend to keep wanting to move on. My standards require a statement of honesty about my lack of long-term interest. That usually busts it with the ladies. I find myself taking comfort in the arms of soiled doves."

"There's som' safe an' soberin' advice."

"A short-term cure for a long-term ailment, I'm afraid," replied Heck as he added another splash to everyone's cups.

Nola lay on the bed of evergreens, listening to the men. Number Four tossed in her sleep, chased by some nightmare only she saw. The firelight reflected on the tall trees. Tom tossed a chunk of wood on the fire and a shower of sparks ascended toward a canopy of brilliant stars.

"What do you think about marriage, Lung Hay?" asked Tom.

"When I was a boy, my father told me that a man without a wife was like a stallion without a fence."

"Well, shit. That sounds pretty good to me," said Tom.

"Nephew, how many stallions ya seen out there on the range? Sure it's dandy there in the beginnin'. All those fillies winkin' at ya. You out there laying claim ta as many as ya can jump. But pretty soon you're spendin' most of your time fightin' off ever' stiff dick in the neighborhood 'til ya get your teeth kicked in or a hock busted bad enough and then you're gummin' hard grass. An' some other swingin' dick 'ill be takin' care of your ladies. No, the Chinese make a good point. Marriage is an institution."

"So's the state penitentiary," chuckled Heck.

"Ah, come on, Hank, it ain't suppose ta be a death sentence. It's about give an' take. Ain't that right, Lung Hay?"

"Chinese say a deaf husband and a blind wife make a good marriage."

"There ya go! Exactly my point," replied Print, pointing with his pocketknife at Lung Hay. "The Chinese are a smart people. I've always said that."

Heck rolled his eyes and Tom shook his head.

"Look, I already admitted that I don't understand women too much. An' I ain't been lucky with 'em. But that don't mean that I can't see the logic in marriage. . . . A little bug juice, if you please," asked Print as he held his cup out to Heck.

"Ah, hell. He's getting wound up now," said Tom, tossing another piece of wood on the fire.

"Livin' out here has changed a lot of things. Suspended the conventions of eastern life, That's probably why you like it so much, Hank, Women plowing land and pannin' for gold. Men sewin' up their own britches, cookin' for themselves. That's well an' fine. It's good for the people an' good for the country. But too much? No, sir. Without women an' marriage, we'd all be shot or drunk ourselves ta death or died of the clap. No, sir."

"Don't think ya can die of the clap, Uncle."

"A small point. You'd wished ya had ever' time ya had ta make water, so I've heard."

Print slipped the figure he was carving back into his vest and closed his pocketknife. "All I'm sayin' is that you two colts are still young enough ta make a run at it. I'm the ol' caballo here. Out there, with the bunged-up hock an' no teeth eatin' prickly pear choy waitin' for the blizzard."

Tom winked at Heck. "Guess we better take you

and old Bob Tate out and shoot you both right now. Sounds like the only kind thing to do."

Print shot his nephew a look that had a smile attached to it, but not much of one. "The blizzard ain't here yet, Nephew."

Heck got up and stretched. He took his cup and dropped it in the washbasin. "Boys, I'm off to the Land of Nod. See you in the morning."

The others watched him head for the woods before turning in. Tom turned to his uncle and said, "Maybe I ought to go to Sacramento or down to Denver and find a rich woman to marry."

Print quit whittling and moved his pipe from one side of his mouth to the other. "My advice would be ta never marry for money, son. Neither of ya will be gettin' or givin' love. You'll both just be rentin' it out. If ya need money that bad, go to a bank. That's what they was invented for."

"Damn. There's no pleasing you tonight."

Print brushed the shavings from his lap. He removed the pipe from his mouth and tapped out the ash. "If you was ever lucky enough ta find a woman that could stand your stubbornness for more 'n three days and in fact ya did get married, it might not work out. But if you never marry, sure as shit draws flies you will be sorry."

Tom said nothing. Print rose and walked over and patted him on the shoulder.

"Why don't ya get yourself some sleep, son. I don't think ya have ta worry 'bout no wedding bells in the next couple a weeks."

Print walked off to the trees to pee. Tom called out to him, "Be careful not to bump into anything out there in the dark, old man."

Print replied, "The best thing I found in my life I bumped inta in the dark."

Print laughed and Tom smiled.

Tom looked across the fire at Lung Hay. "You ever married?"

The Chinaman nodded yes.

"A long time?"

"Many years. Still have wife in China."

"What brought you to America?"

"Gum San."

"Gum San? What's that?"

"Gum San. Gold Mountain. All Chinese hear California was Gold Mountain. Gum San. I leave my young wife with my parents and come to be a rich man. Now my wife is old, my parents are dead, and I am not a rich man."

"Think you'll ever see her again?"

"Maybe. We are old people now."

Tom nodded and they sat in silence. Tom sighed deeply.

"Lung Hay, you play checkers?"

"Oh, yes."

"Good deal. First chance I get, I'm gonna get a board and chips. A helluva lot more civilized than poker."

"Oh, I like poker," said a smiling Lung Hay.

Chapter Twenty-two

A purple skink crawled into the sun and onto a flat rock to warm his reptilian blood in preparation for a breakfast of some juicy bug. Not far away, smoke from Print's campfire curled above the tallest pines. Print was late getting up, and when he did, he felt a headache. He also noticed that none of the girls was next to him. They had stayed the night with Nola. Again Heck had breakfast going and the others were eating. Print made a trip behind a wide tree and then went down to the river to splash water in his face to clear his head. He returned to the group and tipped his hat to Nola.

"Mornin', Miss Johns."

"Morning, Mr. Ritter."

"Honkle Pren," said Number Five.

"That's right, 'Honkle Pren.' How's the head feelin', Lung Hay?"

"Much better, thank you. How is your head?" asked Lung Hay in the most innocent tone.

Print shot him a look but wasn't sure about the question so he let it pass. He took a plate from Heck and clasped a biscuit in his mouth. He found a spot and sat down. He took the biscuit and used it to push food onto his fork.

"I wish som' smart fella would invent a way ta take a couple of hens on the trail. I would surely enjoy some fresh eggs."

"Ya mean the Romans didn't already figger that one out?" asked Tom, with as much of a straight face as he could muster that early in the day.

"You'll hafta excuse my nephew, Miss Johns. He takes great delight in thumbin' his nose at my attempts to impart a drop 'r two of historical knowledge."

"Maybe you should take Miss Johns for a walk and you can tell her all about ornithology and the wonders of city waterworks systems. It makes for facinatin' conversation."

Print started to reply, but food almost fell out of his mouth. He stopped it with the back of his hand, Swallowed and cleared his throat. "Ya can see the task I have before me."

They all cleaned the camp. Tom announced his intention to hunt for more game, and Heck volunteered to check the horses, which were grazing in the meadow. Tom gestured to Sun Foy to ask if she wanted to join him. Lung Hay cleared up the matter, and the girl agreed. Nola went with Lung Hay and the rest of the girls for a walk. Print sat with his hangover and poured another cup.

It wasn't long before his solitude was interrupted by movement across the river. He got up and casually walked to the wagon, where his gun and holster were. He made no attempt to retrieve them but stood and watched a procession of riders and packhorses walk along the opposite bank from this camp. The rider leading the procession was dressed in buckskins.

Print took a quick glance in the wagon bed to find the location of his gun.

The buckskin rider called out, "Hey over there."

Print reached for the big Colt, withdrew it, and slipped it into his waistband.

"Mornin', neighbor," the voice called out.

"Mornin'," Print called back.

"Mind if we cross?"

Print did not reply.

"I'm guiding these folks on a hunting and fishing trip."

The buckskin rider had the horse in the shallows, prepared to cross. Print saw several men, definitely not turned out in local attire, and a woman. He replaced the pistol in the wagon and walked toward the river's edge.

"Come on. Quietly. I got a herd an' mustangs grazin'."

"So I see. Quite a string you got there."

"Come on. Just give the herd a wide berth."

The rider waded on in, followed by the others. Print stood on the water's edge as they forded the shallow crossing. The buckskin man walked his horse out of the water in front of Print.

"Huntin' an' fishin'," commented Print.

"Yes, sir. It's all the rage these days." He reached down and extended his hand to Print. "They're from back East. Dudes, but they're all right. Good people." He bent lower and whispered, "Even if they are Yankees."

Print smiled and turned to walk up the bank.

"Mind if we rest a while? I been pushin' 'em hard since dawn."

"Sure. Just mind the herd."

Soon all were across, and still mounted. The buckskin man did the introductions.

"Name's Yip Dawes."

"Print Ritter."

"Well, Mr. Ritter, this here is Mr. Robert Bentingcourt. That's Mr. William Rice Findley, Mr. G. G. Pollard, and the lovely Mrs. Bentingcourt."

Print tipped his hat to the lady. "How 'bout som' coffee? We got a fresh pot workin'."

"That sounds good. Thank you."

They all dismounted, and an Indian in buckskins took the reins of the horses and led them away. Print watched the man leave.

"That's Kaybo. He's a Mandan–white man cross. He's all right too. He's the packer, tracker, skinner, an' cook," said Yip.

Print kept watching and then turned to his new guests. "Anyone that don't want coffee?" he asked. "Might have ta rinse out a few cups first."

Print started pouring as Kaybo returned with a packhorse and quickly untied several folding chairs and opened them.

"Ain't that handy," remarked Print.

Yip retrieved more cups from the washbasin and soon everyone was sipping hot coffee.

"So huntin' an' fishin' is the thing to do these days?"

"People back home can't get enough of it," said Pollard.

"Where's home?"

"I am originally from Elmira, New York. Mr. Findley and the Bentingcourts are from Boston, where I now live," replied Pollard.

"You a fisherman or a hunter, Miz Bentingcourt?"

"Both, actually. This is our honeymoon. And please call me Eva."

"Well, if you folks want ta camp here for the night, we'd enjoy the company for supper."

"Marvelous," said Bentingcourt "But you must let us provide the repast. Are you on for fish tonight, Mr. Ritter?"

Print shoved his hands deep in his pockets and rocked back on his heels. He looked to Yip. "Why sure. We ain't had fish in at least a week."

"Then if you will excuse us, Mr. Ritter, we have dinner to catch."

Print gestured toward the river. "Help yourself. You fellas need any bait? I could grub up som' worms for ya."

"No, indeed," said Findley. "This is fly-fishing we'll be doing. Wet and dry flies are all we will be using."

Yip and Kaybo started unloading the mules, while the anglers opened leather tubes and took out bamboo sections that they assembled into rods. Bentingcourt struggled into a pair of rubber pants.

"What ya got there, Mr. Bentingcourt?"

"Chest waders made of vulcanized rubber so I can go where the fish are."

The dudes headed for the river as Yip and Kaybo started setting up camp.

Lung Hay, Nola, and the girls returned to find large, elaborate tents up and two collapsible tables set up with numerous chairs. Print did the introductions. And then did it again as Heck walked in.

"Where you been?" asked Print.

"Actually, I took a nap over there in those hemlocks. Too much whisky and too little sleep last night."

Print lifted Number Five and carried her on his hip and started for the riverbank. He pointed to the people by the river's edge. "They do any fly-fishin' back in China?"

Ghing Wa couldn't care less what he was talking about. She just liked to be carried around by the old man. He found a spot on the west side of the bend in the river and lowered the girl. He sat down too. The three men and the woman were strung out along the riverbank with Bentingcourt going into the water wearing his vulcanized rubber pants.

Print told the little girl what the people were doing, and she listened as if she understood him. The long poles bent as they moved back and forth in the air. Gossamer fishing line floated high overhead, and the sun caught the damp line and it looked liked long loops of silver thread moving ever so lightly in the air. The poles moved back and forth like metronomes and Print saw that there was, if not a rhythm, then at least a cadence to what the anglers were doing. He explained this to the girl, and when he filled his pipe and took out the matches, she held out her hand and he let her strike the match and light his pipe. He bent close so she could reach the pipe's bowl. He drew deeply and blew a perfect smoke ring. The girl squealed and tried to put her finger through the smoky circle. She tugged on his shirtsleeve and he blew another. And he said to himself that there was a lot more to life than being worth more than a hundred dollars.

The poles swayed and Print and Ghing Wa were content to sit and watch them. From the top branches of a huge ponderosa an eagle fell, pulling up just before it hit the water, and then skimmed along in front of the fishermen. It hit the water with its talons and stopped on the surface. There was splashing and the bird struggled to get airborne, a big trout in its grasp.

"There goes dinner, boys!" hollered Print.

"God, wasn't that magnificent!" cried Eva Bentingcourt.

"Yes, it was," Print whispered to himself.

"Means the fish are rising," called out Findley.

Means that eagle gets supper tonight, Print said to himself.

Soon they were in the thick of it, reeling in fish. Every time the line hit the water, a fish took it. Yip walked up and sat down next to Print. Ghing Wa had no more pipes to light, so she wandered closer to the water.

"Too hot ta be workin' in buckskins," said Yip.

"I was meanin' ta ask you about them. You look like ya gone native."

"The easterners lap it up. I think of it as a costume."

"A while back we had three rank-lookin' bucks get up in our faces an' wolf us out of a damn fine horse. It ain't exactly Boston out here."

"Hell's fire, man, if I could raise Sittin' Bull hisself up from the dead ta swoop down an' plunk a couple a arrows in their arses, I swear I believe they'd pay me double. They can't get enough of this."

Yip pulled out a pipe and tamped tobacco into it. He offered his pouch to Print, who declined.

"Ya like what you're doin', this fishin', huntin' deal?"

"This? Man, I wouldn't trade this ta be the top rump rider in the finest whorehouse in San Francisco. I done 'bout everything out here ta earn a nickel. Trapping, lumber, pannin'. Even cleaned out piss pots for a hotel down in Julesburg. No, this is the best deal this dog's ever had."

The fishing party was walking toward them, loaded down with big, shiny trout.

The men were preparing the evening meal. Tom had brought back pronghorns and plenty of birds. Print enlisted the help of the girls to pluck and clean the fowl, while Tom and Heck field-dressed the antelope. Yip and Kaybo were at the river's edge, squatting on a long, flat rock, cleaning fish, as the men of the Bentingcourt party watched.

Tom and Heck had rubbed the carcass in pepper and Print took the cuts and skewered them on the spit. First the shank, then the rump, the loin, and the flank. Next the shoulder, rib, and brisket. He took the liver, sliced it into long strips, and had it simmering in a saucepan of bacon fat and wild scallions that Lung Hay and the girls brought back with them. In another pot, huckleberries, with a liberal application of whiskey, were bubbling slowly.

He sent the girls out to pick prairie sage and quizzed Lung Hay on his knowledge of wild mushrooms as opposed to toadstools. The Chinaman assured him no one would be poisoned. Upon the girls' return, he rinsed the birds in water, then stuffed their cavities with prairie sage and wrapped them in muslin.

Kaybo and Yip returned with the cleaned and filleted fish. Kaybo set up shop on the other side of the cook fire. Soon both Print and the other cook were preparing a varied dinner. Kaybo had the advantage of more pots, pans, spices, and condiments at his disposal. Before long the trout were sizzling in pans garnished with various herbs and seasonings. Not to be outdone, Print skewered the quail and doves on sticks to hang above the fire to cook.

Nola walked up, a shawl about her, her face heavily bruised, but the swelling was going down. Print stood, wiping his hands on his pants. He introduced her. "Miss Johns is employed to take care of the girls. She had a nasty spill, but she's on the mend now."

As a dozen birds were roasting over the fire and four large skillets of trout sizzled, a large pot of beans with molasses and strips of bacon on top bubbled. The Dutch oven, buried in the hot coals, was baking biscuits. Pollard hoisted a bottle in the air.

"Some Madeira, ladies and gentlemen?" Pollard started pouring into the extended tin cups.

Lung Hay, Kaybo, and Nola declined.

"Sir, to your hospitality, a virtue for all fellow travelers," said Pollard.

They all toasted, and more Madeira was poured.

"To Robert's honeymoon—before he starts working for a new boss."

They laughed and drinks were downed. Yip stood and held out his cup for a refill. He held it in the air. "To Mrs. Bentingcourt, who skinned a wolf and got a mink."

Robert Bentingcourt stood.

"Now, with gusto and God's good graces, let us devour our hard-won dinner."

Plates and utensils were passed as Print and Kaybo ladled food. Cuts of meat, filets of trout, beans, and golden biscuits were served. The camp fell silent save the clinking sound of plates and forks. Lips and chins shone with drippings from the bird meat. Yip brought bottles of wine to be opened and passed around.

"I'm feeling more like the guest than the host here," said Print.

"Nonsense. Not everyone offers to share their fire with strangers," quipped Bentingcourt.

Heck stabbed a thin slice of lemon from his fish and held it up on the end of his fork.

"How do you get fresh lemons up here on the Divide?"

"Shipped in to Rawlins from Saint Louis. Packed in sawdust, Keeps them fresh," answered Findley.

More food and drink were consumed. Biscuits

sopped up the last of the beans and molasses and bits of trout. Print leaned back. "It don't get much better than that."

"Oh, yes, it does. Kaybo, if you please."

Kaybo had removed a covered dish from the coals and lifted the lid to reveal the contents of a brown-and-golden confection.

"Apple pandowdy, à la Kaybo."

"Say your prayers, boys. I think we just passed through the pearly gates," said Heck.

Fresh plates with the dessert were passed around and all ate in silence. After dinner, more wood was added to the fire as all sat around drinking coffee or sipping some of Bentingcourt's aged port.

"This is a truly magnificent country out here," said Bentingcourt.

"Well, you'd better enjoy it while ya can, 'fore the bankers, lawyers, and politicians ruin it," said Print.

The easterners looked at one another. Finally Pollard spoke up. "I take it you do not care for men of those professions."

"No, sir, I do not. You can take a banker, a politician and a lawyer, shove them in a barrel, kick it down a hill, and there'd be a son of a bitch on top every time. Pardon me, ladies. Too much of Mr. Bentingcourt's fine wine makes me forgetful that we are in the company of such lovely ladies."

"That's quite all right, Mr. Ritter," said Eva Bentingcourt. "You just happened to have dined with two bankers, two lawyers, and a politician. You see, my husband is a banker and a lawyer. Mr. Findley is a banker, and Mr. Pollard is a lawyer and a state assemblyman for the Commonwealth of Massachusetts."

"You'll have to excuse me, ma'am," said Print. "At my age I cannot touch my toes, but I got no problem puttin' my foot in my mouth."

Everyone laughed.

"Why do you feel men of our professions are so bad for your part of the country?" asked Findley.

"You're askin' me ta skate on thin ice after such a wonderful supper."

"We didn't get to be who we are by being thin-skinned, Mr. Ritter. I'm curious. Why are we such a blight?"

Print paused, took out his tobacco pouch, and started to fill his pipe. "I was referring ta the professions in general as opposed ta our present company. From what I seen of men in your profession, they don't care for gamblin'. See, the West was made on gamblin'. The whole country is thick with gamblers. I seen waddies bet a month's wages on who had the most bedbugs in his blankets. I heard a two pistoleros down in Raton that bet all they had as to who could sustain the most nonlethal wounds at twenty paces. I seen a man shoot a coffee can off his wife's head ta collect a fifty-dollar bet. And he done it, too. Course, he was a Mormon and had a solid inventory of wives ta spare."

He struck a match, puffed the pipe, and took a sip of port. "That's just the picayune stuff. Nobody come out here that wasn't gamblin'. Rich or poor. White or colored. They bet against the weather. They bet against locusts, cattle fever, and prairie fires. Cave-ins floating 'cross rivers, child-birthing. Every morning out here ya draw a breath, it is a gamble, and it ain't going to stop. The West will always be a gamble."

Print paused to flick a small piece of tobacco from his tongue. He wasn't sure if he was being entertaining or insulting to his dinner guests but decided to continue wading in.

"What about Lung Hay?" interjected Tom.

Print nodded in agreement while attempting another sip at the same time. "Mr. Lung Hay here came all the way to California to gamble that he'd be a rich man in the goldfields. Now he's gamblin' if he'll ever see his bride back in China. Tom and I are gamblin' we can get these horses 'cross country ta Sheridan. Only person I seen out here that ain't gamblin' is the red man. He's been forced inta a game that he just keeps drawing bad cards from, and his pot is dwindlin' fast.

"It's all one big gamble, cept house odds don't always apply. Sometimes caution can be almost criminal."

"I will drink to that one," said Tom, holding up his tin cup. "Cautious bankers foreclosin' on a man. Timid politicians back East afraid to help the non-voters out in the territories."

"And lawyers sometimes impeding justice and the need for immediate action," added Heck.

"Are we to assume you prefer vigilante justice?" asked Bentingcourt.

Print could tell that Yip was uncomfortable with the way the conversation was going. "One can be as bad as the other," said Print. "There is an element out here that can't abide with the odds and they have no problem adoptin' a more larcenious attitude ta make things fall in their favor."

"So you've seen frontier justice in action?" asked Pollard.

Print looked from Tom to Heck to Yip and nodded.

"Tell us one . . . one that won't incriminate you."

Print relit his pipe and took full advantage of the dramatic pause. "I was privileged ta see the conclusion of a business transaction years ago. Fella name a Ted Arns. Rancher east a Worland was havin' trouble with the unexplained disappearance of som' a his cattle. Now there was a flashy fella that come into that part of the country 'bout the same time Ted and som' a the other ranchers started seein' their inventories dwindle. Now the flashy fella was always turned out in clean pants an' a silk scarf an' a stylish tilt ta his Stetson. Name was Dwayne Fowler. When it came ta brandin', he was said ta be an artist with a runnin' iron."

Print paused for another sip and Tom raised his eyebrows as a signal to hurry it up. "Well, Ted Arns finally tracked the sporty Mr. Fowler down in a saloon in Meeteetse. Back then Meeteetse was a small joint. No sheriff. No magistrate. So Ted called him out right in front of the whisky sippers an' card sharks. He did give him the option ta relocate to a different hemisphere, but a fella that wore his hat the way Dwayne Fowler did wasn't goin' ta be showed up in front of a crowd."

Print peered into his empty cup and made a face. Bentingcourt solved the problem with two fingers of port.

"Fowler said if this wasn't a business issue, it was about respect. Ted Arns disagreed."

Print looked at his audience, milking every dramatic drop that he could. "Fowler was fast in trying to get his point across, but Teddy Arns was more accurate in statin' his case—and the placement of two slugs here an' here," said Print, pointing first to his neck and then to his chest.

"And what happened?" urged Pollard.

"Rancher Arns ended that transaction by putting the flashy Dwayne Fowler inta the 'bills paid' side of the business ledger."

Broad grins were on the faces of all the people

who understood English. Print was beginning to see what Yip meant about their love of western color.

"What about the girls?" asked Eva Bentingcourt.

Print shifted his weight to get more comfortable. "Sometimes I bloviate too much. Let Tom tell that one."

So Tom proceeded to tell the story about the girls and Fender and Cariboo, He left out the part about Big Rump Kate and skirted around Nola's involvement. Kaybo, Sun Foy, and Heck cleared dishes as Tom told the story.

". . . and that Captain Billy Fender, he was a gambler too. He was a miserable son of a bitch. Excuse me, ladies. You'll have to take my word for it. He was the kinda fellow that'd steal his own blankets, but he was a gambler, right up to the moment he cashed out."

The group was silent as they pondered Tom's words.

"Is there a musician in your party, Mrs. Bentingcourt?" asked Heck, "I saw the violin case."

"Mr. Findley is a fine musician," replied Eva.

"Would you honor us, Mr. Findley?" asked Heck.

"I would, Mr. Gilpin, except that I managed to run a fishhook in my thumb the other day and I am afraid that you would regret having to hear me. Do you play, sir?"

"I do, some."

"Then, sir, be my guest, and put a topping on this lovely evening."

Heck retrieved the violin case, took out the instrument, and tuned it. He started to play. All the faces of the party shone in the campfire light as they watched Heck. It was exquisite. Lyrical. As he played, he bowed and winked at the girls. All were transfixed. And when Heck finished, they all applauded.

"Bravo, bravo, Mr. Gilpin. What was that piece?" asked Bentingcourt.

"*Caprice*. By Fritz Kreisler," replied Eva Bentingcourt.

"Indeed it is, ma'am," said Heck, nodding to the lady.

"Who would have thought that we would hear one so contemporary as Kreisler under the stars of Wyoming? Surely that is rarer than fresh lemons," said Eva.

"I heard him play when he toured back in eighty-eight," said Heck as he tuned one of the strings.

"Please, Mr. Gilpin, another piece."

He bowed slightly to Eva. "Ma'am." He turned to the others. "*MacLeish's Waltz.*"

Heck played a haunting melody, a work more emblematic of the times and the region. After a few bars, Bentingcourt stood and reached for his wife's hand. He started to lead her in a waltz. The men backed up and moved to give them space. Eva was radiant. Nola watched her and instinctively covered her bruised face with a hand. Print noticed, struggled to his feet, and extended his hand to Nola.

"Miss Johns, may I?"

She tried to turn away, but Print took her and gently brought her to her feet. The two couples danced around the fire to the slow waltz. Even on the rough ground, they were graceful. Nola averted Print's attempt at eye contact.

"You're lighter than my biscuits, Miss Johns. Positively weightless."

She smiled slightly but shook her head in denial.

"Don't take my word for it."

He stopped and waited for the Bentingcourts to pass, and then he tapped Robert Bentingcourt on the shoulder. They changed partners, and

Bentingcourt danced with Nola around the fire. Heck played on, and then they changed partners again.

"See, I ain't the only one thinks you're a fine dancer, Miss Johns."

Heck drew long notes from the violin, which resonated in the night air. When he finished, Eva curtsied, and Nola followed suit. The men bowed and everyone clapped.

"A perfect topping on the evening, Mr. Gilpin."

Heck bowed.

Slowly the girls got to their feet. Nola escorted them back to the wagon and their pallets. The Bentingcourt party retired. Print banked the fire, and Heck piled the last of the cups into the big washbasin.

"I think I'll go sit with the horses a while," said Tom.

Print placed his blanket close to the fire, removed his boots, and lay back to fall asleep. Kaybo joined him at the fire, spreading his bedroll on the other side. The cream-colored tents blinked out, one by one.

Chapter Twenty-three

The next morning after breakfast, the Bentingcourt party prepared for another day of fishing. Nola had gathered up a bundle of laundry, and Number Three and Number Two followed her with bundles too.

"Anything you want washed, Mr. Ritter?"

"I think I'm fine, thank ya. Mind if I join you? Probably a good idea ta stay downstream of the fishermen."

He picked up little Number Five in his arms and led the way down to the riverbank. He found a spot downstream from the camp with a big, flat rock that jutted out into the water. Soon Nola and the girls were scrubbing laundry and rinsing it at the water's edge. Print found a comfortable spot to sit and watch.

"Ya haven't said what happened back at that hotel room."

Nola continued scrubbing and didn't bother to look up. "I went to check on the girls. . . . I was sent to check on the girls."

She turned and looked at Print. "I worked for Kate Becker, I believe you met her."

She went back to washing. She wiped away a strand of hair that had fallen in front of her face. "She wanted to know what you were up to with these girls. When I got to your room, those men were already there. I tried to stop them, really I did."

"Pretty obvious from what they done to you that you tried."

"We were fortunate that you and your nephew came upon us when you did."

"I appreciate what you did to protect the girls, Miss Johns."

"What you told them last night at supper about how you came to have the girls—is that true?"

Print gave her a questioning look. "Yes, ma'am, one hundred percent true."

"Why did you do it, Mr. Ritter? Take in the girls, I mean."

"What was I supposed to do? Give them a canteen and a tin of crackers and say adios?"

"I wasn't suggesting that, Mr. Ritter, I only wanted to know why you took them with you."

"Miss Johns, I'm a thoroughly failed Christian person, but I wasn't about ta leave them out there in the middle of nowhere. No, sir. And I didn't have no carnal designs on 'em neither, if that's what you was thinkin'."

"I didn't think either of those thoughts, Mr. Ritter."

Print took out his pocketknife and a little figurine of a girl and started to whittle. Nola continued to scrub and rinse the clothes, and the girls took them and spread them on the rock to dry. Print and Nola sat in silence for several minutes.

"It's Mrs. Johns."

There was more silence as Print took the knife blade and ran it against the rock he was sitting on to sharpen it. "How'd ya wind up in the employ of Miss Big Rump?"

"One dance with a girl and you want to know all about her, Mr. Ritter."

Print smiled sheepishly. The girls took more linen to spread on the rocks.

"We came out here from Illinois. Mr. Johns's people had a small farm near Moline. We lived with his folks, working the farm. Kel's—my husband's—ma died and about a year after his papa died. Turns out they left the farm to Kel's sister and her husband. We were left with almost nothing. Kel said he couldn't live in Illinois after that. Said he wanted to make a new start in the West. So we took what little we had and struck out for the 'New Canaan,' so to speak. Spent our first winter in Omaha. Next year we moved to Laramie. Kel got a job freighting supplies to a mining camp up in the Centennial Range. Thirty-seven miles each way. Twice a week. We were making do until he drove the wagon off a switchback.

"They brought him back to Laramie. He survived, but they took both his legs off. We barely had a nest, much less a nest egg. I worked at whatever I could and got a job clerking in a dry goods store. But he'd sit upstairs in the boardinghouse all day. They came to the store the first day of May to tell me he had shot himself."

She paused and looked at Print. He had been looking at her, but he dropped his gaze as if to concentrate on the little figurine he was whittling. With no more washing to spread, the girls were playing down by the water's edge.

"I had no money and there was no going back to Kel's people."

"Families sure can be hard 'n one another."

"You think so, Mr. Ritter?"

"Absolutely. It was family hardness that set Tom an' I on this course for Wyoming."

"Maybe if I'd been as brave as my husband, I would have put an end to it right there. But I was young and scared. Fear and hunger will make a person do things they never pictured for themselves. You sure you really want to hear this?"

"You tell me as much or as little as ya like. I ain't a judge or a preacher."

She looked out across the water, away from Print. "I started there in Laramie. Then it was Walcott, Medicine Bow, Rawlins, all over, wherever the mines were hitting pay dirt or the cattle were selling." She spoke in a level voice devoid of emotion.

She turned to look Print right in the eyes. "It's a rough trade, Mr. Ritter. Easy enough for you men, but rough if you're on the receiving end."

She looked back out across the water. "I was in Rock Springs. A man split my scalp with a bottle and dumped me out the back door. It was around the middle of November. They found me the next morning. My hair was frozen to the ground."

Again she turned to look at Print. "They had to cut my hair off."

Even Print could not hold her gaze, and he looked away.

"You know what a whore with no hair is worth in this world, Mr. Ritter? Not much."

Print looked up into the sky at the sound of a hawk keening high above them.

"Thing is, sometimes even a bald-headed whore wants to keep living. Your hair grows out. Life goes on. But time's against you."

Print interjected. "Nothin' more unforgivin' than time."

Nola continued. "You feel it setting in like a hard freeze. You start out in the parlor houses if you're young and have any looks at all. But youth and beauty start to go fast. I never understood how something that God meant to be so wonderful could wear a woman out so fast. Soon you're at the rooming house at the end of town. Next stop are the cribs down the line. Finally, if you haven't been killed or done yourself in, it's the hog ranch. Ever pay a visit to a hog ranch, Mr. Ritter?"

Print, who was looking down at the little figurine, raised his head to meet her eyes. He shook his head.

"That's the last rung. I'm about halfway down that ladder.

"Still think you want to go dancing with me, Mr. Ritter?"

Print looked down at the palm of his left hand while he rubbed it with his right thumb, "I guess you're down on men."

"I don't hate all men. Most of you aren't bad. They just wanted to pop their cork. A lot of lonely men in the West. I believe most wanted a brief, bright moment of companionship. I had a miner pay me just to watch me hang laundry on a clothesline. Never touched me. And he was a young man, too. In the end, I think it's as much about being lonesome as anything. Sure, you want to pop your cork. That's natural. We do too."

Print shifted his weight and turned to look upstream.

"Does that make you uncomfortable, Mr. Ritter? The idea that women want it just as much as you fellows? Why shouldn't we? There ought to be some payoff for the pain of childbirth. What isn't much of a bargain is being kicked and hit and cut up. It's not natural, and it doesn't fit the definition of companionship. There's no creature on the face of the earth lonelier than a whore, Mr. Ritter."

Ritter looked up at her. "You think you could call me Print?"

Nola ignored the question and brushed back an errant wisp of hair from her face. She rose and gathered up the laundry. The girls returned from the shallows to help her. Print gathered up Number Five in his arms and followed Nola back to the wagon.

Just as she reached the top of the riverbank, Print spoke to her back. "You're the best dancer I ever twirled with."

Nola stopped and stood for a long moment. She turned to face him. "You don't scare easy, do you, Mr. Ritter? . . . Print."

She turned and continued walking back to the camp.

Print said nothing, and simply shifted the little girl to his other hip, following Nola and the girls back to camp. Soon he was joined by Bentingcourt returning from the riverbank.

"Mr. Ritter, we are going to move upstream a few miles before nightfall. I wanted to thank you for your hospitality. Please take this and enjoy it as the memory of our brief visit."

He handed three bottles of Scotch to Print.

Findley stepped forward and held out his violin case for Heck. "Mr. Gilpin, thank you for last night's recital."

Heck, with a look of surprise, said, "I couldn't. That's much too generous."

"Sir, you must. The image of you playing out under the stars of this western sky will warm the long winter nights in Boston for me. Please."

Heck took the violin case and bowed slightly.

They all stood around the camp and watched as Yip led the party back across the river.

"They're going to make me have to say nice

things about Yankees," Print said. With his hands jammed in his pockets, Print turned to face Tom and Heck. "Much as I'm enjoying this spot, figure we ought to strike out in the morning. Can't count on summer holding on forever."

That evening, after supper, while Nola went about collecting the pots, the girls sat on a blanket, watching Heck run rosin down the length of the bow, with the violin lying beside him.

"I think I'll take advantage of all this fresh water and give these pots a good scrubbing," said Nola.

"Let me give you a hand," said Print, standing up to help.

Print took a heavy iron skillet and a stewpot and followed Nola. You could hear Heck in the background, tuning the violin.

At the river Nola knelt and took a handful of river sand and started to scour the pots. Print took a position on a rock and rolled himself a smoke. Faint strains of Heck's violin could be heard in the background.

"I didn't notice you smoking cigarettes before."

"Once in a while, a night like this calls for a good smoke."

The full moon reflected on the rippling water.

She paused at scrubbing the pots. She rose and walked over to a rock and sat down and removed her shoes. She raised her skirt, rolled down her stockings, and soaked her feet in the cool water. Print got up, walked over, and sat down beside her.

"Oh, that feels good. You ought to try it, Mr. Ritter . . . excuse me, Print."

Print flipped the last of his smoke into the river and proceeded to remove his boots and socks.

"Do you really think women are so puzzling? I heard you talking the other night."

"Oh, that. You mean about the Rosetta stone? No. Maybe I just had bad luck."

"What was it you really wanted from women?"

"I see this is going to be a two-smoke night." Print reached into his shirt pocket to take out his makings. He took the paper, filled it with tobacco, and then rolled the cigarette. He lit up and took a deep draw while Nola watched.

"Same as most fellows, I suppose. What did you call it—a bright, brief moment? How 'bout a partner, a companion? Somebody to keep your feet warm at night."

Nola splashed her feet in the water in response.

"I would like to have known just once in my life that I was truly and deeply loved by a woman, a woman with a heart as true as a rancher's wife."

"You're quite the romantic."

"Romance is for pikers. I ain't talkin' 'bout infatuation. I'm talkin' 'bout something way beyond romance. Bone deep. You just feel it between the two of you."

Print brought his feet out of the water and looked at them in the moonlight. He gestured with his feet. "If you stub the right toe, the left one feels it."

Nola raised her feet out of the water and held them next to Print's.

"Ain't no he or she or you or me. You're both just one."

"You sound like an expert on the subject."

"Me? Nah. Hell, I don't know what I'm talkin' 'bout half the time. But I do believe it does happen to the lucky few."

"But not to most folks?"

"No. That's why there's so many hard-edged and fearful people out there. It's like livin' your life without salt."

"You don't seem to be lacking any salt in your diet, you know, all hard-edged and scared."

"Oh, I can get spooked, same as everyone else."

"Really? When?"

Print paused to think for a moment. "I get rousted out of my sleep sometimes for nature's call. I find there's something frightnin' about that hour of the night. There ain't no foolin' yourself about what you've done and what you haven't done with your life."

"What do you do?"

"Well, I try like hell to get back to sleep."

They sat for a moment in silence.

"So, have you given up on women?"

"No, ma'am. But I figure I got about as much chance of findin' that gal as becomin' the King of Siam."

Nola laughed. "I have a hard time seeing you as the King of Siam, Mr. Ritter."

"Sure you just can't you call me Print? Everybody else calls me Mr. Ritter."

She looked at him for a moment, smiled, and then said, "I like to think that when I say it, it has a different ring to it."

A broad grin came across Print's face as he looked out onto the water. Then he looked back at her.

"You have a unique sense of humor, Miz Johns. Shall we go?"

Print took his feet out of the water, and as he did, Nola grabbed his ankle. She dried his foot with the hem of her dress, then the other. They put on their boots and shoes. Print stood to help Nola up. They faced one another and Print reached for her face. She drew back.

"I'd pay forty dollars just ta watch you hang laundry any time, Miz Johns."

Slowly he reached again. She didn't resist. He let

her hair down and, with a Braille-like touch, ran his fingers over the long white scar on her scalp. He held her head in his hands and drew her to him and kissed the scar.

"Yer a good woman, Miz Johns, you really are."

With her arms at her sides, she rested her head on his chest. They gathered the pots and pans and turned to the sleeping camp.

Where the meadow met the riverbank, she stopped and put the pots down. Print turned and she took the pans from him and put them on the ground too. She untied his kerchief and slipped the suspenders off his shoulders and opened his shirt. She unbuttoned the top of her dress and clothes fell like flags on a field of surrender.

His white body was the color of soap as he lay on the meadow grass. He shivered, and when he felt her body next to his, he shivered again. She pulled him close to her, and she rolled on top of him. She looked down at him and her hair hung down on his cheeks. He couldn't see her face but saw the Great Milky Way in the night sky behind her. It looked like a bride's veil on her. He shook violently, he felt so cold. She kissed his face and held her lips next to his ear and soothed him.

They moved in a pantomime that was older than the river that ran beside them. They moved alone and they moved together. Then they passed through each other into nothingness. No river. No horses. No stars. He felt himself falling endlessly backward into oblivion.

Chapter Twenty-four

Print was up an hour before the first light appeared in the east. A front had rolled in during the night and left a skin of frost on the camp. He walked over to where the saddle horses were picketed and brushed the crystals off Bob Tate's mane. He sniffed the air; it smelled of horse. He stroked the chestnut's mane and neck. He couldn't ever remember a horse that smelled bad. Unlike the countless humans he had come across. The boys in butternut wool from a summer of marching and the metallic sweat of fear. Miners so drunk they soiled themselves. Whiskey-sick cowboys. The hermits up in the big woods and their huts so rancid that he always slept outside. The Russians who had drifted south from the Yukon and as far as Kamchatka, following the timber trade, smelling of tinned fish and rotten teeth. The gamey tang of the doughy whores. The cheap cologne, their own musk, and the sweat of other men. He doubled-up the cinch strap and flopped the stirrup down. Yes, horses smelled just fine to him.

When the sun came up it burned off the frost, but the day remained cool and sunny. A big magpie alighted on the bough of a hemlock. The bough swayed under its weight. In its beak was a purple skink.

Print joined Tom at the fire, where a pot of coffee was working.

"Bit of fall in the air," said Print.

"All the more reason to push on. I don't want to get trapped in these passes," said Tom.

"We can wheel them once or twice," said Print, "and then we'll send them on."

They broke camp, and Sun Foy, at the reins of the wagon with Lung Hay on one side and little Number Five on the other, steered the wagon to the edge of the meadow as the men went about bunching up the herd. Nola and the other girls sat in the back of the wagon, watching. Number Four was sitting on the edge, her legs dangling off.

Print signaled to Tom and Heck to start the horses. They started turning the herd in a large counterclockwise circle. As it picked up momentum, the men continued to keep the herd tightened up. Print broke away and went over to the wagon and said, "We're going to pull out. You all stay behind us."

And then, as an afterthought, he turned and looked back at where they camped and said, "I'd like to try that fly-fishing some day."

He rode back to the wheeling herd of galloping horses. He signaled for Tom and Heck to circle one more time and then let them go.

Number Four kept watching the horses, then turned to see the people in the front. Just like that, Ye Fung jumped off the back of the wagon. She stood for a moment, looked back again at the girls, then dashed straight into the thundering herd. The first horse dodged her to the side and missed her. But then, a second later, another horse hit her, sending her flying into the air, and she fell into the dirt and dust of the pounding hooves.

Tom saw what happened and gigged his horse around the edge of the turning herd to where the girl disappeared. He swept in, low in the saddle, and grabbed at the girl. He grasped her clothing and pulled her up and across his saddle and pulled out of the churning horses.

Tom cleared the herd, the limp body across the pommel of his saddle. He swung out of the stirrups and lowered Ye Fung to the ground.

A stunned Print rode up to Tom and joined him on the ground. Heck kept looking across the backs of the horses from the other side of the turning herd, which was slowly starting to come to a halt now that the other riders weren't there to keep them going. Nola jumped from the wagon and ran to the men and the lifeless form before them. Sun Foy thrust the reins at Lung Hay and followed her, while the rest of the girls looked on in shock.

The climbing sun had warmed the day as the men went about digging a grave. The girls, along with Lung Hay, had pulled tufts of tall grass to use to line the bottom of the grave. Tom and Print picked up the blanket at either end that held Ye Fung and gently lowered her into the hole. Tom pulled back the blanket that covered her face. He bit his bottom lip and covered it again. He rose, and he and Print started to fill in the dirt. When they were through, Print said to him, "Anything you want to say?"

"I already said it."

Print nodded. He looked at the girls. They came forward and knelt, placing a bunch of Indian paintbrush at the foot of the grave. Print removed his hat, and the other men did too.

"We're all travelers in this world," he said, "from

the sweetgrass to the packinghouse. Birth 'til death, we travel between the eternities."

He put his hat back on, turned, and started to walk off, and said, "Nephew."

The sun was directly overhead when at last the herd moved out, followed by the wagon and riders. A light wind ruffled the bunch of Indian paintbrush left at the foot of the fresh grave on the bend of the Snake River.

Chapter Twenty-five

They had been on the move for three days when the herd crested a flattened-out hill. In the distance, they saw a building that sat in the open country by itself. The mounted men tightened up the herd as they drew closer. The building was a low-slung affair made up of a half-dozen stalls facing the intersection of two dusty drovers' trails.

It was really an intersection from nowhere and to nowhere. Several horses, saddled, waited in a corral in the back. A man in a bloody apron was butchering a steer suspended from a tripod of poles. Several women came out of the stalls. Hard, tragic beings. They were the worst of whoredom. The toothless, the diseased. Cankered shells of what were once women. There was a sign that said "Runyon's."

Print pushed his horse into the lead, passing Tom. "Keep 'em movin', Tom, I don't want 'em stoppin' here."

Print pulled up ahead and was greeted by the man in the bloody apron.

"You folks going to put up for the night?"

"We got two hours of daylight 'fore we call it a day," said Print.

"How about some fresh beef? You can put your herd in the big corral out back. My gals could sure use some money."

"We're shy on time today. Gotta grease a few more miles 'fore we make camp."

Print pushed his horse forward to keep up with the lead mares. Soon the wagon rolled past and Tom stopped to make sure it continued on. Nola and Lung Hay looked out as the wagon glided like a ferry passing a dock of passengers waiting to board. The sad women waved at them and the girls that were looking out the back. The man in the bloody apron stepped forward.

"See you travel with your own girls."

Tom turned in the saddle and looked at the girls peering out of the back. "They're my nieces," he said coldly.

With a blood-caked hand, the butcher grabbed the reins of Tom's horse. "Mister, you must have a strange-looking brother-in-law."

Tom leaned low in the saddle and in a whisper said, "Get your hands off my horse 'fore I blow a hole in your liver, fella."

The butcher let go of the reins and backed up. Horse and rider moved on.

"Go on. We don't need you cheap-ass people 'round here anyway," said the aproned man.

Tom stopped his horse, his back to the man, and cocked his head as if to hear more. The butcher turned and walked away, and Tom moved on.

A tragic old hag was standing in one of the doorways. She called out, "Hey, cowboy, how about a ride? Come on. Won't take long. You won't even have to take your boots off. Come on. Us professional ladies got to eat too, you know."

From within one of the darkened stalls of the hog ranch, heavy breathing and groaning could be heard, and a creaking bed. A figure rose in the darkened stall, leaving an old, world-weary woman on the mattress. The figure watched the last of Print's procession go by. And the shadow on the wall showed a man, one arm against the wall and a head with unusually large ears.

The faces of other women from hell could be seen peering out of the darkness of the stalls as Nola and the girls looked at them. The dust rolled up behind the departing wagon. The Ritter-Harte party moved eastward, away from this ignominious spot where two cattle trails crossed in the middle of nowhere out on the prairie.

Print pushed them along 'til almost sunset as he wanted to put as much distance between the herd and the hog ranch they'd passed. As they went about setting up camp, the girls went out looking for wood for the fire. Suddenly, there was a cry and then whimpering.

Tom and Nola ran to where the girls had gathered around little Number Five. Lung Hay followed close behind. Ghing Wa had stepped into a gopher hole and twisted her ankle. Lung Hay pushed through everyone and said, "Please, let me look. I want to look at her."

He knelt and carefully touched her leg, from the knee to the calf to the ankle. He turned to Sun Foy and said to her in Mandarin, *"Please, I need you to hold her. Please hold her strong."*

Tom knelt on the other side of the girl as Lung Hay removed the slipper, then slowly removed the binding around her foot. What was revealed was a tiny, deformed foot, toes broken and bent under and mashed up into the sole of the foot. All of the adults except Lung Hay were taken aback.

Lung Hay turned to Sun Foy and said, *"We are lucky. It is just a sprain."*

Print rode up, dismounted, and walked over, bent low and looked. "Sweet Jesus. What the hell is that?"

Lung Hay, without looking up, said, "It is an ancient custom," to which Tom replied, "And they call us barbarians."

Lung Hay rubbed the ankle carefully. "It is not broken. Please hold her tight," he said to Sun Foy.

Lung Hay carefully bound up the foot again. The little girl was in great pain. She grabbed Tom's hand, and he stroked her brow. Lung Hay talked quietly to the little girl.

"What did you say to her?" asked Print.

"I told her she would be all right. I told her Ghing Wa was a brave girl."

"Ghing Wa?"

"Yes. Ghing Wa, that is her name. Ghing Wa."

"How come you never told me that?" asked Print.

"Why, you never asked."

Lung Hay turned and pointed to each one of the girls. "Sun Foy. Ghee Moon. Mai Ling. Ghing Wa."

Tom mouthed the words. "Sun Foy."

Print pointed to the little girl on the ground. "Ghing Wa?"

"Yes, Ghing Wa," repeated Lung Hay.

"And the little one that was killed by the horses?"

"Ye Fung." Lung Hay nodded.

Print repeated the name. "Ye Fung."

"She did not die from horses. She died from shame," said Lung Hay, looking directly at Print.

Print sat up late that night, and he thought about why he hadn't asked Lung Hay the girls' names before. And he thought about the little Chinese girl whom he barely knew, and her rash death.

He recalled the years out on the trail and how talk would drift to the war and the younger boys wanted to hear all about it. He had sat and listened to some fellows that wolfed and bragged about battles they'd been in and what a high time they had. There were the others who never talked about it and would get up and walk away from the fire rather than listen or talk. He talked some, but not much. He figured that if a man had not been there, then it was a waste of air to go on about it.

And he didn't want to talk to any Yankees about it. He didn't hate them, but he sure found most to be tedious at times. Thing is, they were always right. Not that they thought they were right—most of the time they *were* right. At least on things like commerce and efficiency of all things. He found they missed the mark on people most of the time. They were naturals at telling other folks what to do. He decided that they had been that way ever since the first one tiptoed over Plymouth Rock. He didn't expect them to be changing much in the next couple of hundred years.

The boys would ask him if he was afraid before the fights. Yes, he said, he was afraid.

The one time he was scared down to his toenails was an afternoon engagement against a battery on a hill overlooking the Rapidan. They were ordered up the hill to take out the four-gun battery. He was in the second or third line and they were almost on top of the placement when a shell from one of their own howitzers hit the magazine on the Yankee caisson and exploded as the first line breached the guns.

In slow motion he saw a leg, from boot to hip, turning in the air, end over end, hit a fellow in the line in front of him and knock the lad's head half off. The fellow must have been leaning into the incline of the hill because it didn't knock him over. The impact had straightened him up, the head hung back between his shoulder blades, and the soldier then sank to his knees and toppled over. He had seen worse gore—surely at the hospital. But the incident was so random. So violent.

Except for the time a quartermaster's wagon ran over his foot and smashed it and they sent him to the hospital in Richmond, he was never touched. It was the strange and utterly random way the boy died that afternoon on the Rapidan that still filled Print with fear.

Chapter Twenty-six

Early the next morning, before the sun was up, Tom and Sun Foy sat in the short grass away from camp, on a small rise facing the east. It was cold. Tom didn't mind it, but Sun Foy shivered slightly. He looked out at the prairie as they sat in silence.

Just before the sun broke over the horizon, he held a finger to his lips. A covey of doves broke out and rose from a nearby clump of cottonwoods. Then another covey. Tom got up and extended a hand to help Sun Foy up. They picked up two buckets and walked toward the bushes.

Later, when they walked back into camp with the buckets full of water, Tom asked Lung Hay to tell her that "the birds fly to water in the evening and from water in the morning." Lung Hay translated, and Sun Foy nodded.

The day was hot as the herd and wagon moved across what seemed like the endless expanse. They were now out on the buffalo range, long, rolling hills that went on for as far as the eye could see. In the afternoon the sky to the west darkened as magnificent columns of a thunderhead built and rolled down toward them. Soon the skies opened up on them and the rain fell in sheets. There was thunder and lightning; the darkness was lit by blinding flashes that hung the scene in suspended animation. And then more darkness. The procession came to a halt. The horses bunched up, their tails turned into the storm. The riders were in slickers, and rain poured off the brims of their hats. Sun Foy parked herself on the little horse next to Tom, hair plastered to her face. Tom took off his hat and put it on her head. Nola and the girls and Lung Hay huddled in the wagon as rain poured down the canvas sides. And then it lightened, and then it stopped and the storm was gone. The sun returned and the prairie was washed and puddled.

"Damn, if the Old Man didn't toss his hammer down the canyon walls that time!" yelled Tom to Heck as they started the horses up again.

"Smell that sage? You don't find that back in Philadelphia," replied Heck.

Sun Foy's soaked shirt revealed her breasts. Tom was staring at her. She looked at him, knowing that he was. She had a benign look on her face that was neither shy nor offended. He looked at her face and then averted his eyes.

The wagon moved on, following the herd as it trailed the departing storm.

Print was on point, and in the late afternoon, he saw something off to the herd's right. He waved Heck up to his side. "Hank, keep 'em movin' on. I'll be right back."

Print loped over to a piece of planking sticking out of the ground. It might have been a floorboard of a wagon. The ground in front of it had been tunneled and dug up. Probably coyotes, thought Print. The sole of a boot green with mold lay several feet away. Someone had carved into the wood plank "A Texas Cowboy."

Print called for a break an hour later as he wanted to give the herd a lot of time to graze. After making camp, Tom, on the little red roan, was playing with Sun Foy and Mai Ling. He was trying to separate them by cutting them with his horse. The cow pony feinted left and then right. He backed up and stopped. Then he jumped forward again, the giggling girls dodging one way and then the other. Tom smiled and then uncoiled his riata. He swept left and laid a loop over Sun Foy. He gently hauled in his rope, bringing her to the pony's side. She smiled at him as he loosened the loop and removed it from her.

Heck was sitting on a nail keg with Ghee Moon next to him. The violin sat in his lap, and he showed her how to draw the bow across the strings, and he placed her fingers on the correct frets with the other hand. She slowly drew the bow across and a soft, sad sound was heard.

After dinner Nola and Print collected the pots and walked to the little creek they'd camped by.

"Never knew Uncle Print to take such an interest in dish washing."

Heck chuckled. "Wasn't he the one that said something about bringing a strong man to his knees? Think he left out the part about going to the river."

At the side of the creek, Print and Nola both knelt, scrubbing and rinsing the pots.

"You're quite the domestic cowhand, Mr. Ritter—I mean Print."

"No, you're right. I do like the way you say way 'Mr. Ritter.'"

"What are you going to do with the girls?"

Print wiped his hands on his pants and started to roll a smoke. "We got seven, maybe eight days 'til

Sheridan. I still have time to get it figured out. What about you, Miz Johns? You made any plans?"

Nola said nothing. She continued washing the pots.

"You don't have to go shy on me."

She stopped and looked at him. "Like you said, it's seven, eight days until we get to Sheridan. I have time, too. Now, if you'll excuse me, the only clothes I now own are the ones I was wearing when I left Cariboo. I need to do some washing."

Print was at a complete loss. He stood and then took the pots and headed back to the wagon. At one point, he turned around to look back and saw Nola undressing, her strong back and wide hips in the starlight. He lingered a moment and then moved on. As he walked back into the camp, Lung Hay and Tom looked up.

"Not much skillet cleaning tonight, Uncle."

Print shot him a frosty look, dropped the pots by the fire, and went to get his bedroll. In the background, Heck was playing a rendition of *Aura Lee.*

The fire was crackling in the predawn light, the coffeepot perking in the coals.

"Where's Uncle Print?"

"He walked out of here way before daylight. He's prickly this morning," said Heck.

"He must've got some dust up his nose," replied Tom.

Both men looked at Nola. Nola looked at them and simply said, "No salt."

Neither of the men understood what she meant.

"Well, before we pull out, I'm going to go scare up some game for tonight while we wait for him."

Tom and Sun Foy lay side by side behind a large clump of Russian thistle in the short grass out on the buffalo range. A hundred yards in front of them was a small group of pronghorns. Tom eased the carbine forward and placed it beside Sun Foy. He reached around her to steady the butt against her shoulder. He placed her index finger in the trigger guard, and then he helped her aim. He had his arm around her. Their cheeks touched momentarily and he pulled back. Sun Foy looked down the barrel. Tom leaned close to help her sight. He breathed in her scent and smelled her hair and he forgot about the pronghorn.

Suddenly the carbine roared. The recoil hit Sun Foy hard. She was wide-eyed and stunned. For a long moment Tom held her to him, his eyes closed, his cheek against her hair.

Tom was dressing out the pronghorn back at camp, the girls watching him skin the hide from the carcass, when Print rode back in. He dismounted, loosened the cinch on Bob Tate, and saw a group of mounted men approaching the camp from the east. Tom saw the men too. He stabbed his knife into the ground several times to clean it and then sheathed it. He rubbed grass and dirt on his bloody hands. The girls scurried to the wagon.

"Company coming, Uncle."

Tom drifted over to the picket line to blend in with the horses. Nola and Lung Hay joined the girls by the wagon, and Heck moved back from the fire as Print walked toward the men.

Five mounted men and a packhorse came to a halt in front of Print.

"Morning, folks. I'm Bill Miller, marshal out of Sheridan. These are my deputies: Dick, Doug, Don, and Dana McNeary."

"That's handy," said Print.

"Who's the jigger boss here?"

Print said nothing. "You men care for coffee?"

"Thank you. So, you the honcho here?"

"My name's Print Ritter. This is my party."

"Good-looking bunch of horses you got there, Mr. Ritter."

"Yep."

"You got papers on them, I suppose."

"You bet. . . . You got a badge, I suppose?"

The men dismounted.

"No need to get puffed up," Miller replied as he pulled back the left side of his coat to reveal the brass badge. "I should be eating ham and eggs at The Blue Goose back in Sheridan instead of sleeping on the ground, eating jerky, and looking for horse thieves."

Nola had come forward with cups for the men and then poured from the pot. The men tipped their hats to Nola. The one called Don took his off and then replaced it.

"Thank you, ma'am," said Miller, and then he turned to Print. "I'm after a rough lot run by a fellow name of Big Ears Bywaters." He smiled and shook his head. "You can't be on the wrong side of the law and not have some ridiculous name attached to your reputation these days."

"Well, if I run into him, I'll give him your regards, marshal."

"It ain't a name he responds to well. Don't let that name fool you. He's trickier than a redheaded woman. They steal horses 'round here and tail them up to Alberta. Sell them to the Metis renegades. Then kype horses up there and bring them south to sell. Been pretty active down Carbon County way. I'm surprised Big Ears ain't paid you a visit. They say he can hear a horse at twenty miles."

The marshal pulled on his earlobe.

"Point taken," said Print.

"Steer clear, if you can. They're all well garnished with weapons."

Print pointed to his horses. "These horses are from John Day country. I'm deliverin' 'em to William and Malcolm Moncrieffe in Sheridan."

"The Moncrieffe brothers? You can't touch them with a million. They'll pay good money too—if you get them there."

"You want to see my papers?" asked Print.

Miller handed back his coffee cup and mounted up. "That won't be necessary."

"Good luck locatin' Mr. Big Ears."

"My plan is to catch up with them soon enough. Then I'll put the kibosh on them." He patted the coiled rope on his saddle. "We'll straighten them out and make good citizens out of them. With any luck I'll be wearing his ears on my watch chain."

The rest of the men handed their cups back and mounted up too. The marshal turned to go, then wheeled the horse toward them again.

"Folks don't take to yamping livestock in Carbon County."

He tipped the brim of his hat to the women. "Ladies." The riders departed.

Tom walked out from the picket line and was joined by Heck.

"Ambitious fellow," said Tom.

Print stuck his hands in his pants pockets. "All the more reason ta get these horses there soon as we can. We'll all sit a double watch from here on out."

It was a moonless night. The camp was sound asleep. The horses browsed on the short grass. Tails switched. Tom and Heck were out nighthawking. They slowly circled the herd, in opposite directions. They didn't tighten it up too much, but they didn't want any of the horses straying. As they passed one another, they stopped and Heck said, "I been meaning to ask you about what you did back there in the hotel. Pretty hard on that fellow, weren't you?"

"You think so? There's men that had a lot worse done to them."

They walked on in a long circle away from one another until they met up on the other side of the herd and stopped again.

"My uncle told me about a time he was down in Elko years ago. He and some hands caught a fellow that had raped a woman. He didn't get far."

"Did they hang him?" asked Heck.

"No, they prunced him."

"Did what?"

"They prunced him," said Tom. "They cut his nut sack off."

"Oh. Did he die?"

"No. He just got fat and grew old."

The men pushed their horses on as they circled around the herd again.

By noon the next day, the herd had made good time. They had found water twice, and Print intended to move the herd along until it was dark. Still in a bad mood from his conversation with Nola the other evening, he turned in the saddle to look back and saw that Tom had fallen way behind. He turned Bob Tate and loped around the side of the herd and back to meet Tom.

"What's the problem?" he yelled to Tom as he pulled up.

"Nothing. I just feel like we're being dogged."

Print looked over Tom's shoulder and beyond. "Ah, that marshal's got ya jumpy."

"Maybe," replied Tom. "I'm not sure. Why don't

you push on for an early camp? Pick a good site for us. I'm going to hang back and stretch out the distance for you. Then I'll close up quickly."

Print agreed and loped back to the herd.

It was evening, and Print had picked a spot to camp that was in a small coolie. There was a rock outcropping on either side a hundred yards up. Print had built a big campfire and was sitting in front of it whittling, the wagon behind him and no one else in sight. He heard footsteps coming up from behind him. He knew it was his nephew, Tom.

"Stay in the dark and pick a good spot. Up in the rocks to the left would be the best."

"Where's Heck?" asked Tom.

"He's up in the rocks on the right. He's got the rest of 'em up there well hid."

"Where are you going to sit?"

"I'm gonna sit right here."

"Like a big piece of cheese waiting for the rats to show up?"

"Well, let's not make it Swiss cheese. We can't shoot it out with these fellas. We're going to have to face 'em, listen to what they have to say."

"Then what?" asked Tom.

"We'll find a spot and we'll play it by ear."

Print pulled out a tattered copy of *The Writings of Anatole France* and read by the fire.

An hour later he could hear the sound of horses walking in from the darkness. One rider emerged; several others were visible in the half-light. He rode his horse into the firelight. He was tall and thin with a pinched face and very large ears.

"Evenin'. Saw your fire. Got some coffee to spare?"

Print closed his book and placed it beside him. "We're fresh out of coffee."

"Too late for supper?"

"Supper's over."

"Where are the rest of your people?"

"That's none of your concern, mister."

The pinch-faced man started to dismount.

"Whoa, there," said Print. He waved his finger back and forth to indicate no.

"Ain't a friendly camp you're running here, mister." The rider settled back in the saddle.

"You been cutting my sign all day and now you ride in here at night with a hard lot. What did you expect?"

"Well, I thought you might want to do some horse business."

"I ain't in the horse business."

"What business you in then?"

"You got shit in your ears, mister? I told ya, my business is none of your concern."

"I come in here peaceful. All I wanted to do was some horse business and be respectable."

"Respectable?" Print looked the rider up and down and then the riders behind him. He shook his head and chuckled. "Fella, my daddy told me a long time ago you can't shine shit."

"I ought to burn you down right where you sit, mister. You ain't going to talk to me that way and live."

Print said nothing.

"I ain't afraid of you."

"You should be," said Print. "See, I'm in the blanket business."

"Blanket business?"

"Yeah. I sell blankets, mostly ta the tribes in need of smallpox and typhoid."

The men behind the pinch-faced man looked at one another and muttered.

"I ain't afraid of no blanket," said the pinch-faced man.

"Like I said, you should be. Ya ever seen a white man's face after he's had the pox? With those dinner plates you got for ears, I figured you might have heard the name of Smallpox Bob."

Print stood and walked over to pick up a saddle blanket. Coming from up high, out in the darkness, they could hear the distinct sound of a round being jacked into a carbine. Big Ears looked up and then back at Print. And then they heard the same sound come from the right. Big Ears and his men looked left, and then back to the right again, and then at Print.

"I didn't ride in on the turnip wagon, Mr. Big Ears."

Print walked toward the riders with the blanket extended. The horses behind Bywaters started snorting and backing up, and two of the men turned their horses and started to trot away. Print stopped and looked over at Big Ears.

"Tonight's your night, old man," said Bywaters, "but I'm going to make a point of meeting you again."

Print shook the blanket again, and the rest of the riders spun their horses and bolted into the night. Big Ears simply backed his horse up slowly, turned it slowly, and walked into the darkness. Print watched him leave and listened to the footfall of the horse until it was gone. He took a bucket of water and doused the fire. Soon he could hear Tom coming down out of the rocks. And then Heck and the rest of them joined him in the darkness.

"Where'd you come up with that stuff about the smallpox?" asked Tom.

Print smiled slightly, "Books, son. Readin' books.

"I don't think we'll sleep tonight. We need to put some distance on these fellas."

Print tightened the cinch on Bob Tate and mounted. He took up a position at the rear of the herd as they moved out, realizing that there was now more at stake.

Books indeed, he thought. Books and memories, memories that hurt and haunted him, at times so bad he couldn't eat and couldn't talk. He had worked hard in the beginning not to think of the woman and the little girl. He thought he was losing his mind. He drank alone and he drank with others. He wanted to take it out on the working girls, but he couldn't. He couldn't slap them. He couldn't have them. In the end, all he could do was bury his face deep in the big Swede's breasts and cry. Afterward he was ashamed, and she told him not to be. That he would be surprised how many men had shed tears on her bosom.

He drank again, then sobered up and made inquiries. Someone said they had gone to Laramie. When he got there, he was told they had left for Denver. Denver was big, and all he found was someone who knew someone and that they had heard she was going south. How far? Maybe Springer or Las Cruces. He wired his old boss Mr. Wallop, who had told Print that he would help. And he did. Print took the money the old man sent and drifted south along the eastern front. Over Raton Pass to Cimarron and then to Springer. No one had heard of them, and he knew they hadn't been there. But he kept going. Wagon Mound and Las Vegas. In Tularosa he almost died from the mescal. Between there and Las Cruces he pulled up and camped and looked at the line of blue mountains that stretched into old Mexico.

He said to himself that he was a fool and that he probably always had been a fool. He had gotten into the wrong deal and he knew it from the start. And that was why he was a fool. He looked at those blue mountains for two days, and then he turned that skinny cow pony around and started back. He didn't drink. In Santa Rosa he bought a book, Barnes's *New National Reader.* When his mind drifted back to the woman and the girl, he stopped and got down, sat on the ground, and started reading. After that he'd saddle up and move on until thoughts of them overcame him, and then he'd stop and read some more. He read Hawthorne, Hardy, Richard Dana, Cooper, and Dickens. He quoted Tennyson. He memorized Gray's *Elegy Written in a Country Church Yard,* reciting it over and over to the cow pony. He didn't drink for two years, until he knew he didn't have to drink. He bought another book, Irving's *Tales of the Alhambra.* He swapped that one out for the writings of Bret Harte. Robbie Burns and Carlyle were pretty tough sledding, but he couldn't get enough of Kipling. He made it back and worked off the money he'd borrowed from Mr. Wallop.

He came to believe that the little girl had got him reading. That it was somehow a bond between them. Every time he started feeling sorry for himself or wondering what she would look like or where she might be, he reached for a book.

Chapter Twenty-seven

The herd moved over the rolling hills of the old buffalo range. With the failing light of a rustler's moon, it looked like chain mail sliding over the country. The wagon tottered along behind.

They pushed on all night and through the day and stopped only briefly for a cold meal and coffee. That night they camped on the banks of the Tongue River and had a proper supper.

"We're getting close to Sheridan, aren't we, Mr. Ritter?" said Heck as he put his plate and fork in the washbasin.

"We should be at the Moncrieffes' by tomorrow afternoon."

Everyone looked surprised. Nola got up to gather the pans and tin plates, and Print went to lend her a hand. They walked off toward the river again.

"There's somethin' to be said for eatin' off clean dishes every night," said Print.

"I don't mind doing the dishes," she replied.

"I don't mind helpin'. I enjoy your company."

"You mean you enjoy my company 'til we get to Sheridan."

"No, I do not mean that. Look, I'm old enough to

have owed your daddy money. I tried to tread lightly around you. You probably had your fill of men. You had no need, I felt, of my sniffing around."

She threw the handful of sand into the water and looked at him.

"Sniffing around? Look at me, Mr. Ritter. I've had countless sweaty men in my life. I can't change that fact. But none of them, not one of them, did I let in here," she said, touching her chest.

"I didn't mean to insult you."

"There's a big difference between selling it and offering it, Mr. Ritter. Why don't you go have a smoke and leave me alone?"

The next day Print was out on the point, way ahead of the lead mare, the flea-bitten gray, and her lieutenants. He was in a foul mood, and he spent much of the time thinking about Nola and last night. Off in the distance he saw a small group that was on a course that would intersect theirs. It looked like a skiff out on the ocean. As they drew closer, he could see that it was a small group of tired-looking Indians. As they drew abreast of them, he saw an old man lying on a travois pulled by a raw-boned Indian pony. A woman and a little boy were mounted on another pony, and a slightly older boy walked.

Print raised up in the stirrups, turned, and called for Tom to stop the herd. Shortly he was joined by Heck and Tom, and the wagon drew up behind them. Heck eased his horse forward and, using sign language and various dialects, asked, "Where are you coming from?"

The woman looked at him for a while and then said in perfect English, "We are Brule Sioux from the Rosebud Agency."

Print was taken aback by her English. "Well, why ain't you there?"

The woman looked at him. "The buffalo wallows are empty. All our horses have been taken."

"You speak pretty good English," said Tom.

"My name is Cecilia Spotted Calf. My father was a peace chief. I was sent to the East to your school. He died, so I came back to help my grandfather."

"Then you oughta know it ain't safe out here."

"My grandfather wants to die in the North, where there are no whites. Soon the Cheyenne and the Arickaree, and even our enemies, the Blackfoot and the Crow, will be gone. Then our voices will be in the rocks and the grass, and we will wait for the time when our Great Father inclines his ear upon us and we will tell him our story."

"Well, Miss Spotted Calf, we got some jerky and supplies," said Print. "We'd like to help you out if we could. Heck, see what you can get for these people."

Cecilia Spotted Calf looked at the girls. And they looked back at her.

Sun Foy whispered to Mai Ling, *"She could be our sister."*

Heck gave them a bundle of food.

"That ought to get you where you're going," said Tom.

"Better steer clear of the wolfers and the whiskey traders," Heck said.

The woman stopped and turned her pony to look back.

"If anyone asks about ya', we'll tell them you're headed south and west," said Print.

Cecilia Spotted Calf turned her pony to the trail and they moved on.

Meeting the bedraggled Indians had cast a pall over Print's party. Print, Tom, and Heck got the herd going and they trailed behind it for a ways.

"It's an old story," said Print. "Egyptians done it to the Israelites. Romans done it to the Egyptians.

Mongols done it to the Romans. We did it to the Negroes. Now everyone's doin' it to the red man."

"We call them savages for takin' scalps, but look at Cold Harbor," said Heck.

"I've been north and seen the blood on the rocks. Their enemies lost more than their scalps, and they stole and trafficked in a hell of a lot more human freight than my grandpappy ever did," replied Print.

"You don't think they've been given a pretty raw deal?" said Heck.

"Worse than raw," added Tom.

"Well, of course they have. It ain't that simple. Can you honestly imagine a world today with all of us piled up in Europe and them havin' a grand time here, chasm' buffalo? No, sir.

"Humanity sometimes walks forward on heavy boots. Now that's a cold, hard fact," said Print.

"Well, I don't want to be around when their Great Father lends an ear to their story," said Tom.

Print stopped his horse, looked at him, and said, "Oh, you will be. We'll all be there. And that's a cold, hard fact, too."

Later in the day Print pulled up the herd. He motioned for Tom and Heck to join him, and then he waved his arm for Sun Foy to bring the wagon up. When they were all together and the men still mounted, Print addressed them.

"Well, folks, we got a decision we gotta make. We're almost there. Those fellas back there, I suspect, are still followin' us. What I propose is that, Heck, you take the wagon, Mr. Lung Hay, and the girls, and you proceed on down the track here. Tom and I'll take the herd. Now, you see that over there? It's too small to be a mountain and too big to be a hill."

Print was pointing to a large outcrop in the distance. "That's the whale's back."

When Tom looked at it for a while, he could see that indeed it looked like the back of a big whale breaching the surface of the prairie.

"Now, here's the deal. You all go on down the track. Tom and I will take the horses. You can't tell from here, but there's actually a river cut down into the ground. We'll bring the horses down in that, and if the water ain't too high, we can snake our way along that 'til we get to the tail of the whale's back. We'll go up over the spine, drop down, and meet you on the other side. I don't think that those fellas are as interested in that wagon and the girls as much as they are in these horses. But it's a risk. If we all go down the track, there's a chance we'll lose the herd, and there will be spilt blood too. The only other thing to do is to ditch the wagon and put everybody up on horseback. But I don't like the idea of everybody mounted going over the whale's back. Do you think you can handle it?"

"Yes, sir, I do."

"Miz Johns?"

She nodded.

"Lung Hay?"

"Yes," he said.

"All right. You probably won't need it, but here, take this." Print slid his rifle out of its scabbard and handed it over to Miz Johns. "If ya have any problems at all, you're on your own for the next fifteen miles. We'll meet ya or you'll meet us on the other side. Think it's the safest thing for all concerned."

Tom and Print waited as they watched the wagon move on down the trail, and then they got the herd going. They slipped in along a forest of ponderosas, and they followed it for a half a mile. Then they dropped down into the river. There wasn't much water in it, and there were high banks, so the horses couldn't go anywhere except upstream. Print led the way, and Tom brought up the rear. They snaked their way up that river. It turned and it bent and it turned again. Then, when they looked out of the walls of the river and saw the whale's back, they drove them up a bank into a small clearing. Print led the way up the hill. It wasn't a mountain, but it sure wasn't a hill, either. It was steep and it was narrow in the spine, and he just trudged on with Bob Tate. The flea-bitten mare and the other mares followed, and everybody pretty much fell into line as they went right up over the spine. Toward the back of the herd, some got nervous and started pushing to keep up with the leaders and that started about twenty of them scrambling and slipping. Print and Tom could not get to them and had to let them sort it out for themselves. Before it was over, two slid on their sides downslope. Tom was on the rear of the herd, and as he passed, he could hear the two whinnying down below to the herd as it continued on.

Tom and Print picked their way all the way 'til sunset. Then, as the sky turned purple and darkened, they dropped down the far side. It was dark when they saw the canvas top of the wagon in the distance.

When they arrived at the wagon, Print gathered them together. "Everything all right?"

"Yes, Mr. Ritter," said Nola as she handed the rifle back to Print.

"Hate ta have to ask this, but I think we really should push on through the night. Think it's the safest thing we could do. It's the last night. I want ta get these horses in the Moncrieffes' pens, and I want ta get all of you ta Sheridan. So we'll move on one more night and then we'll be done with it."

So, slowly, they pushed the herd on. The herd was tired and they hadn't grazed much for the last day.

But they had been watered, so they moved on into the night. The little wagon swayed along behind them.

The night was ink-colored. The dawn was rose. And by midday, the sky was yellow. The herd crested a low rise, and down before them in the distance lay the Moncrieffes' spread. Print conferred with Tom and Heck.

"I think I'm goin' on in to give the Moncrieffes a heads-up. You boys bring 'em on in slowly." Print turned and loped off on the big chestnut.

Print passed under the lodgepole entrance of the Quarter Circle A Ranch. The gate was adorned in elk antlers. He rode up to the front yard of a white ranch house and was met on the lawn by a moustached man who was wearing a blend of English country, cavalry twill, and western attire.

"Mr. Moncrieffe?"

"I am. Malcolm Moncrieffe," said the man with a strong Scottish accent.

"My name's Ritter, Prentice Ritter. I wired you in April about bringin' horses from John Day."

"Ah ha," said Moncrieffe. "The man from Oregon. Welcome. We've been following your journey with anticipation, Mr. Ritter."

"I'm not sure I understand, Mr. Moncrieffe."

"I received correspondence and packages from a Mr. Bentingcourt in Boston, and just the other day, Marshal Miller wired me from Cody asking about you. That's more news than I get from my family in Scotland.

"Sorry you just missed my brother. He's off the ranch on business."

"Where would you like me to put these cavvies, Mr. Moncrieffe?"

"We'll put them in the south pasture, over there," the Scotsman said, gesturing to the poorman's gate that was coiled and laying on the ground. "Keep them separated from the others for a week. I'll get my boys to lend you a hand."

Print and the Moncrieffes' hands rode toward the approaching herd. The Moncrieffe spread was a vast grid of corrals, large paddocks, and pastures, and there were literally thousands of horses there. The Ritter-Harte herd started picking up its pace as they got closer. There was excitement in the air, and soon the herd was galloping, then thundering. Print and the Moncrieffes' cowboys split to either side as the herd rolled at them. Heck and Tom were trying to keep them closed in, but to no avail. The wall of galloping horses thundered toward the south pasture. Print and the hands formed a moving line to try and turn them in. Finally, the lead mares buckled, turned to the right, and swept inside a huge pasture. Inside, the horses were leaping and bucking and rearing. Tom, Heck, and the mounted riders pushed in the stragglers. Two Moncrieffe cowboys secured the poorman's gate as the dust-covered wagon rolled up moments later.

Print and Tom rode over to Malcolm Moncrieffe. "Mr. Moncrieffe, my nephew, Tom Harte."

Moncrieffe looked past Print at the wagon's occupants. Turning in the saddle, Print followed his gaze and noted, "The rest of my party."

"You put on quite a show, Mr. Harte."

"Tried to keep 'em in good flesh, sir. This is first-rate stock you're getting. No yew necks, no pin ears, no pig eyes. Three weeks, they'll be fat as ticks."

"Let's get you settled in, and then we'll do some business."

The ranch office was a small building off to the side of the main ranch house. Inside, Malcolm and Print talked.

"This draft is drawn on the Stockmen and

Merchants Bank in Denver, but our bank in Sheridan will honor it."

"Couple of times back there, I wasn't sure this transaction was goin' ta happen," said Print.

"That's a good deal of money, Mr. Ritter. Will you buy more horses?"

"Not really sure. I'm thinkin' of gettin' some land."

"Hard to go wrong with land. You might want to talk to Oliver Wollop, my cousin. He's got his finger on the pulse of the state's politics. Good thing to know when you're buying land."

"I think I knew his daddy, or it mighta been his uncle." Changing topics, he said, "If we're through here, I think I'm gonna take my crew inta town for some shoppin' and a bath. We'll see you again in the morning."

The wagon rolled down the main street of Sheridan with the mounted men behind it. They pulled up in front of one of the storefronts. Everyone dismounted. Print walked over to Nola.

"Miz Johns, I want you ta outfit yourself and the girls for all your requirements. Don't go thin on the expenses. I'll be back ta settle up. Think we'll go have a drink and then a bath and a shave."

Later, when Print, Tom, and Heck caught up with Nola, the girls were all dressed in little denim trousers, shirts, and straw hats.

"That's what they wanted, Mr. Ritter. I got them dresses too, shoes, everything. I got myself two dresses, if you don't mind."

"Of course, not. That's what I wanted."

The next morning, in the pens at the Moncrieffes', Tom was helping the ranch hands work some horses. Sun Foy watched as he roped the colts. Malcolm Moncrieffe, Print, Heck, and the girls were watching through the poles of the corral.

"Your nephew seems to have a way with horses," said Malcolm Moncrieffe.

"He always has."

"Not an overly talkative lad, though."

"For sure. What's your plan for all this stock you bought?"

"We're in partnership with our cousin Oliver. We're supplying mounts for the British army. We've already shipped over twenty thousand horses to South Africa for their war."

"That's one hell of a lot of horseflesh."

"Not nearly enough, from the reports we get. They're calling for upward of a half a million animals. Horses and mules, that is. Between the Brits and your Spanish-American dustup, the price of horseflesh is going through the roof. But enough talk. We're having a picnic this afternoon. I hope you'll all join us, as we don't have guests here at the ranch that often."

As the tables were being prepared, the ranch hands got up a game of baseball. The men played with big three-fingered mitts. They invited some of the girls to join them.

Print sought out Tom. "Tom, you got a moment?"

"Sure."

They walked off to the side, and Print took a thick envelope from inside his vest pocket and handed it over.

"Your share of the proceeds an' then some. That should square it between you and your ma."

Tom looked inside, surprised at the amount of cash it contained. "What about you?"

Print, with his hand palm down, passed it between them. "More than square," he said.

They shook hands and Print walked off. Tom

watched him for a long time as he walked away, and then he returned to watch the game.

One cowboy playing shortstop was paying extra attention to Sun Foy. He was standing behind her with his arm around her, showing her how to catch the ball. Tom turned back once again to look for Print and then turned back to Sun Foy and the cowboy. Tom walked to his horse, mounted up, and trotted over to home plate.

"Gimme that bat."

A bewildered cowboy looked up at Tom and handed it over. Tom centered his pony over the home plate.

"Come on. Toss it in here."

A smiling ranch hand complied and gave a slow, easy pitch across the plate. Tom stood up in the stirrups and swatted the ball out across the lawn in the direction of the cottonwoods. His pony jumped out, rounding first base, then second. He aimed the pony at the cowboy who'd been helping Sun Foy and almost bowled him over, the ranch hand having to dive for the dirt. There was a smile on Sun Foy's face as Tom headed for home. He crossed the plate, waved his hat high in the air, "Yee haw!"

And he kept on going. Tom spun the horse around and raced back to home plate and brought the horse up short. He swung down out of the saddle at the same time the dinner bell rang. He walked his horse over to the hitching rail, loosened the cinch as Sun Foy joined him, and they walked toward the picnic tables set up in the backyard.

It was quite a spread, and the girls and Nola and Lung Hay and the ranch hands all enjoyed the afternoon. But Print was nowhere to be seen. When finally Tom asked Malcolm Moncrieffe where his uncle was, Moncrieffe told him that he had gone back into town to do some business.

Chapter Twenty-eight

Print had the big chestnut in a good trot going down the road to Sheridan. The weather was good, and his mind was elsewhere. At one point he eased back to a walk and checked his pocket watch. He opened it up, shut it, put it back in his pocket, and turned in the saddle. He thought he heard horses. Barely visible in the distance behind him, he saw dust from a rider. . . . Print looked forward, scanned the skyline, and moved on. Five minutes later, Print looked back and saw that the rider was closing on him. He fanned Bob Tate with his hat, and they raced along the dirt road for a mile, leaving billowing dust behind them. He kept looking over his shoulder and didn't see the three riders who rode up out of the blind ditch to block the road until he was almost on top of them. He pulled Bob Tate up hard. With the late afternoon sun on his face, he saw that one of the riders had the unmistakable silhouette of a pair of big ears.

"Well, I told you we'd be together again."

Print rested his forearm on the saddle horn, his horse blowing hard.

"You a praying man?"

"Not much."

Big Ears looked up at the sky as if to tell the time. "You will be, time I leave my mark on you."

They escorted Print and his horse off the road and down to a thicket of cottonwoods. There they stripped him down to his long johns and seated him astride the trunk of a blown-over tree. Big Ears fingered through the horse money and then stuffed Print's money belt into a saddlebag and removed a small fencing hammer from the other side. It was the kind used to repair barbed-wire fencing. He took out some sixteen-penny nails as well and placed them between his teeth.

"Thanks for the donation, old man. First thing I'm going to do is nail your credentials to this log. Then I'm going to push you over backward. We're gonna to see how much sand you really got. Then you're going to find out how good I really am with a running iron."

Two of the rustlers stepped up to grab each of Print's arms. Big Ears straddled the log to face him, and he sat and took a nail from his mouth.

"You're going to wish the Mandan squaws got hold of you, time I get through with you, mister blanket man."

Big Ears got ready to set a nail between Print's legs. Print mumbled under his breath.

"What'd you say to me, old man?" said Big Ears as he leaned close to Print's face.

With all the strength he had, Print head-butted Big Ears, bringing his forehead square on the bridge of the man's nose with a fierce thud. Big Ears rocked backward, screaming, blood pouring down his face. He stood up and with all his strength hit Print under the right eye with his fist. The force knocked Print over.

Big Ears sputtered through blood flowing from

his mouth. "All right, blanket man, you just booked yourself a ticket to hell. You're going to leave this world a miserable, old, toothless man."

Print was splattered with blood as Big Ears spit out his words. The men set Print back upright on the log. Big Ears wiped the blood from his mouth with the back of his sleeve, the hammer in the other hand. Print looked up at him, his right eye already swollen shut.

Suddenly the chest of Ed "Big Ears" Bywaters opened up. It exploded, though there was no sound, and he and his entrails were pitched onto Print. There was the delayed sound of a distant rifle report. Then confusion, as the men scrambled. Print struggled to get out from underneath the dead and mangled Big Ears Bywaters. A rustler took a slug in his thigh and screamed, cursing. The other man mounted. There was gunfire. Print wiggled out from underneath the dead body. The outlaw in the saddle aimed at Print. Print rolled over and over in the dust as the rider fired at him from his hysterical, turning horse. Then the rider was blown out of the saddle and hit the ground hard. Print rolled up as close as he could to the log in hopes that he wouldn't get stepped on by the scrambling horses.

Print tried to get his bearings. He looked around and saw a man against a tree. He was shot in the leg and the gut and bleeding badly. Their eyes met and locked. A rifle roared behind Print and the man's head snapped backward as the back of his scalp flew away. Then there was silence. Print lay back and looked up to see Tom looking down at him. Tom bent down and grabbed his uncle and lifted him to his feet. Print held onto Tom at the shoulders as he tried to gain his balance. A big gash ran down the side of his jaw below his ear and down his neck. They looked at each other as if they might embrace. Breathing heavily Print simply nodded.

A piano played in one of the saloons on the darkened front street of Sheridan as the two riders led three horses with bodies strapped across the saddles. The rider stopped in front of the marshal's office. A light glowed inside. Tom dismounted, and a tired Print, his eye swollen shut, sat astride his horse, unable to move.

Marshal Miller and Deputy McNeary were inside playing cribbage when Tom entered, and they looked up at him. Tom said nothing. He took a wadded-up handkerchief and placed it on the table between the two men. The marshal and his deputy just looked at him. Then, gingerly, Bill Miller opened the kerchief. Inside were two large, bloody ears.

"My uncle said they were for your watch chain, marshal."

Miller and the deputy looked up at Tom, then back at the handkerchief. Tom simply turned and walked out into the night.

There was a dry wind blowing out of the West when Print walked out onto the veranda the following afternoon. He watched the Chinese girls as they attempted to play croquet. Nola was sitting on a bench, watching them too. He stepped off the veranda and walked across the lawn to Nola.

"Evening," said Print.

"Good evening, Mr. Ritter. How's your eye feeling?"

"Oh, I can't see much right now, but it'll be all right." Print reached for his makings.

"Every time I talk to you these days, you seem to have a sudden urge for tobacco, Mr. Ritter."

"I had a long talk with Lung Hay," he said. "I proposed that you take the girls to San Francisco. He says there's a place there that will look after them in a more permanent way."

"And you volunteered my services."

Print said nothing.

"That's very generous of you. Thank you. If Ghing Wa is fit to travel, I'll make plans to leave immediately."

"No need to rush off."

"No need to delay either. I can be ready by tomorrow, if necessary."

An awful silence fell between the two of them. Both were prideful and both were hurting.

"Nola," he said. He realized it was the first time he had ever addressed her by her first name. "My one attempt at havin' a family and settlin' down turned out badly. The truth is, I'm neither brave enough nor strong enough to go that way again."

She said nothing. She got up and walked back to the house, leaving Print to watch the girls as they played on the lawn.

Three days later the fickle weather of early autunm in Wyoming had changed again. It was cold and overcast and threatened snow. Everyone was assembled in front of the Sheridan-Laramie stage line. Ghing Wa was lifted into the coach, then Ghee Moon and Mai Ling. They were all very quiet.

An embarrassed Tom motioned for Lung Hay to join him as he stood beside Sun Foy. "Could you translate for me?"

"Yes."

"I thought I had this all worked out."

Lung Hay started to translate, but Tom cut him off. "No, wait. This ain't easy."

Tom looked at Sun Foy. "I ain't got much. Well,

that's not right. Actually I got a pretty good wad of dough now."

Lung Hay translated.

"I don't even know how to get in touch with you. I want to know what happens to you. I . . . I . . . I want to know you had a good life."

He took a step backward, and Lung Hay helped Sun Foy into the coach.

Then Nola walked out of the stage office to the waiting coach and Print. He took his hat off and faced her. She turned to him.

"Most men are afraid of failure in this world. It seems like some are afraid of success. Good-bye, Mr. Ritter."

She kissed him on the cheek, then quickly stepped into the coach and looked away.

A bareheaded, black-eyed Print put his hat on and watched as they shut the door, and with it his life.

Chapter Twenty-nine

The Royal Coachman landed lightly on the pool between the bank and the quiet run that diverged from the fast current of the river. In the cool water a fat trout swept its tail back and forth, considering the fly that had landed on the surface.

It was the middle of September 1915 on the Snake River, and a wagon passed under the entrance of lodgepoles adorned with moose and elk antlers. A sign hung below the cross pole, "Siam Bend." Lung Hay walked out from the vegetable garden at the side of a log house. It was long with a stone chimney at either end. Two dormer windows protruded from the shake roof. A veranda ran the length of its front. It faced the river, where Print was fishing.

Lung Hay, a hoe in hand, walked to the wagon to meet the driver, who handed him a packet of mail and several parcels. Down by the river, Print was casting. The wagon turned around in front of the log cabin and passed Ye Fung's grave. Print stayed in the river until almost dark, as it was a good time to fish since the fish were biting.

Later, inside the log cabin, he sat in a deep, stuffed chair and read the mail. There was a blue envelope with a San Francisco postage mark on it. He put on his spectacles, opened the letter, and read.

Dear Mr. Ritter,

I hope this letter finds you well. I am embarrassed that it has been so long since last I wrote to you.

Summer must almost be over at Siam Bend. You have no idea how it touched me to learn the name you have given that point on the river.

I seem so preoccupied these days with time. You told me right there on the river that nothing was more unforgiving than time. You would not recognize me now, as time can be ruthless, especially to women.

You, on the other hand, I am sure, are as stout and straight as a ridgepole. You also have Lung Hay to keep a mindful eye on you. Ghee Moon, Mai Ling, and Ghing Wa have grown into wonderful young ladies. I see them often and they always ask after you.

I do so hope that I can visit you. Lung Hay is better at writing letters and the girls tell me everything about your fishing camp. Promise me that you will not laugh at an old woman when I tell you that she wants to sit with you by the river and splash her feet in the water.

There are so many things that one wishes they might change about their lives. I know for me, one would have been to be less prideful when we were last together.

It is my fear of time and how it stands between us that prompts me to write to you this evening. I want to say without shame or guilt that it is you and only you who will abide in me in my final hour.

Thank you, Mr. Ritter, for giving me back my life, even if I could not share it with you.

With warmest thoughts,
Nola Johns

Late in the night, Prentice Ritter had fallen asleep and the letter rested on his chest. The lamp beside him on the table was burning low. An ancient Lung Hay shuffled into the room and silently placed the letter on the table and turned the lamp out. Print opened his eyes. They fluttered. He woke momentarily and looked at Lung Hay and then dozed off. Lung Hay went and took a seat in a chair across from him and waited for the morning light to fill the room.

Epilogue

If you have no family or friends to aid you, and no prospect opened to you there, turn your face to the great West, and there build up a home and fortune.

—*Horace Greeley*

Nola Johns died in the influenza epidemic of 1918. She was buried at Siam Bend on the Snake River, next to Ye Fung.

Lung Hay never returned to his wife. He died in 1921 and was buried at Siam Bend.

Prentice Ritter joined them in 1924.

Heck Gilpin escorted the herd from Sheridan to Capetown. He later settled in the Republic of South Africa.

Mai Ling stayed at the Cameron House in San Francisco and worked with Donaldina Cameron in her continuing efforts to rescue young Chinese girls from the privations of the slave trade.

Ghing Wa graduated from Stanford University

School of Medicine and returned with Ghee Moon to China and started a hospital. They were lost in the turmoil of Mao Tse-tung's revolution.

Tom Harte married Sun Foy. Their grandchildren still ranch in Wyoming.

ACKNOWLEDGMENTS

I would like to thank the late Waldo Haythorn and Beldora Haythorn of Arthur, Nebraska, Maxine Brocius Bushong, Major James Rumpler, and Doug Gardiner for so many stories that helped in the writing of this book. Thank you to Horton Foote and Ulu Grosbard for vetting the story in its early stages. I would like to thank the Cameron House in San Francisco for help in researching the history of Donaldina Cameron and the trafficking of Chinese girls. Special thanks to Mark Stewart of Lippan, Texas, and the entire Bews family of Longview, Alberta, Canada, for making sure I didn't sound like a dude; to Scott Cooper and Wes Morrissey for telling me when I missed the mark; and to Dave Barron, who helped me find Bob Baron and Fulcrum Publishing; to Sam Scinta, its associate publisher, who spent long hours on the book's development; and to the hardworking team at Fulcrum, who made this book a reality.

I want to thank Luciana Duvall for her encouragement in writing this story, and most of all my friend Robert Selden Duvall, who told me to "write that story down" and was there to help me, from start to finish. Thank you, Bobby.